Donor

Enjoy!

Emma Barrett-Brown

Emma Barrett-Brown

Donor

First Published Independently via KDP
2020 ©Emma Barrett, Plymouth UK

Printed and Bound by KDP – Kindle Direct Publishing October 2020, Plymouth, Devon.
Cover Design by Emma Barrett-Brown ©2020
Cover models: Natasha Crystal Berry, (**https://www.facebook.com/tashaltmodel**) and @MadMatt

This book is for Jay
And for Tabs, who I hope is going to love it!

Prologue

Roaring strains of deafening heavy metal music permeated the night, creating a blanketing wall of sound which Beatrice Morgan's throbbing brain couldn't quite take in. Crashing guitars, flashing lights, snatches of normality between the blurred dizzy spells. All around was a sea of chaos. Half-naked bumbling bodies throwing themselves around drunkenly on the tiny black sea of lino created for such a purpose like twitching mutants which sweated and writhed. People laughing, shouting along with disjointed chords and screamed lyrics. Usually Bree would be out there with them, engaged in the stampede but not that night, that night it was all too much. As well as the music and the ruckus from the dancefloor, there was the hubbub of a hundred voices chattering too, and around the bar, understaffed as ever, was a crowd of hopefuls calling and waving glasses, trying to attract attention. Bree grasped the tall, black-painted table she was sitting at and tried to concentrate on her companion as well as trying not to slide off of the smooth and slippery plastic stool she sat on. The man – she didn't know his name – was fairly handsome with over-the-top eye-liner and a cheeky grin. Bree liked him. He'd bought her a drink, asked her all about herself. Too much about herself? Had she told him about Danny? She didn't remember.

Bree's shoulders slumped, her mind racing in a drunken haze. She looked down at her fancy Chanel watch but the numbers all moved about in a blur. Bree blinked, had she really drunk that much? In the distance, Angie and Pete – her besties – were a blurred outline as they stood rowing in a dark alcove by the back door where people had spilled out to smoke. Pretty normal really, they were always fighting. Bree was too far gone to be able to wave them over, besides… her companion was cute… wasn't he? It was hard to tell in the smoke from the dancefloor but he looked a bit like Danny.

A wound reopened somewhere within.

The thunderous guitars of the heavy music pounded on, the people happy in their fool's dance – fuelled more by alcohol than drugs, in alt places like this. Bree's companion was leaning in closer, smiling, laughing. Bree pulled back slightly. Her head swam again, her heart hurt. On the table sat her mobile phone and the dregs of her last drink – one of far, far too many apparently, put on Daddy's credit card. Daddy wouldn't mind – he never did. The phone was part of the cause of the problem though, that evil little electronic messenger with it's heart-breaking buzz, it's innocent voice a smokescreen for the dire news it held. Danny wanted to break up, it had displayed on the old flip-out screen. He didn't want her anymore. Bree glanced to the phone, then back to her companion.

'I need a smoke!' she mouthed to her companion, more for the fresh air and need to escape than for the nicotine but he seemed not to notice and so carried on talking, words she could barely make out. His hair was long, like Danny, and his clothing dark – but that's where the similarities ended. He was older, his face harder than Danny's boyish demeanour, he was too open too, talking too much. Danny was the quiet type – a musician and a poet. Bree adored him. Her eyes fell to the phone again, to the "Sorry Baby" text which no amount of alcohol could erase. She lurched in her seat, trying to clear her mind and concentrate on her current situation. The lights were upsetting her now, flickering and dancing across the slick floor with its pile of sweaty, exhilarated performers. Each one seemed lost in their own little skit with arms moving effortlessly in time to the music. Minds lost in the dance, fuelled with exhilaration, adrenaline and of course, cheap beer and sours shots. Bree looked about desperately for Angie and Pete, but her friends seemed to have vanished into the ether.

The man beside her was still talking. Bree glanced up again and saw his lips curl into a smile. As pretty as he was, that smile was cruel. There was a strange twinkle in his eye too, a silver light which burned, just momentarily, shining bright and then fading to nothingness. The room spun around Bree again, crashing through her mind and making her feel brittle, ill.

'What...?' she gasped.

'I said, it's very loud in here, isn't it?' he said, half-speaking and half-mouthing the words.

Bree tried to smile and made to excuse herself to the bathroom where she could be sick, but the man stood, slipped an arm about her shoulders and helped her down from the stool. He smelled like cloves and dust.

'Come on, let's go somewhere quieter,' he shouted.

'No,' her voice quivered, but he seemed to have no trouble hearing her, 'I feel sick.'

'Then I'll drive you home.'

The man's words seemed oddly stretched, blurred, and Bree could barely make them out. She frowned, trying to make sense of it all, somehow. Her whole body swayed again and her head was beginning to thud. Had she really, actually, drunk *that* much? Her companion had matched her drink for drink and he still seemed sober.

'Y-you can't drive...' she stuttered out as she indicated his empty beer glass. The man just shrugged and slipped an arm behind her back, pulling her with him on feet which barely moved by themselves.

'Stop! Please... I need my phone! Danny... I just broke up with Danny! I don't... don't want...' Bree mumbled, pushing against his weight to try to free herself, but the man was insistent, his hand on her arm strong. Across the room, she spied Angie dancing, alone, spinning about and waving her arms above her head. Bree screamed her friend's name, tried to pull free from her companion. Her meagre, drunken strength was no match for his grip on her, though, and he dragged her away with an inhuman ease through a sea of people who didn't notice. At the last moment, Angie looked up, but was then swallowed in a sea of hot, sweaty faces. The man continued to walk Bree, slowly and steadily, to the door. At the entrance, he exchanged a few words with the doorman, and then laughed. Bree's brain was fuzzy to the extreme, pounding. The man walked her out onto the road, past all the people smoking, and then off down a back street, behind the club. Bree groaned and tried once again to push him off, but when he did finally release her, she slumped helplessly against the wall, her legs barely holding her and one ankle screaming in pain as her foot slipped sideways in her heeled shoe. Her companion laughed and ruffled her hair, still speaking gently as though he had not just kidnapped her from the nightclub.

'Come on, Beatrice,' he said, 'it's time to go.'

How did he know her full name? Did she tell him her name? 'Are you mates with Danny?' she managed.

'Hush,' he said, then took her arm again, dragging her onwards.

In a few more steps, Bree caught sight of a black BMW parked in behind one of the buildings there. Once more she tried to scream but it came out only as a low moan. The man pulled her onwards, and then opened the door. Bree slumped onto the back seat.

'Please... oh god...' she moaned, but the man climbed in beside her without a word. He smiled, and there she saw his teeth beginning to extend. Bree started, and then gasped as his eyes began to burn with a silver glow. Within her, something pulled, a memory, but then it was quashed as the man moved in closer.

'What...?' she murmured, but it was too late for realisation, as the man moved forward and slipped those elongated, hideous fangs into the white flesh of her shoulder.

Everything went black. It was to stay black for some time.

1

Reuben Chamberlain sat in a small, darkened study at the back of a house which had once been a parsonage, out in the wilds of Cornwall. What was left of the church was a ruin now, standing alone on the edge of a cliff which gave way to a steep drop down into the waves. The village it had served had died with the depletion of the mine which had fuelled its economy, leaving the place abandoned and solitary. Reuben didn't mind the lack of locals. Being what he was, it was easier to hide himself and his little family of misfits that way.

On the table before him was a newspaper clipping, one of several documenting the same story. Beatrice Morgan. Local socialite's kid, snatched from a nightclub. It was a high-profile case; the media were going nuts and you could hardly walk a mile through any city in the south of England without seeing a poster or flier with her face on it. Reuben's eyes scanned the clipping. Poor kid. They wouldn't find her. Not the human authorities who were currently pestering all the local sex-offenders and other persons of note. Her recently ex-boyfriend was a person of interest, and her friend's boyfriend had been arrested, but they were barking up the wrong tree.

Reuben sighed and leaned back in the chair. Of course, he had no evidence that the kin *were* involved either, other than a gut feeling… but then, on the other hand, Reuben's gut feelings weren't usually something to ignore. He scanned over the clipping one last time, and then stood up. The kitchen of the parsonage was a fairly small one, with an old Aga still instead of a modern stove; not that the occupants of the house ate much, not since Lucy – Reuben's last human companion – had passed on, anyway. The wallpaper was blue and faded, and the furnishings old, not fitted like a modern kitchen aside from one unit with the sink set in and a few scruffy cupboards above. The whole place was shabby these days, since Lucy's death, but it was good enough for Reuben and his ragtag band of drinkers.

Reuben stretched and then picked up the clipping. To his right was a door which led to a narrow winding set of stairs to the rooms on the side of the house – Reuben often thought that the house could have done with at least one floor holding more than one room, rather than the higgledy-piggledy mash up of floors it was, some of which were only accessible by one of the two sets of stairs. Whomever had designed the house, back in the day, certainly had had an odd vision. Reuben headed up the stairs, and across a small square landing to where a vamp named Joshua sat in front of a heat-spewing desktop computer. This room was fairly small, and held a smaller window than the others, less light to glare on a screen.

'Hey?' about normal for Josh as a greeting. His blue eyes were glued to the screen where some sort of game was displayed. His scruffy blond curls were cropped close again as he did sometimes and his clothing was casual, modern. He'd worn glasses as a human and even still, sometimes Reuben caught him putting a hand to the bridge of his nose where they'd once sat.

'Hey, I don't suppose you could run this one for me?' Reuben asked, passing Josh the clipping. Reuben, a drinker born in the 1700s, had no head at all for computers and the gadgetry of the modern era – but Josh, having been brought over to the kin in the 90s, was not just more tech-savvy but actually enjoyed messing about with the damn machines. An eternity spent playing computer games! Reuben despaired of it a little, but it wasn't his place to scold; he looked after the kids but he wasn't their father, nor even their blood-sire. Most of them, his band of misfits, were fairly new to this life of darkness, those were the ones that needed him the most. As they aged, they'd wonder off onto their own paths, and that was fine too. Let the bigger clans deal with the older ones, they tended to be messier of the mind anyway and Reuben didn't really have much time for that – he was messy enough himself. He still obeyed the rules – just about, but more than anything he tried to avoid others like him, unless he was working. Life was easier as a free agent.

'Yeah sure, what do you wanna know?'

'I'm not sure. Anything you can find out.'

'Ok, gimme an hour,' the younger lad said, taking the clipping and putting it down beside him, 'wanna beat my level first…'

Reuben opened his mouth to argue, but decided not to bother – Josh would get to it, he always did. Reuben instead retreated back down the stairs and went into the kitchen where Isabelle – another of his little family – had snuck in and was just getting started on some knitting. She was a fair bit less coherent than Josh – well, than any of them – but then the way she'd been born into the life would do that to a person. She was pretty enough, with her dark blond hair which fell over her shoulder and which was in danger of being incorporated into her knitting, and her freckled face. Reuben could see why they'd taken her. Once upon a time, before he'd seen the error of his ways, Reuben might have done the same. Izzy didn't acknowledge him at first, but held her face close to the stitches, counting them out aloud – fairly common practice for her. She liked order, liked consistency. Reuben didn't pause but moved past her to put on the kettle. Drinkers didn't have to necessarily eat or drink human food, but that didn't mean they couldn't and Reuben had always been partial to a cuppa.

'Tea?' he asked.

'I thought I heard you walking about,' Izzy replied, ignoring the offer, '...and there was cut up newspaper here again. It was messy. I threw it away.'

'Sorry, I'll try to keep it tidier for you, I'm working on a new case.'

'You call them cases – you mean a new abduction?'

'Yes.'

'Morgan? The rich girl?'

'Yes... that one struck you too hmm?'

'A little. It doesn't feel right.'

'Agreed. Have you fed? You look a little peaky.'

'Not yet.'

Reuben flicked the kettle back off. This was something Izzy often forgot to do, and it was something much more important. Without feeding – "drinking" – the blood pangs kicked in and with somebody whose sanity was as fragile as Izzy's, that could be lethal. Reuben paused in front of a small mirror which hung by the door to pull his shoulder-length black hair into a ponytail. Lots of the old myths about drinkers weren't true and the whole lack of reflection thing was one of those... just like the garlic, crosses and so on.

'Come on, then,' he said, putting on his long black leather coat, a genuine 80s artifact, 'come with me, we'll go together before I start my training for the evening...'

Izzy looked almost longingly at her knitting, but then nodded and put it down. A glance at the clock showed Reuben it was just gone midnight. Plenty of time to find somebody to feed from and be home before daybreak. He held out his hand to Izzy and she took it, allowing him to lead her out into the grounds of the old house. Outside, the parsonage wasn't too shabby, old red brick which was made darker by the lack of any outside lights, and broken cobbles but without too many weeds. Andy, another of the family, was older than the others and could tolerate the daylight more in line with Reuben – he tended to the gardens in the late afternoons when the sun was retreating and the sky dusky. He'd once had a house and gardens of his own – before his turning – and claimed he enjoyed the upkeep of the grounds. Reuben wasn't quite sure he understood that one either. His family were all immortal, they had eternity, and they spent it playing games, knitting, and gardening... but then, who was he to judge? He'd hardly spent his own years on earth particularly well. Izzy stood by the door, waiting as Reuben opened up the garage and unlocked his car – a Mercedes SLK convertible – a fairly swish ride he'd taken from one of the last groups of rogue drinkers he'd put to bed. It wasn't even stolen either, so he'd just registered the documents to the fake name that Josh had set up for him online. Josh certainly made life easier in that respect, he knew his way around modern life in a way Reuben couldn't have fathomed. Before Josh, he'd had to rely on Lucy for a lot of that sort of thing but even she'd struggled to keep everything current and legal. He didn't need much though; he had a driver's licence with the wrong name on it and a passport in case he needed to travel. The group didn't bother with bank accounts and the like – they didn't have enough between them to really worry about that. The house was something which needed to be managed, but until recently he'd had that put into Lucy's name too and then she'd willed it to her "grandson" who happened to share a name with the fake ID Reuben carried. That imaginary grandson would be in his sixties now though, so Reuben would have to consider how it was going to be passed down again this time. The influence helped, but Reuben didn't like to fuck with human minds if he could help it.

The car started with a little growl and Reuben flicked on the lights, showing Izzy's form coming to close the door behind him. The garage he'd had newly built, using the influence to make the builders forget him after they'd erected it – pockets full of cash but nothing on the books. Izzy pulled down the door behind him, and then clambered into the car. As ever when he pushed her to feed, her eyes were dim and her lips pressed. Izzy, like all of them, knew what it meant to be the victim. At least they could blot it out for their own feeds though, that was a blessing at least. Neither of them had been given that blessing when they were turned but poor Izzy, she'd had it worse.

Reuben patted her arm, 'Come on, let's get this over with,' he soothed, and then turned the car towards the gate.

2

In her dreams, Bree saw Danny, felt his kisses and his soft hands on her skin. Despite that he played guitar, his fingers never held the hardened callouses of some musicians, no, they were always soft. She sobbed, but his voice whispered gently, telling her not to be afraid, that it was all just a bad dream and when she opened her eyes, he'd be there waiting to hold her, just like always.

But he wasn't.

Bree's eyes opened to find it was daylight. She glanced at the curtains and realised they weren't hers. The room was unfamiliar, stale and old, and she was alone. Then she really woke up, consciousness seeping in like the twisted, half-mangled memories of a decent hangover, not that she really knew that much about that at seventeen years of age. Her head swam, her lungs felt too full, like she'd been smoking too much, or had been somewhere dusty for some time. She moaned and tried to sit up, but there found resistance in the pounding of her skull on the hard floor.

Bree tried again to move her body and found that she couldn't – at all. Clarity drew in.

She was gagged, bound, lying in the corner of a room.

To her left was a bed. It was a double and made up, albeit with dirty off-white sheets. The bed was a divan, with drawers underneath and behind it was a tall headboard which she suspected wasn't attached to the bed. The window opposite where she lay was an old-style one, not double glazed, and the green paint around it was coming off in flakes.

Panic began to build. Bree's fingers, bound as they were beneath her bodyweight, began to scrabble on the hard boards, feeling for something to grip, to pull at, but gaining nothing more than the sharp spike of a splinter piercing the flesh. Her eyes darted about, looking for something, anything to give her a clue as to where she was but the other furniture in the room was tatty, unused. There was a wardrobe made of what looked like pine, but it was rotting where it stood, as was the drawer set next to it. The rug on which her bottom half lay was sat was thick, soft, and had probably once been expensive, but it was filthy and ragged, an odd shade of purple. In a half-dream, she glanced down at herself – dressed in a long blue dress which looked a bit like a prom-dress, rather than the jeans she'd been wearing the night before. There was blood on the front of the dress, her blood, she guessed, and some on the floor beside her. Bree murmured aloud, the sound echoing. Her throat screamed, a sharp and urgent pain which caused her to try to put a hand up, forgetting in her sudden shock that they were bound behind her. She murmured again and inhaled a mouthful of rag-dust and dry-mouth.

'Oh god,' she murmured, behind the gag, 'oh god, oh god!'

Her jaw ached and her eyes were dry as shit. Where was she? Wriggling, slowly, Bree managed to get herself onto her front. The ropes cut into the flesh of her wrists and she moaned again, trying desperately to get loose from her bonds but having little joy. Footsteps sounded suddenly from without and then the door opened. A figure paused for a long moment, and then walked past her and pulled the curtains closed. Bree stared up at the man who had her prisoner. His face was somewhat hidden but she could see his boots, hiking ones – expensive, and the blue jeans he wore with them. He glanced down and she was met with an unknown face framed by shaggy brown hair. Not even recognisable by the partial memories from the club the night before, no, this man was a complete stranger. Bree tried again to speak through the gag but the man administered a hard kick to her belly.

'Shush!' he said, actually pronouncing the word, rather than making the hiss. His eyes stared with a hardness which tore through her. 'Shush, there's a good girl,' the accent was northern, but not coarse or strong.

Bree curled up as best she could into a ball. Tears of panic leaked from her eyes. More footsteps, sounding as though they were on a set of stairs, and then another voice drifted in. In her haziness, she felt there was something familiar about that voice, probably the guy from the club.

'Is she awake?'

'Yeah,' that was the first man.

'Well, feel free, before I put her back to sleep. She won't remember,' the other voice said.

'Much obliged,' the man in the room replied, then knelt down beside her and took her chin in his hand. 'Did you hear that, little one?' he asked. 'I've been given permission for a taste.'

Bree stared, frozen. The man smiled again, almost charming, but then his face began to change. It was only subtle, a shifting of the jaw, and then an odd glow to the eyes. Bree whimpered and pulled herself backwards, pressing against the wall as the man opened his mouth, showing her his teeth. They were nothing human. The canines had grown a little, not like the huge, over-sized cartoonish fangs of the vampires of Hollywood, but just enough so that she knew he'd have no trouble breaking the skin. The other teeth too, looked sharper, more pointed – like a cat's teeth. Bree murmured again as he moved closer, almost a whimper, and tried to wriggle back but she was no match for him. The man's hand took her arm, the grip firm enough to cause pain. He lifted her by her shoulder and pulled her body up to him. Bree struggled but nonetheless she felt the sharpness at her neck, like before, and then the pain like somebody stabbing her throat. The man drank deeply from the wound, a devil's kiss. Bree began to moan, crying tears of agony as the man teased at her throat, suckling and licking like a babe at the bosom of his mother. His teeth tore again and his hands restrained her head, stopping any movement she might have made. For a moment he pulled away and she heard his sigh of pleasure, but then he went back to it.

Just as consciousness threatened to fail, the man pulled away. He wiped his mouth with the back of his hand and then looked down onto Bree, grinning a grin which showed her the blood on his lips; her blood. Her neck hurt, a pain which went right down into her shoulder and as her head thumped back down onto the floor she saw stars.

'You're such a good girl,' the drinker whispered. 'Such a good girl.'

'That's enough!' the voice from without barked. 'Leave her alone now.'

The blood drinker sighed and rolled his eyes at Bree, as though the other voice was spoiling some mutual fun, then pulled the rag out of her lips to kiss them. Bree gagged but he intended only the one kiss and then lifted her and threw her down on the bed in the corner of the room. Dust flew and Bree's sharp breath at being just dropped down led her to inhale a nose-full. She coughed a few times and then curled back up as much as her aching limbs would allow. Wetness by her ear warned her that she was still bleeding and she was pretty sure the dress had slipped at the top, baring her body to the room. The drinker left and was replaced by a new shadow. Bree didn't even look up, didn't even want to see the figure that stood there behind her.

'Now listen, Beatrice,' a voice spoke, 'you're going to forget…'

When Bree awoke again the light was different, more evening than the darkness of night. The sound of laughter came to her ears from below, and then a few strains of music. Some sort of party?

'Why can't Mama keep the damn noise down? Doesn't she remember I'm sleeping above?' she thought, jumbled, and it wasn't until she tried to sit up in bed and found her hands still bound behind her that she suddenly realised she was not at home, not a child tucked up in her own bed but a young woman of seventeen, and still a prisoner. Bree groaned, tears spilling down her face, and pulled herself out of the bed. Her legs weren't tied, nor was she tied to the bed, just her hands bound behind her back.

As carefully as she could, being sure not to make any noise, she put her feet onto the manky carpet and let her weight fall onto them. Then she frowned. Manky carpet? Where was the rug? The bare floorboards? Then she realised something else – she was wearing a different dress. White, thick cotton with little cherries embroidered onto it. Very girly, very unlike her own clothing and a complete change from the previous night. Bree shuddered and looked around. The furniture, other than the bed, was gone – and even that was different, not a divan, but a wooden frame.

From below, Bree heard a whoop of laughter, followed by the blaring of the stereo being turned up. Music she didn't recognise. She shuddered again and repressed tears, she had to keep a clear head if she was going to escape but everything seemed surreal, blurred and other-worldly, a bit like the time Pete had let her try a bit of one of his stinky cannabis cigarettes. Trying to hold on to sensible thought, Bree looked about herself. There was no mirror in the room where she could get a look at the ropes binding her hands. Her grandfather had been a keen sailor and had been happy to teach the tricks of the trade to his granddaughter in the absence of a grandson so she was good with knots, but she needed to get a look at it first. Thinking to use the glass, she moved to the window. The curtains were drawn but she managed to pull them aside using her head and teeth, and then looked out. There was no usable reflection, really, but Bree could at least gain some intel on the place. She was on the second floor of a building. Outside was a little garden and some trees, more going off into the distance? Ok, so she was in a small building in or near the woods. But which woods though? How long had she been out cold in the back of that car? Whoever these people were had obviously moved her at least once during the day when she was out cold, drugged up and hallucinating, but how far had they taken her?

Panic tried to set in again, but Bree pushed it back, promising herself she'd allow it later when she was free. She had only been out a couple days at most, whilst whatever drugs they'd pumped into her had been at work, and since that time she'd now awoken twice – once at night, and now, in evening. So, a day, maybe a night and a day… unless she'd slept through the first day in which case it was two nights and two days. She couldn't be too far from where she'd started. She wondered if Angie or her parents had raised the alarm yet, if anybody was looking for her. Surely her mother would have even if Angie was too scared of getting in trouble for taking Bree to the club! Behind her, as she thought things through, her hands were working on the knots which held them together. They were well-tied but they were giving, slowly. Bree tried to remain calm, to just ignore the noise from below. She was almost free when the sound of footsteps on the stairs came to her ears.

'Oh fuck! *Fuck!*' she muttered, losing some of her calm. She pulled at the bonds behind her back with more desperation, pulling them tighter rather than looser in her panic. The fear finally broke through and she felt warm tears wash down her face as the door clicked, a key in the old lock, and then swung open, revealing yet another stranger. This one was older-looking, with grey in his chestnut locks and a bit of a beard. He was casually wearing black jeans and a black knitted jumper which was ragged at the sleeves.

'Please, no!' she whispered. 'Please god, leave me alone.'

'I'm hardly God,' the man laughed, smiling that horrible smile, 'but I suppose to you I must be of that ilk.'

Panicky tears salted Bree's lips, even as she tried to repress them.

'Just let me go,' she whispered, 'I have... have a family, a friend who was with me last night! They'll be looking for me.'

'Oh, will they indeed?' The man smirked and put out a hand to grip her arm.

'Please!' Bree screamed, composure leaving her, 'Please! Don't!' but the man was immobile, and her struggles just caused his fingers to close around her arm more firmly, dragging her along with him. His strength was of the like she had never before known and she felt her stomach turn over in fear, feeling for a moment like she would actually vomit. Her captor was relentless: Bree fell to her knees; he picked her back up again. Bree struggled to escape; he just gripped her harder as he marched her from the room and down a set of old wooden stairs. His hand was strong on her arm and no matter how she struggled, she knew it no good. Bree just wasn't as strong as he was. At the bottom of the stairs, the man pushed an old rotten door and she peered inside.

The sound of Bree's scream cut through the air like a siren calling out its warning. She pushed backwards, trying to escape as her eyes took in the scene before her. There were three men and a woman sat around the room, all of them looking over at her as her captor dragged her inside. There was no carpet and the floor was littered with ashtrays, empty wine and beer bottles, even a crisp packet or two. That wasn't the cause of her scream though, that was for the fixture in the corner of the room. It was a cage. A real cage, like you see in all the movies. It was made of steel bars, about shoulder height. Even that wouldn't have been so bad if it wasn't occupied. Of the two people inside, one was obviously dead, had been for days by the look of it. His face, if indeed he was male – it was hard to tell – was cracking, purple in some places but with a green spot on the side of his cheek. The skin was starting to pull tight, but the bloating wasn't yet done. The stink of the decay filled the room and there was a puddle of liquid in the bottom of the cage. Almost worse, the other occupant was still alive. Bree supposed he must have been her age, seventeen or so. Thin, blond, completely glazed as he stared out at them. The living boy was in rags. His t-shirt might once have held a logo, some band, she guessed, although she could not make out what it had been. He was covered in blood, both old and new, as well as what could have been the liquid seeping from his gruesome cell-mate. He did not react when they brought her in, not even a flicker of emotion in his dull eyes.

Bree screamed again, trying to pull back.

'Shut her up, Jonas!' the woman spoke. 'That noise goes right through me...'

The woman was probably the most attractive of the people in the room, long curls which cascaded down her back in a stunning shade of red which must have been a dye-job. She was dressed in black leather with black paint on her eyes and lips.

A stereotype realised.

The three men were all dressed in more simple clothing than that of the woman. The eldest-looking of them was the one from the night before. In his forties perhaps, maybe late thirties; he wore a white shirt and blue jeans with hiking boots. His hair was short but not too short, so that it framed his face in a style only a decade out of date, his eyes were old, grave and cruel. Both of his companions were younger. The youngest looked perhaps twenty, stern face surrounded by a loose blond mop. His clothing was more casual still, blue jeans, t-shirt, trainers. The third and final man in the room was sat on a chair behind the others. His hair was pulled into a ponytail, a fairly dark shade of brown. His eyes seemed to twinkle, his lips pulled into what must have been a fake smile, and his clothing was just thrown on, rather than worn: black t-shirt and combat jeans, black short-sleeved over-shirt and bare arms. He appeared thirty-ish, perhaps. The guy from the club was absent.

'Oh, now what do we have here?' the long-haired man asked, 'Where'd you find this one, Jonas?'

'This one's a resident here. She belongs to the boss man but we've been given the honour of looking after her,' he said 'we're allowed to taste, as long as we don't kill her.'

The long-haired man stood and walked with the grace of a cat to her side. He stroked her face with long trailing fingers, and then slipped one onto her pulse. Almost gently, his lips went to her throat. This time, though, she was expecting the pain and so was ready to tense for it. Still the shock of it nearly floored her, and her captor, Jonas apparently, had to hold her up for his buddy. The man drank for a minute or two, but he was gentler than the others who had tasted her blood, his lips caressing rather than biting and pulling at the flesh. After a minute, he pulled away.

'Not for me,' he said, shaking his head, and then moved to sit back down. The woman cackled and held out her hand to Jonas for Bree. He handed her over as though she were a doll. Bree let loose another scream, terrified, as suddenly she was surrounded by them, each biting into her flesh, pulling her limbs about. Her consciousness wavered in her terror. Her whole body screamed, juddering as the pain and panic combined. Bree allowed herself to go limp, expecting oblivion, but then a voice from behind them stilled the assault. '…annnd I think that's just about enough…'

'What?' the others all seemed confused as the long-haired one spoke, the gentle biter.

'I said, I think that's about enough,' he said. 'Release the girl…'

'Or what?' that was the one named as Jonas.

Bree watched in a desperate hope, as the long-haired guy looked from one to the other of them. His lips were pressed, his eyes like steel.

'Because if you don't, I am going to kill every last one of you, and then I am going to take the girl anyway,' he said.

3

Reuben stood up, steeling himself for what was about to come. The girl, Beatrice Morgan, stared at him with as much fear as she did any of the others. That was ok, he'd be afraid too if he'd lived her life over the past ten years. Ten years. He could scarcely believe she was still alive after so long. He'd found her by accident in the end too, after so long searching, on what should have just been a routine easy job. There'd been some uprisings in drinker activity lately. There always was when a big nest was cleared and that was the case then – thanks to Hugh!

Hugh Haverly was one of the local authorities, a changer – werewolf – but with a drinker for a brother. The pair kept the peace and took out those who disturbed it, where they could. Despite how he'd had many offers to join the Haverly clan, Reuben tried to keep his distance here he could. Even still, sometimes he mucked in – like when they'd gone up against the last nest, the Orchard Estate. There he'd helped out where he could, done some babysitting of the Haverly place whilst the elders of the clan had gone out to fight. The place was full of younglings who needed guidance when the old man was away and so Reuben helped out when he couldn't get out of it. Hugh Haverly was an odd one, and his brother, Samuel, with him, but they were fair and paid well for his services. Of them both,

Reuben had the most respect – love even – for Samuel. A lot of the clan even thought they were blood kin due to that man taking Reuben in at his worst time, back when the blood thirst had been so strong and he so little in control. He wasn't Sam's kin, but he'd rather that was believed than everyone know the alternative about how he'd been made. Hugh knew, of course, Hugh could sniff out most things but as far as Reuben knew, Hugh was the only one who knew his secrets. Reuben was fairly sure that some of the stuff which had gone down in the taking of the Orchard nest was directly related to that knowledge, but as nobody ever said anything to him, he couldn't know for sure. Either way, it had gone down easily enough in the end. Once more a nest-leader had been slain and the nest had dispersed. As ever, though, with the death of the old boss, several new nests had tried to take shape locally and the old man needed some outside help with getting them cleared – this place was suspected to be one of those.

Reuben had been ready to enter the little cottage out on the moors where this little group were holed up with guns blazing, a quick easy clear-up, but then his instincts had warned him to play it safer. There was something about this nest, something he didn't understand but which led to him approaching with caution, gaining admittance and going undercover – something he did sometimes. It was always worth trusting his instincts – Reuben, as a human, had had "the sight" and when turned, although dulled, the abilities had never left him.

He'd spotted Beatrice on his second night there, about a month ago. She wasn't one of the playthings they had in the living area, not one of the expendables, but was kept mostly hidden, used and drank from only by the elites of the nest, of which there seemed to be two. Reuben had been tempted to try to sneak her out then, and then again when they'd let the other girl in the cage die. The lad in there – Reuben didn't know his name – had declined after that to the living comatose state he was now. Reuben's hopes of saving him had died with the

'Sure there is. We're a race, not a cult.'

'I just want to go home,' she whispered. The knife wobbled in her hand. 'I just want…'

'I know, here, give me that,' the man stepped in and took the wobbling blade from her hand without too much trouble. He patted her shoulder awkwardly, then stepped back. 'Ok, you stay here whilst I case the rest of the place. Ninety percent sure you're safe down here now.'

The man moved to check the piles of clothing, grabbing at jewellery and watches and throwing them into his backpack.

'You're stealing their things?'

'Well… yeah… Gonna torch the place so it would be a waste not to – money is money where I come from.'

Once the bodies were clean, Bree's rescuer set off towards the main door. Bree followed. Ninety percent sure of safety wasn't good enough for her, and this guy at least seemed able, and willing, to offer her some protection. Her mind couldn't quite accept what was going on around her yet but she went with it – what other choice did she have?

'Oh!' the man said suddenly, stopping and holding out a bloodied hand, 'I'm Reuben.'

'Kind of an old-fashioned name,' Bree said, not taking it.

'I'm kind of an old-fashioned guy, and you are Beatrice, aren't you? Beatrice Morgan?'

'I… how do you know my name?'

Reuben paused and a crease took his brow. 'I'll explain that later,' he deferred. 'Is it Beatrice? Bea?'

'Bree, mostly…'

'Brie, as in the cheese,' he said, smiling to himself. 'Well, Brie, shall we?'

Bree nodded and followed him as he made his way up the back staircase. She avoided the first room there though, the one where she'd been held. Wild horses wouldn't have convinced her to go back in there. Reuben didn't let it stop him though and came out holding a small box. He opened it and showed her the content. A Chanel watch which was no longer ticking and a gold necklace with a tiny heart on it set with a ruby. Danny had given it to her on their first date.

'Mine,' she whispered.

'I thought they might be. Here, take them back!'

Bree did so without comment and then followed Reuben into the next room. He seemed intent on searching every nook and cranny, picking up anything which could be seen to be valuable and throwing it into his rucksack. Wanting to be useful, but also wanting to be out of that terrible place as quickly as possible, Bree helped. She found two rings on one dresser and then a purse containing several hundred pounds thrown down in what was obviously one of the women's rooms. Other than her little cell, the rest of the house was carpeted, and some of the rooms were nicely decorated too, unlike downstairs. In one room, painted blue and with a full set of furniture, she happened to pull open a drawer, and there found piles and piles of banknotes. Reuben came up behind her.

'Jackpot!' he grinned, 'Most of us bloodsuckers have one of these somewhere – we don't trust banks, see? Hard to withdraw money when you haven't aged in a hundred or more years...'

'Is this really real?' Bree whispered, still half-convinced she was dreaming, hallucinating, or... something.

'The money...'

'No, I mean the... everything – this...'

'What do you think?' Reuben asked.

'I just... I don't ...'

Reuben turned her to face him, a gentle hand on her arm. 'It's all real,' he said softly, 'I'm sorry. Now come on, bag up this money and let's go rescue that boy downstairs.'

5

The road was grey and featureless, despite that they drove through the beautiful Cornish countryside. Reuben's fingers gripped tight to the wheel; his palms pressed so that the skin felt pulled tight. His lips were taut too and his eyes he forced to look straight ahead rather than down at the sleeping girl in the passenger seat. He was angry, angrier than ever he'd been on behalf of a human being... well for some time, anyway, and angry was not a good state for Reuben. The glory of finally finding the girl held nothing to the fury he felt at her treatment, at her memory loss. Somebody had definitely been fucking with her mind, that much was obvious. The poor kid was traumatised, broken and if his suspicions were correct, finding out how long she'd been gone was going to be another blow, one he wasn't quite sure how to tackle. Reuben inhaled the scent of car air-freshener and soot from the house they'd left aflame behind them. His lungs burned for the rate he was pulling in oxygen and he knew he was coming close to needing a proper feed.

Dangerous.

She was worth it though, lying there hunkered down in her seat with her eyes closed, peaceful at last. Reuben glanced into the back seat at the boy. He was even further gone, gazing out into the darkness of the night with that same glazed look on his face. Unease weighed heavily on Reuben. Over the previous ten years, the strange impulse that there was more to Beatrice's disappearance than met the eye hadn't left him, and now, with her rescue and the strange state of her memories, the worry grew even stronger, the voices within which guided him grew louder.

Reuben's "voices" were something which had existed before the curse which he'd had thrust upon him. Before the torture which had birthed him to what he was now. A strange sort of pre-cognition which he had, in a different time, considered to be the word of God. It had started when he was a boy, with the slightest of things and had escalated from there. A garden party where he'd told "Mama" that a certain gentleman was unwell, having been told such from the instinct within. That same man had died later that night in his sleep. Other, smaller instances – knowing what was inside a gift before opened, knowing what supper was to be before it was served. The voices themselves spoke rarely, as in audible words, but they gave Reuben insight, instincts which he knew were not his own. Now, through enlightenment, he knew they were closer to spirit guides, and that he'd probably held the power for mediumship, but back when he was a boy such a concept had not even existed. Such sight, in the late eighteenth century, was dangerous and could have led to his persecution but Reuben's father, a scholar, had thought quickly and had heralded him touched by God, before the taint of witchcraft was raised. As such, he was placed in an order of Catholic monks to be schooled, from whence he had returned convinced that God indeed was talking through him, guiding his movements, so that when a child was lost, people came to him for assistance, or, when a fortune was on the brink, a few words from him could save a family from an uncomfortable fate.

Reuben sighed and tried to wade back through the memories, back to the present. For so long after his love of his god had been stripped from him he'd been so angry with the world, and therefore so careless in it. He'd done things, many things, he wasn't proud of in his time. This was the time of redemption though, the time of rebalancing and putting his misfortune to good use. He might not believe in God anymore, but he believed in karma, and it was time to re-balance his by going enough good to blot out the awful things he'd done previously.

If that was possible.

Reuben's eyes flit to his passengers again, despite that he was driving. The boy might be past saving. There was little left of what he had been, robbed by trauma. Most likely the family would suggest they abandon him somewhere he'd be found and taken to a hospital. After being in such a profoundly damaged state, it wouldn't overly matter to their secrecy if, should he ever come around, he began spewing forth tales of vampires... he'd be considered insane anyway. Sad but pragmatic. Reuben prided himself on his ability to think sensibly in the face of disaster.

Bree was properly asleep now, albeit only lightly, with her dark blond hair pressed against the damp glass of the window. She wasn't overly emaciated as far as he could tell, certainly not plump as she'd been in the picture on the missing poster, but not gaunt. Her hair looked soft, clean and brushed – had they done that? For some reason, that thought turned his stomach. She was dressed in a dirty white dress, nothing else. He'd have to find her some clothing, and he was going to burn that damn dress once she no longer had need of it. Again, the anger was building but Reuben repressed it. He wouldn't likely have time to meditate or train tonight, so he'd have to exert discipline in keeping his thoughts straight.

G

Bree raised her eyes and looked up at Laniton Church and Parsonage for the first time. The parsonage must have been a couple of hundred years old at least, set onto a bit of a hill in the middle of the countryside. There were trees around the back, but one side seemed to let out onto a clifftop where the ruins of the church were just visible. All about were small blue flowers which littered the rough, un-mowed grass at the front of the property, but the place wasn't necessarily run-down, just tired. There was a green gate which Bree guessed led to the church-path, and the rest of the property was lined by a rickety wire fence. The driveway they'd come up was not a long one, but enough to set the house back off the road so that it felt nestled in the countryside and cosy.

'This was the rectory, once,' Reuben said. 'It's not much now, but it used to be pretty nice.'

'I see.'

Bree looked up over the flaky white and green paint, the front lit up by the headlights but the edges fading darker in the poor light, despite that dawn was coming in fast. She cast an eye over Reuben. Myth said that with the sun he'd be dust. He in turn did seem to be somewhat in a hurry to get inside, so maybe that one was true. The darkness still laced about them though, tinted as it was with the first lights of a dawn about to break. Reuben exited the vehicle and came around to open her door for her before moving to the back seat to unbuckle their silent, traumatized friend. Bree could have run then, maybe some people would have, but instead she just stood staring at the beautiful surroundings she'd been brought to. The lawn, overgrown for sure but still lush and green even in the darkness, stretched on until it met a tall fence which spanned the grounds, and behind this, she could see thick trees too. All around was the scent of pine which denoted the thick woodland through which they'd driven, mingled in with the gentle fragrance of flowers, maybe lavender, that Bree couldn't quite see for the darkness.

From behind came a slight scuffle and when she turned, Bree saw that Reuben was helping the boy from the car. The poor traumatised kid was stick thin; he'd been in that cage for some time. Bree wondered morbidly what his life had been. How long had he been there? How long had the other person in with him been dead? Did they know each other? Had they been friends?

'Let's call you Joe,' Reuben said to the boy, 'I bet they robbed you of your name, didn't they? So I'll give you a new one, Joe, until you can tell us who you really are.'

The boy didn't bat an eyelid. With pressed lips Reuben waved his hand in front of Joe's eyes, and then looked at Bree. 'There's nothing left – poor bastard.'

A noise at the door, and then there was a strange woman standing there. She wasn't much past her teens, if at all. Her face was round with reddish looking skin that was sprinkled with freckles. Her eyes looked green-ish grey, but that might just have been the light, and her hair was loose, dark blond and whilst not matted, not brushed either. She was dressed in black denim dungarees with a pale pink jumper underneath but the clothing looked worn, grubby. She glanced nervously out at the car, but then smiled.

'At last!' she said, 'Reu!'

'Ah, Izzy,' Reuben said easily, beckoning the girl over. 'Izzy, this is Bree…'

'Bree? Not Beatrice? Morgan?' the girl asked, her whole stature was awkward, as though she was on the verge of running away.

'How do you know my name?'

'I remember you from… from the newspaper…' Izzy trailed off and looked to Reuben.

'Yeah… we'll get into that in a bit. This guy we are going to call Joe until we decide how to proceed best with him.'

The girl shuffled from one foot to another and then shrugged and went back inside, attention lost.

'Don't mind her mannerisms,' Reuben said, his voice gentle, 'She was turned against her will and never recovered fully. She was a prisoner like you… I think she might have been a little feeble-minded even before they started on her… sorry, archaic term, my apologies… either way, she certainly isn't at her full capacity now. When I pulled her out of the hell they kept her locked in, she begged me to kill her. She'd been their prisoner for some years, and they'd had… much fun at her expense. I would have considered her request, but I guess I thought I could help her – not that I don't believe in mercy-killings, but… but it wasn't her time. I still don't think she's over what happened, although she's better than she was before so I suppose my decision was the correct one.'

Whilst he spoke, Reuben was leading Joe up towards the house, Bree wondered if Reuben's opinions on the boy were the same as for the poor girl – would he issue a "mercy killing"? She really hoped not, didn't want to go back to terror being her natural emotion. Unable to really do anything else, she stepped towards the open door to the house, following Reuben's lead but hesitating to enter the strange house with this strange creature who so easily confessed to not being human.

'Listen, I know you're drained and rightfully terrified,' Reuben said, glancing over and perhaps reading her hesitation in her face, 'It eases now, I promise. You are safe here and as soon as I can, I am going to take you home to your mum, ok?'

'Ok,' she said.

Reuben nodded and then walked towards into the dark doorway, leading Joe with him.

Inside, the house was welcoming. There obviously wasn't a huge amount of money to keep the place flawless, but it was cosy, clean and uncluttered. Reuben threw his bag down by a staircase which led up from the front corridor and led Bree and Joe into a room off the side, opposite where the staircase went up. Inside was a small kitchen area. It held the standard, an old cooker, built-in cabinets, and a sink set in under a window. A bottle of washing up liquid sat by the sink which seemed suddenly so ordinary to Bree that her confusion deepened. At the edge of the room was a breakfast nook, rather than a dining table – the room probably wasn't big enough for that – which was something like a booth from a restaurant, high backed wooden bench chairs by a fairly large table, enough to seat six. Bree took herself to this piece of furniture and sat down.

The house itself was deathly quiet and still. A light shone outside from above, showing that somebody must be using the rooms upstairs. Maybe the odd girl, Izzy was up there, but there was no sound of footsteps or creaking boards. Reuben guided Joe to the seat opposite, and then flicked on the kettle.

'Tea or coffee?' he asked, another fragment of the ordinary in a disordered experience.

'Tea,' she whispered.

'Regular or fruit?'

'Regular.'

'Milk? Sugar?'

Bree burst into tears.

The outburst was as shocking to her as it must have been to Reuben and Joe – if Joe was even still in there. Reuben moved back to her side and crouched so that he was at her height rather than take the seat next to hers. His fingers pressed hers and his teeth, ordinary teeth, not the monster fangs now, chewed at his bottom lip as his eyes ran over her face.

'There, that's better, right?' he asked softly.

Bree nodded, still allowing the tears to fall and dissolve the lump she'd carried in her breast since her rescue. Reuben rummaged in his pocket and came up with an old-fashioned cotton hanky which he used to dab the tears until they stilled somewhat.

'So... sugar and slash or milk... in your tea?' he asked again, his voice gentle.

'I... er... I...' Bree sniffed a few times, trying to control the hiccup of the residue of sobbing.

'It's ok, take your time.'

'Both,' she finally managed, 'both... please... two – er – two sugars...'

'Good girl,' Reuben's eyes remained sympathetic but his lips gave a small smile. He stood and went back to his tea-making as though nothing had happened.

The mug was hot when Reuben slipped it between Bree's shaking fingers, the smell of it enough to make her stomach growl audibly. Reuben heard it.

'There's some bread that's not mouldy yet if you think you could manage it? Toasted maybe?'

Bree shook her head, she had no idea when she'd last eaten, but she didn't feel starved and the knots in her stomach were too huge to try to fit food around.

As Bree calmed, her eyes cast about finding more points to focus on, the old clock on the wall, kinda dirty, modern plastic, but still ticking away. The little clicking sound it made was almost comforting, rhythmic. There was a calendar on the far wall, but it was two months out of date, the ornate lettering of "March" yellowing slightly, tattered at the edges. Bree's eyes focussed there, and then her forehead furrowed. Her eyes were misreading the date, she really must be tired but for a minute she was sure it read 2018. She squinted at it to try to bring the small numbers into focus but her eyes just blurred more, too tired for all that. She sighed, shook her head to clear the confusion and took another sip of hot tea. It was very sweet, certainly more than two sugars.

For the time-being, Bree lapsed back into silence as Reuben tried to get a reaction from Joe for the hot tea he'd placed before him. His only reward was a slight movement of the boy's eyes towards the cup, where they then loitered. Bree looked down into her own cup, the tiredness was kicking in again, overtaking her form and making her eyes feel droopy. Reuben glanced up at her and was about to speak when the kitchen door opened, shocking Bree back to standing with a little gasp of fear.

'Calm,' Reuben said softly, as she spun about, stepping backwards so that her legs were pushed against the hard wood of the bench. In close to panic, she stared at the guy in the doorway. He looked to be mid-twenties maybe, his build was tubby but not fat and his hair was dark blond, curls which were tight around his ears. His clothing was more modern, skate shoes, baggy jeans, fairly tight t-shirt with the name of a band Bree didn't recognise emblazoned across the front of it.

'Oh! Hey, didn't realise you had company,' the guy said, smiling a goofy grin, 'sorry dude...'

'That's ok, Bree, this is Joshua, Josh, this is Bree.'

'Bree?' the guy said, coming further into the room and flicking on the still-hot kettle to re-boil it, 'Odd name – do I know it?'

'Beatrice "Bree" *Morgan*,' Reuben said, emphasis on the surname, 'She's a victim of a kidnapping...'

'Ah! Beatrice... yes,' the guy said, the sympathy sounding genuine at least as he stirred cheap instant coffee into his cup and added a dollop of milk, 'I'll head back up, catch ya's...'

'Goodnight,' Reuben said softly

Bree exhaled slowly, still feeling a bit frazzled, like a rabbit in the headlights, but forced herself to sit back down. Her tea had splashed onto the table but there was still some in the cup so she gulped at it in an attempt to calm herself.

'My apologies for your startle – I didn't realise Josh was home otherwise I would have warned you,' Reuben said, 'Are you all right?'

Bree nodded, inhaled again and then forced the odd calm back upon herself. 'So are there more than the two of you here?' she finally managed, and was proud to hear her voice didn't sound too wobbly.

'Oh, my apologies, yes! Five of us, in fact.'

'Five? All…'

'All drinkers, yes. Me and Izzy and Josh, and also Jessie and Andy from time to time. We also have an associate in London, Chris, who sometimes stays with us. It might be that you don't meet everybody though, this is a base – people come and go…Sometimes we don't see each other for weeks, sometimes we're all home and it's cramped as hell…'

'Oh, ok.'

'Everybody here is safe, though,' he added. 'Most have had experiences not too different from yours, but that they were turned for whatever reasons.'

'And so you all just live here… together?'

'Like I said, this is a base – the closest thing to home any of us have anymore.'

Bree nodded again and then looked at Joe, he was looking at her, but still with those dull expressionless eyes. 'What about him?' she asked.

'I've been pondering that. I think the best thing for him is to give him to the authorities. I think I'll probably drive him back to the city tomorrow night and drop him in a hospital lobby or something if I can't get through to him.'

Bree nodded and finished the now fairly cool dregs of her tea. Her reflection looked back up at her, oddly distorted so that her face was thinner, older. She stared a moment, then glanced up at the window but the light was not right to catch a reflection there.

'You could take me home at the same time?'

'Maybe. Get some sleep first though. The sun's coming up so I can't go anywhere for a while.'

'I... I guess I could do with some sleep,' she said, 'is there somewhere...?'

Reuben stood and carried the cups to the sink; his own and Bree's he rinsed, Joe's he emptied down the drain first. This done he came back to the table.

'There are only six rooms here,' he said, 'I'll put Joe in the spare room and you in mine...'

'In yours?' Bree felt her stomach tighten again.

'Yes, I'll take the couch up there, it's in the same room but I promise I won't snore...'

'I... uh... the same room?'

'I will be a gentleman, I promise,' he said, 'I need to be up there because the drapes are thick enough to hold out the sunlight even when it's highest at noon, they are not so good downstairs anymore, they need replacing really but I... anyway, never mind...'

'So you are hurt by the sunlight, then?'

'Yes... not all at once, like the movies, but over time it can be dangerous, especially if I were to try to sleep in it.'

'Oh. Why can't I sleep downstairs, then?'

'I don't want you to stay down here alone in case, ah, somebody else comes in and startles you again, or in case you decide to go off wondering and get lost outside in the countryside...'

'I'm still a prisoner, then?' She asked, her lips pressing together.

'I wish you would not see it as such, but just for this one night, I think it safer you remain where I can keep an eye on you.'

Bree nodded again, and then sighed, 'ok, fair dos, ok,' she said, defeated. 'One night!'

'One Night, Reuben agreed.

Reuben led Bree up to the top floor of the house, flicking on and off light switches as they went. Joe walked with them, led by a hand on his arm from Reuben.

'Odd design, this house,' Reuben said, 'there's this staircase which goes up to the north-facing rooms but there's no access to the south-facing rooms from up here, to get to them you go through the pantry and up the back steps. This is my part of the house, so it'll be quieter here.'

Bree nodded, mute once more, exhausted.

'Joe,' Reuben said, pausing in the middle of a panel-lined corridor by a wooden door, 'I am going to put you in here. I am going to lock the door, do you understand? Just for your own safety...'

Bree's lips pressed again, her belly knotting up once more at the idea of the poor lad being locked in again. Reuben went inside the room with Joe whilst Bree lingered outside but she could still hear him speaking in a soothing tone to the lad, telling him where the toilet was, apparently in the closet, and then re-emerging.

'He'll likely piss where he stands...' she said.

'Well, I've sat him down, so at least he'll piss where he sits...' Reuben replied, the vulgarity somehow sounding wrong on his lips, 'Come, my room is the next door – we're up in the attics but it's not dusty or anything, it's a proper room...'

Bree swallowed the fear and followed Reuben through a wooden door and then up a thin staircase to another door, the stairs made for an uncomfortably dark corridor, lit only by a single bulb and once again nerves rushed Bree.

'This is us,' Reuben said, 'let me go in first?'

Bree nodded, he probably wanted to pick up used clothing or whatever, she thought. At least she was conscious, at least nobody was trying to hurt her! She could trust Reuben – she had to, she had no other choice!

Reuben came back out after a few moments and led her inside by the hand, a gentle, kind touch which she didn't mind. Inside, the room smelled like a hippy shop: incense and old used candles. Reuben's space was very tidy, more so than he'd have been able to do in the two minutes he'd been in the room before her. It was quite clutter free, too, with only the odd knick-knack here and there: a statue of an odd Chinese style frog on the windowsill, an ashtray with the dregs of a used cone on the dresser. Of personals, there was a bottle of brut aftershave and a hairbrush on the bedside table. The room itself was fairly large, but seemed less so for the short, sloping ceiling. A modern sofa was pulled up against the one window of the room, where the bottom of the sloping roof met the wall, this sofa was a metal framed pull out bed, made up with blue blankets which could be seen despite that it was folded away. The bed was wooden with four tall posts, but no canopy. It too was made up in blue, with four soft-looking pillows. The dresser had no mirror, but there was something wedged down to the side which might have been one, perhaps it was broken and needed fixing.

Reuben led her to the sofa and sat her down beside him.

'I know you're exhausted,' he said, 'and I am going to let you sleep in just a minute, but first there is something we need to discuss.'

'What?' she murmured.

'In a second, before you sleep. I would imagine you are going to ask me where the bathroom is, and when you go in there, you are going to want to see your reflection...'

An odd fear walked stiletto heels up Bree's spine. Her mind flashed to the car-window, to her reflection in her tea and then to the oddly blurred calendar. A shiver ran all the way through her.

'Bree... I think you are already beginning to realise...' he added, holding her eye, 'on some level at least?'

The fear increased. Bree's eyes moved down to her hands. They were her hands, not the hands of a woman, the hands of a girl! There were old scars though, on her wrists, one on the back of her hand. Wounds which had obviously had time to heal.

'How long?' she asked, her tone dull.

'Just answer me this,' Reuben said gently, 'what year is it? Bree? How old are you?'

'It's 2008,' she whispered, knowing she was wrong, 'and I'm seventeen.'

Reuben's eyes showed sorrow, he did not speak but he did not need to.

'It's not 2008, is it?'

'I'm sorry.'

'How long?'

'I…'

'How long?' Her voice rose, anguish in her tone.

'Nearly eleven years,' Reuben almost whispered, 'Ten years and ten months ago, your parents issued a missing person's report. Your movements were traced to a nightclub where you'd gone with a friend. Then nothing. The only thing they had was your mobile phone which you left on a table and the testimony of your friend and your ex-boyfriend. Some people – him included – thought you'd committed suicide because… because of the breakup.'

Bree's eyes filled with tears but she didn't collapse, held herself strong. Somehow, on a deeper, more hidden level, she'd already known it. That was why she wasn't terrified, that was why she knew what they were… even if her consciousness had been blotted out, her subconscious knew.

'There was a massive media campaign,' Reuben continued, 'your face on every lamppost all over the city, your name all over the news. Your boyfriend, I don't recall his name, was questioned, but it was a false lead. After that they had nothing.'

'They questioned Danny? Oh god!'

'They released him though, he wasn't under arrest for very long. There were no other real suspects, there wouldn't be I guess. Amongst my kind there is an order of us, of those like me, who… who try to help people like you. I knew as soon as I saw the posters that you had been taken by what we call the

Kin, but as much as I tried to, I couldn't find you... I'm so sorry it took me so long.'

Bree's shoulders slumped, her tears building up again but this time tiredness helped her to repress them. She rubbed her eyes and then closed them. The world grew further away, slowly, the darkness becoming more than a mere distraction but a soft pillow to fall into. Bree's body sought sleep. Too wrought to really hold out any longer despite it all. She shuffled a bit and then felt Reuben's hand on her arm again.

'Do you want the memories back?' he asked softly. 'Amongst my kind, gifts differ. I don't have the ability to return them to you but I might be able to find somebody who can...'

'Bree looked down at her filthy body, remembering her nakedness under the cotton dress she wore. She shook her head. 'I think I'm better off not knowing,' she whispered.

'I understand. Should you ever change your mind, you let me know.'

'Ok.'

'Come,' he said, his voice pulling in like a distant echo. 'Let's get you to bed?'

Reuben moved to the dresser and pulled off his shirt. He pulled out a faded black t-shirt which he put on, and then, as though an after-thought, he pulled out another and threw it to her along with a pair of his boxers.

'It's a bit intimate, since we just met,' he said, 'but they're clean...'

Bree nodded, her only other choice was to sleep in the blood-stained dress she'd arrived in. Bree used the bathroom with the lights off, too tired to face her reflection yet, and then Reuben slipped into the bathroom and came back out in just boxers and t-shirt. Bree, who had just climbed into bed, averted her eyes as he walked to the sofa, grabbed the pully which pulled it out to a bed, already made, and then climbed in there.

'Goodnight...' she managed, sleep coming again as Reuben flicked the lights with by the window from where he sat in bed.

'Goodnight Bree,' he replied.
'Thank you…'
'You are so very welcome. Go to sleep Bree…'

7

Reuben closed his eyes and snuggled down on the hard sofa-bed. There, once again his job was done, the victim was saved and he could rest. Another stitch in the never-ending tapestry that was his self-prescribed penance. Every life saved was one closer to his own salvation too, one step closer to amending for some of the crimes he'd committed when he was young in the blood. Inside his mind, the memories began to flood again, memories which were hard pressed to push back. He'd not meditated in days, missed most of his training, and so he was vulnerable to it, the crushing voices he somehow knew he'd never really repress.

Reuben pulled in a deep breath, trying to sooth his inner demons with the soft rhythmic sound of the girl's breathing. He'd saved her! He had done it when all others had given up, just like the other times. Once again he'd proved the gift was just that, a gift! Not the curse of the drinker, but the gift of the saviour. Not God, not anymore… Reuben's preacher days were long gone, but if ever he had or did believe in a higher power, he had to believe that he walked the path of redemption. As long as he maintained control, that was! The meditation helped, as did the martial arts he practiced, usually day in and day out. He had turned to a different form of belief and practice many years earlier, an odd combination of Buddhism, Druidism and other such philosophies which gave more of a gentle, open approach to religion than the Catholic faith of his youth. Not that he truly followed any path now but his own. Age had jaded him against most religion, against most belief, but what he had was at least something. Everybody needed something to strive for, to cling to. Reuben's mind bought him the image of another man, a man with the physical appearance of an twenty year old but a soul so very much older. He tried to push the image away. Now was no time to allow that face to haunt him, the memory of a love both forbidden and unwanted.

'God doesn't exist,' those pretty, almost feminine, lips had stated, time and time again, 'You're better off without him Ben. Live for pleasure, live for the thrill – there's nothing after, not for us.'

And for a time, Reuben had obeyed him, had given in to hedonism. He'd struggle now, because of that, to ever fully make up for some of the things he'd done. That didn't mean he couldn't try though, and now the girl sleeping so quietly in his bed was proof of the worth of what he did.

Reuben wriggled down a bit snugger in the pillows. He yawned and tried to resist the urge to toss and turn in the sheets as sometimes he did when sleep eluded him. As he was drifting off, Bree made a strangled sound and then murmured something that Reuben couldn't quite catch. She rolled over violently with another murmur and then let out a strange half-cry, half-whimper. Reuben dreaded to think what must haunt her mind now, what ordeals lay locked away there to taint her dreams. Poor kid. He allowed his eyes to follow her movements for a moment, then stood and moved to her side. Reuben paused, he hated to use any influence over an already broken mind but he had to help, if he could. Somewhat tentative, he put down a hand on her hair. Despite her ragged and run-down appearance, her hair was soft and clean… washed. Again that struck him as odd, twisting his guts.

'Hush Bree, sleep peacefully,' he murmured, allowing his demon to use his form and exert influence over the sleeping girl, 'let the fear go for now.'

It was the very least he could do, to still the demons so that she could sleep. Bree's breathing regulated almost at once, her body's judders smoothing out until she seemed more peaceful again. Reuben found a small smile – there in the hell that was his existence, there were some perks to being what he was. Satisfied, he went back to his bed and closed his eyes.

8

Bree was awoken by the sound of movement in the room. When she opened her eyes though, the light didn't change, darkness blanketing down on her form. Then the ordeal came back and for a brief moment she lay completely still, convinced that her rescue was the dream, and that she was now awakening to more torture and fear. Rather than fight, her limbs went heavy, her heart thudding at ten million miles an hour and her breath coming as a pant. She had no idea where she was, and the panic clouded the memories of Reuben and his dark, drape-covered windows.

'Are you awake, Bree?' his gentle voice in the darkness helped to pull her back to the true waking world.

'Reuben?'

'Yeah. Good morning – well, evening!'

The sound of a swish and then the curtains pulled to show the final dregs of sunlight vanishing on the horizon. Bree sat up and shook the last of the sleep from her body, that had to be a good 12 hours at least, maybe more if the colour of the sky was any indication. Reuben was dressed again, jeans and a long-sleeved t-shirt both in black, at least as far as she could tell for the dark light of the room. His hair was pulled away into a ponytail again and seemed to shimmer in the last dregs of light from the window. Wet, she realised, she must have slept through him showering. The air smelled more strongly of that heavy, powdery scent too, she realised, the fine haze of an incense cone or stick having been recently burned.

'Hi,' she finally managed.

'How're you feeling now?'

Bree swung her legs out of bed and stretched, enjoying the soft pile of the rug under her feet. 'Ok... better... I slept well, I think.'

'Good. I thought you could shower, then we'll have something to eat? I'd like to know you're rested and fed, then I'll take you home to your mother...'

Bree's chest suddenly hurt for all the emotion. She sighed, letting loose some of the pressure, and then nodded and stood. 'I'm not hungry, but I'll shower – do you have anything I can wear?' she asked. 'I really, really don't want to put that dress they had me in back on...'

Reuben glanced at the offending item, laid in a pile on the floor where she'd changed for bed.

'Izzy will have something I'm sure. If not, we're not far off a similar size, you can have something of mine.

'Thanks. Before I go in there. Do you have a mirror?'

Reuben eyed her for a long moment, then nodded and opened a drawer to remove a small oval shaving mirror. Bree took it and looked onto her face. She bit her lip so hard it hurt. Her once chubby, freckled face was thin, pointed and with tired, hollow eyes. Her long dirty-blond locks were, if anything, thicker and she guessed that her captor must have liked her hair, for it seemed treated and well-cared for. Bree shuddered at the very thought of those monsters brushing and washing her hair. Reuben gently touched her shoulder and she looked up at him.

'You all right?'

Almost desperately, she looked down at her hands, still chubby, still little girl hands. They were the only part of her untouched by age she'd not lived. She didn't have it in her to reply, but nodded anyway, allowing the tears to drip then following their reflection down her alien face in the mirror.

'You're a sweet kid,' Reuben said softly after a few moments. 'I'm sorry for what has happened to you.'

'Thank you. I…how about that shower?' Bree's desire was more to escape those worried brown eyes, than anything else, but her bladder could do with emptying – she'd not peed all day – and she was filthy from head to toe.

'Through that door,' he indicated the wooden door to her left. 'It used to be a closet so it's cosy but it works.'

Bree stepped into the bathroom, finding it oddly anachronistic with its lit mirror and tiled floor. As Reuben had said, it was a small space, but large enough for the shower and toilet, a small sink too behind the door with a toothbrush, of all things, sat in a glass on the edge of it. Vampires still had to clean their teeth then, huh? It was another of those odd moments of normality which, more than anything, pressed home how alien the situation really was.

Bree let out a long exhale, peed, and then got up and glanced in the mirrored medicine cabinet above the sink. That same reflection looked back. It was too weird, too wrong. She stripped off and looked at her naked form. It could have been worse. Unlike poor Joe, she'd obviously been fed enough to keep her body looking healthy. Her arms and waist looked a little thinner, but not too much so. There were a few scars, but they too were minimal, mainly about her wrists. Her face was much thinner, but that was more through age than through emaciation. Her hair was still full of lustre, thick and luxurious and smelling of peaches. Suddenly the scent made her stomach churn and she stepped into the shower and threw on the water, allowing it to become as hot as she could bear.

Finally, when her skin was raw and her eyes bloodshot from the heat. Bree stumbled out and used the towel to dry herself off, then wrapped it about her. It was wide and warm, big enough to swamp her slight figure. She was fine until her eye caught sight of her reflection again but then it was as though the sight of her hair brought back the smell of peaches and she gagged. A sob built up within, hurting her chest to repress and so she allowed the tears as she threw open the medicine cabinet and rummaged about. Her fingers found what they were looking for almost at once, and she brought the scissors out and looked at them, then closed the cabinet. The sound of the hair snipping was almost therapeutic. Bree watched as the first lock fell free, and then with a deep breath, she grabbed another handful and snipped again, and then again, the long hair falling all about her on the floor.

'Bree, are you all right in there?' Reuben's voice was accompanied by a soft knock. Bree stared at the mirror, at the mess of chin-length hair she had left and then almost folded with crying. Another knock, and then the sound of the handle turning. She'd not locked the door – how was that for psychology?

'What on earth…' Reuben asked from behind her.

'I couldn't get the smell out,' she whispered, still making gasping little sobbing sounds. She turned her face to Reuben and watched his brow wrinkle in sympathy. He came to her side and despite that she was clad only in a towel, he put a comforting arm about her.

'Hush, poor kid,' he murmured, then stood her back up straight, 'What a mess you've made of this – do you want me to have a go?'

The very idea of another man touching her hair made Bree's skin crawl and she shook her head and turned back to the mirror, 'I can do it,' she said, and then lifted the scissors again.

The garden was cool in the dimmed twilight, the long grass was damp and soft, soothing to Bree's still bare feet. Izzy had donated her a pair of jeans, bra and pants, which she wore with one of Reuben's long-sleeved black t-shirts, but there had been no shoes in her size to be had so Bree was left shoeless still.

The night air was still fairly chill, despite that – she was told – it was now May and the summer was drawing in. Reuben was inside just getting ready to leave. Poor Joe was already buckled in too, ready to be dropped off at the nearest hospital. She'd probably end up there too, she realised, poked and prodded to try to force the memories back to her – but at least she'd be with her parents, her little brother, Angie, Danny even, maybe… Did those old friends still think of her? She hoped so. If they were even still about, that was. All of a sudden, it struck Bree that despite how she had no memories of the past ten years, those people all seemed so distant. Danny's betrayal, his breaking up with her, that had literally just been the previous day, to her broken mind, and yet the heartache of it had faded. She couldn't remember Angie's voice, her mother's scent…

'Are you ready?' Reuben's voice pulled her back to the present, damn the man, he was as quiet as a cat when he moved!

'I… er, yes! I think so.'

'Reuben nodded and opened the car door for her, settling her inside and then clambering in next to her.

'How far… how far are we?'

'About forty miles or so.'

'Ok.'

'Things are going to be very different when you get home,' Reuben warned, still not starting the car.

'I just want my family! Mama and Daddy and… and… my brother and my friends…'

Reuben seemed to be in inner turmoil about something, then let out another breath and spoke. 'Bree, I don't know if I am really the person who should be telling you this…' he said, 'but… but your father – he passed away a few years ago.'

The word hit Bree like a truck, pulling a gasp of pain from within her. 'What? I…' her hands gripped her knees so tightly it hurt but for a moment she couldn't unclench them. Bree had always been a "daddy's girl", her whole life. Her mother was shrill and busy, her father was – had been – kind and daft, more eager to play with the kids, to make up silly games and tell tall stories.

Reuben turned to face her, his eyes shining with sympathy, 'He... he committed suicide... I'm sorry...'

'Because of me?' Bree's voice was a wail, pain overwhelming every sense.

'Because of the bastards who took you,' Reuben put out his hand but she didn't take it, lost in the swirl of new pain, 'Because the police, after two years, ceased their investigation because there were no leads. Your family threw a funeral life celebration for you and all your friends spoke. It was on the news on the television... your abduction was given closure so your family could go on but I guess... I guess your father couldn't bear to...'

Bree's chest heaved again and then she was choked by heavy, painful rasping sobs which wracked her whole form. Reuben sat still and quiet for a moment, but then put a hand on her arm. In the back seat, Joe seemed to stir, taking Reuben's attention momentarily but then he came back to her.

'I'm so sorry for your loss,' he said finally. 'Perhaps it will help to consider that after death, he was likely spared the agony of not knowing what happened to you, and there he will have been comforted that at least you still lived, and that your rescue was moving ever closer.'

Bree nodded, mopping up the wetness on her face. 'Take me home?' she whispered.

Bree sank back into silence, counting the miles as the car detoured slightly to drop off Joe, then headed towards home. Bree's house was a large one on the edge of the city, gated and off a short private road. Thankfully the gate stood open. At the front, there was a garage and enough parking for two cars. The roses which she had played in as a child grew still, starting to come into bud or bloom which gave off the sweet scent of rosewater which she remembered so well. Bree cast her eyes over them, and then to the front door. Her mother had obviously had some work done, and the brown wooden door of her previous memory was gone, replaced by a uniform plastic double-glazed door. The windows too were new, double-glazed, although they were somewhat more in keeping with the building for their brown frames. Bree lost her breath and turned to Reuben. He was staring out into the distance – some help!

'Reuben…'

'Come on, let's go,' he said, unclipping his seatbelt with a snap which seemed to permeate the silence.

'I'm nervous…'

Reuben glanced at her face, in the darkness his features were a little dimmed but she could see the concern in his eyes. 'I know, best to get it done, though.'

'What if I don't fit in anymore – they will have moved on and…'

'Don't think like that, they are still your family.'

'I know, but how can I ever go back to… and never speak again of… of what I know?'

'It'll get easier, as time passes…'

'I guess,' Bree whispered, and then unclipped her own seatbelt.

Bree's family house was a typical city home. It was large, in the nicer area, and surrounded by a hedge of conifers on two sides, a wooden fence on the others. It was a fairly modern house, yellow-bricked and cheerful-looking sat on the green, perfectly mown lawns. Everything looked much the same, and although Bree's mind told her that it wasn't, that the swing-set which had still been shiny and new when she left was now old and unused, that the flowers in the beds had changed, she could almost believe that she really had only been gone for several days.

'Reuben,' Bree whispered again, 'help me? Come to the door?'

Reuben put a supporting hand on her shoulder, thought for a moment and then nodded. He had changed his clothes before leaving, his hair was brushed, tucked behind his ears and he was wearing smart casuals, black trousers, white shirt, black waistcoat. He'd washed the blood out from under his nails too, but not until she'd pointed it out. He looked acceptable enough to be delivering her home.

Bree got out of the car first, followed by Reuben. She took a deep breath, and then walked the few steps to the door

'Well, here goes,' she said softly and rang the doorbell.

Bree's mother screamed when she opened the door, an actual scream of bloodcurdling panicked shock. Her face went ghostly pale and then she burst into tears. Bree had no idea what to do, what to say. Reuben stepped forward at once to see to her mother, but the older woman batted him off and put a hand on each side of Bree's face.

'Oh, by god,' she whispered, 'Oh, it's you! It's really you! My baby! My baby!' and then she was wailing, and hugging Bree, and wailing some more. Bree hugged her back, her own tears flowing easily down her cheeks. Reuben stepped back, Bree felt him go, but it wasn't until the car started that she realised he was actually making a break for it. Her mother's head snapped up.

'Who is he? Is he the one who…?'

'No Mama,' Bree whispered, 'he… he found me… wondering out on the moors… a-and brought me home. He's a good man, just doesn't want any of the glory I suppose.'

Bree's mother looked out after the car again for a long moment, and then nodded. 'Just look at you!' She whispered, 'Where have you been?'

'I don't know,' Bree replied, 'I honestly have no idea…'

Things at home were very different. The police came, of course they did, questioning Bree over and over until she was too tired to think. Her disappearance had been a high-profile case and she knew they were under a lot of pressure. She just repeated the same story over and over, she'd gone to a club, realised she was being drugged too late to escape and then had woken up on the moors in clothing which was not her own, some eleven years later. There she had hitched a ride with a man, no she didn't know his name, or who he was, and he'd brought her home at her request. Yes, she believed he'd recognised her, no, she had no way to contact him, no, he'd not told her about the case.

Her mother's age upset Bree. Her parents had been older when they'd had her, in their early forties and now her mother suddenly seemed so much closer to old age. Her hair was obviously dyed red – likely to cover the grey, and prettily styled into a bob about her chin. Perhaps the stress had caused those extra lines, those creases in her old papery skin, but still it hurt Bree to see her so aged. Her brother too, was older, no longer living at home but close enough to be summoned, with a wife and a job in the local offices which ran the business her father had once managed. He was like a stranger to her now, a man where last she'd seen him he'd been a pimpled and bratty boy.

The hardest thing about those first hours, though, was finding an answer to all the questions – not of her whereabouts but of her emotions. *Are you all right?'* being the very worst of them because, without her lost memories, she kind-of was all right. Not happy, not well, but all right. The other was her mother's almost whispered question, asked at least twice a day: *'Did you miss me, baby?'*

How could she explain? No, she didn't miss her. She didn't remember anything. She supposed she probably had thought of them, wanted them, but even those memories were gone. All she had was flashes and nothing frustrated her more than the urging of her mother, of the doctors and police: *'Do try to remember...'* as though she was wilfully not remembering. In the end though, she was taken up to a bedroom: not her own – that was long gone she suspected – and left alone to rest. The silence was bliss.

9

The city at night was never as quiet as Reuben remembered it. Bright electric lights everywhere despite that it was past three am. Too many for a small city, really. Two days had passed since he'd dropped Bree home, and finally Reuben was giving in to the urge to feed. He pulled the car up into a multi storey next to a toyshop and stepped out. The carpark was very dim, with just a few faded lights running along the edge by the slope where the cars entered, and a few more by the exit. Being the time it was, he got a space on the ground floor, though, probably safer for the car than the even more secluded higher levels. He used the electric remote to set the alarm too, just in case. He wasn't overly attached to the vehicle but it would be a hassle to acquire a new one.

Reuben pulled the hood of his hoodie out of the back of his leather trench-coat as he stepped out into the night. It wasn't raining but it was cold and he'd rather people didn't see his face and remember it. He was leaving the car behind too for the same reasons, despite that he'd have a good twenty-minute walk through the city centre and out to the more residential areas past the university to where he was headed. It was better to be safe than sorry. He'd not accidentally killed whilst feeding in more years than he could count, but to do what he did, you had to account for every possibility. "*It's impossible to say you will never kill again,*" Sam Haverly – his one-time mentor – had said to him, "*but you can try. It's always best to make sure you have taken every precaution anyway, though!*" Sam had spoken wisely, more realistic in some ways than his brother, Hugh, who had banned all killing outright.

The house was one on a terrace, grey stony effect, with a modern floor and a tiny yard out the front. The front door was double-glazed where once, when Reuben had first begun to visit, it had been red-painted wood. As he opened the rusty wrought-iron gate, a dog began to growl but Reuben was used to "Perro", his hostess's big German shepherd. He didn't mind the dog, it was always locked away when its mistress was about her business anyway, and Reuben fully endorsed Gabi having protection in case she needed it. Mindful of the hour, Reuben murmured through the door to Perro to be shush, and then knocked. Gabi would know it was him, he was the only visitor who came so late, and more so one of the few which didn't send Perro into an uncontrollable frenzy of barking. Reuben's influence worked well on dogs – it was part of his unique gift.

For a long moment there was silence. Reuben lay a hand on the rough brick by the door and let his fingers caress the grains whilst he waited. His heart thudded as footsteps sounded, and then a few words murmured at the dog in Lithuanian. From the other side of the door came a shuffle, and then the sound of a chain.

'Oo isit?' Her accent cut off the "wh" in who, in a manner Reuben always found charming.

'It's me, Gabi,' he murmured.

'Ah, Mister Ben! Come…' she said, pushing the door open and then turning her back to him to shoo the dog behind the gate. Gabi was an attractive woman, about thirty-five or six. She was dressed in a nightgown with her long ash blond bleached hair loose around her. Her body was very thin, and the hallway stank of cigarette smoke. Reuben stepped in behind her and closed the door.

'Are you free tonight?' he asked.

At once she turned about and pressed her lithe little form to his. Reuben closed his eyes and tried not to drink in the scent of cigarettes and cheap vodka. Her hair was soft though, newly brushed so that it was a little flyaway. It smelled like cheap supermarket brand shampoo, but that was better than some.

'Always free for Mr Ben,' she smiled. Of course she was. He paid her well for her "services".

Reuben pushed through his distaste at what he was about to do and kissed her, pressing his lips to hers and probing with his tongue the way she liked. The kiss he allowed for a moment, then lifted her up to carry her upstairs, making her laugh as ever the gesture did. Sometimes her husband lurked below so he preferred to do his business upstairs where he wouldn't be disturbed.

Gabi's bedroom was always messy, but never dirty – she knew well enough to know her clients wouldn't like that. The sheets were always clean and the little walk-in bathroom always scrubbed. Reuben carried her to the bed and laid her down. Her hands moved to unbutton him, then paused – almost remembering – as often she did.

'There, I see the memory stirs,' Reuben murmured, trying to be gentle, 'remember if you need to, but I want you to stay very calm, very still and very quiet.' As he spoke, the demon began to show, making his eyes glow that gentle silver. His teeth were growing in too, the demon within realising that it was about to be fed.

Gabi's body tensed, her eyes widening. Reuben gently pulled her hair away from her throat and nuzzled her there.

'No fear,' he murmured, 'Just a little bite, a tiny pain, and then I will be done.'

Gabi murmured in fear, but didn't scream or cry, locked in his influence. Reuben allowed his teeth to grow in properly, and then with a whispered apology, sank them into the soft flesh of her throat. The blood was thick and rich, spurting a little from where he'd bitten the vein. It was a stark contrast from the silky smooth skin as it spilled out and began to trickle down over her shoulder. Reuben caught the beads which trailed loose on his finger – it would be no good to get blood on the bedsheets – and then put his lips down to taste the thick heady liquid. As he drank, he gently stroked Gabi's hair, his hand soothing as best he could. Once the demon was satiated, he pulled back and rummaged in his pocket for his penknife. The knife was not the one he used to kill, but a custom-made item with a short silver blade which he used to open his own tough old flesh. This item he used to cut open his finger and to let the blood well there. He pressed the wound so a few drops spilled down onto Gabi's torn throat, then gently rubbed them in. At once, the wound began to close. Reuben put his lips back down and suckled away the last of the now cooling red juices, cleaning the wound until it was properly closed.

Gabi's whole body was stiff, frightened. Reuben murmured for her to stay put, and then went for a washcloth to wipe away the last dregs, and to clean his own face of her blood, then came back and lifted her form into his lap. He kissed her frightened brow, and then allowed the demon to surface again.

'Gabriella,' he whispered into her ear, 'You and I just made love, much as we have many times before. You will not remember what I just did and instead will simply remember a sweet tumble in the sheets. When I leave you in a minute, you'll carry on as though I were just another punter – you will shower, get dressed, and then count the money I will leave on your dresser. You won't be afraid, you won't be glum, and you won't remember the pain. Do you understand?'

Gabi nodded.

'Good girl,' he purred, then rummaged in his pocket for the wad of the banknotes Bree had found. He counted out two hundred, then paused and counted out another fifty – it was highly unlikely that Gabi ever saw a sum like that left for her on a normal day and he didn't really need the money. Reuben left the bank notes on the counter and then got up and let himself out. Downstairs, as he passed, he heard the sound of a game show playing on the television. Her husband was there then, at least he wasn't leaving her alone. Reuben patted the head of the dog who looked out at him over the gate and then quietly let himself out.

The walk back to the city centre where he'd left his car was a slow thoughtful one for Reuben. As ever, the guilt and disgust built up within him, blinding him to the sights of the city he would normally have enjoyed: a stray cat sitting on a wall with a stolen chicken carcass, the lights of a party down in one of the basements and so on. Gabi wasn't the only prostitute he used to feed, there were three in his address book, and sometimes – not often – but sometimes, he'd make a visit to one of the underpasses where the homeless slept and leave some poor unfortunate with a clouded memory and a fat wad in their pocket. There weren't so many homeless now though, especially here. This was a small city, without all the noise and dirt of some but still the odd house had a tv or music blaring and, just as he approached the city centre, two people stood screaming abuse at each other. Reuben kept his head down and crept past, half lost in the shadows. Back at his car, he paused. Usually after a feed, he hurried home but today he didn't want to be thrust back to normality just yet. He wasn't sure entirely what was causing it, but he felt more down than he had in years, more lost in his own thoughts. A session of combat training might help, but that would mean going home. He paused a moment longer at the car but then turned and walked away from it.

Outside, Reuben had two choices, to walk back into the main area of the city or head off down a side road towards the coast. This piece of coast didn't have beaches as such, but there was a pretty coastline along one side with a green and lots of little side paths which led down to the water. Reuben took the latter and headed down towards the sea. It was another ten minutes or so of walking before the scent in the air turned salty, and the sounds of seagulls overhead intensified. Reuben slipped off the main road and down to the water's edge. He was almost in tears he couldn't explain. He found a quiet spot to sit down, hidden from the world but still within the earshot of a group of youths who seemed to be having quite the party further along the cliff. Reuben sighed and rummaged in his pocket for his penknife. Back at the beginning of the change, when he'd seen the error of his ways and had made a bid for redemption, then he'd felt this same feeling – the remorse and self-disgust after a feed. The anger at what had been done to him and the painful memories of his life before, his life with Damien.

Absently, Reuben opened the penknife and ran the blade over his own flesh, making the blood pool. The pain was sharp and instant. Back when he was a younger man, a lot of the monks he had grown up amongst had indulged in the practice of self-flagellation – whipping of their own skin in order to appease God. Reuben never had, his own self-inflicted wounds had begun in a world after that, a unjust punishment on a body which wouldn't hold the scars, wouldn't allow for the blood to flow longer than a minute or two. Reuben cut again and again, the bite of the knife bringing forth a grunt as he hit the bone and pulled back. Then, realising what he was doing, he dropped the knife. It hit the floor with a metallic clang and there lay, dripping its ruby red cargo onto the concrete steps.

'Why? Why now?' he whispered to himself. It had been years since the depression had taken him, since he'd cut himself so violently.

The sea did not answer, but before Reuben's eyes, the image of the girl floated, of Bree Morgan.

'No,' he said, still talking to himself, to the demon, 'no, she's gone home. She deserves her life back now!'

Still her face lingered, but then vanished into the ether as the voices of the youths came closer. Reuben shook off his arm, removing the last few splashes of blood. The wound was healed already, with ought but a red mark to show where the knife had bounced off of the bone. By the time he got home, that too would be gone.

It took several weeks for Bree to get really sick of normality. At first, it was bliss to be home with her mother and Scott – her brother, whilst heavy and uncomfortable to see all the changes, especially since her father had passed. His chair no longer sat in its place by the fire, his tools no longer scattered the yard. There was no chocolate spread (his favourite) in the fridge, and nor were his slippers always in the way at the foot of the stairs. In other respects, though, things were much the same. Her mother was still the local darling, attending all sorts of parties and dinner dates. She was in the WI now, and helped with planning the local fairs and events. Scott popped in every Sunday and they had a lunch around the same dining table as ever with him and his wife Cherie, who hadn't yet produced any children but seemed to be planning to. Bree, on the other hand, was very much changed. Where before, her mother's prattle washed over her, sometimes even interested her, now Bree found it dull and irritating. Now that she knew what was different in the world, the whole concept of normality was somehow alien.

On the third week of her return, Bree was finally issued a psychiatrist to try to help her to remember what had happened, police on standby in case she came up with anything new, but

the office was hot and so over-freshened with chemical air-
fresheners that it just gave Bree a headache. She left with false
smiles and assurances that everything was all well, and was
given a prescription for some short-term meds which she
wasn't entirely sure she needed.

Life was lonely too. After a stilted and uncomfortable
coffee with Angie she'd not really felt the urge to reconnect
with her old friends, and Danny's phone number – which she'd
dialled with a thudding heart – had been dead. Nobody really
knew where he was, and the rest had moved on without her.

The main problem, Bree realised as the days passed,
wasn't that she was traumatised, more that her knowledge of
what lurked beneath the surface had opened up a curiosity in
her, one which could not be abated by shoving normality down
her throat. With this in mind, she decided, some six weeks after
her return home, to try to track Reuben down.

Without an address, Bree knew she wouldn't get far so
spent a few hours online on her mother's very modern, light
and compact laptop, trying to find the house. More difficult
than she'd hoped as it didn't seem to be listed anywhere, even
on Google Maps. Eventually though, she used her basic
knowledge of the location and the satellite view of Maps to
locate the church and its adjoining rectory, and jotted down the
closest address to it. Laniton wasn't too far, not really, a short
taxi trip down to the city centre, just in time for the hustle and
bustle of the shops closing and people beginning the march
homewards after work. Then a train – just for half an hour –
and then another taxi – all of which could be billed to her
mother's gifted plastic; Bree hadn't figured out any finances of
her own yet.

Her mother wasn't impressed though, 'Do you even know
who he is? Do you know he wasn't the one who took you?'

'Yeah, I know.'

'How?'

'Because he doesn't frighten me, Mama. He's kind. He was
good to me and I didn't even thank him…'

Her mother didn't look convinced but had handed her one of those strange smartphones that everyone seemed to carry. It was all a bit sci-fi for Bree but she took it and put it in her pocket.

It was close to dark by the time the taxi pulled up to Laniton. Bree paid, stepped out of the car and opened the gate. There was something of a driveway leading up to the house and now that the dusk was breaking, Bree felt more nervous about it. She'd come this far, though, and so set on up the path to the little house which was hidden away there.

'Hello Beatrice,' a voice from behind made her jump as she raised her hand to knock. She spun about to see the geeky looking one, Joshua, stood behind her.

'Oh! I... er.. hi...'

'Can I help you?'

'I'm... err... I came looking for.. for Reuben... I wanted to... I...'

Joshua watched her stutter for a moment with a creased brow, then nodded, 'erm, ok – follow me.'

Bree's heart had taken up like a mallet in her chest. She'd forgotten just how weird Reuben's housemates were. Josh led her away from the house and towards a copse of trees. She followed but on high alert, ready to run if need be.

'He's training down there,' Josh said, pointing to a break in the trees. 'See the path?'

'Oh, ok – I... thanks?' Bree said, but he was already walking away.

As the trees thinned to a glade, Bree caught sight of Reuben's figure dancing with the shadows. She stepped back into the trees to watch. Josh had said that Reuben was 'training' but she'd had no idea his art of choice was something so beautiful. It was some form of martial art, she could tell that, but such a graceful fluid set of movements that it could have been a dance. Bree could see the concentration on his features even in the dark as he posed one movement to another, holding each one for a few moments as he did so. His hair was pulled away in a tail, and his plain black vest and soft trousers pulled tight to show the definition of muscles. Martial arts take a lifetime to master, but Reuben had had that and more, and it showed. Bree was spellbound by him, couldn't take her eyes off of those graceful, almost cat-like movements. She eyed the way his muscles moved, how his face remained serene but his eyes glimmered with steely concentration. A bead of sweat formed and rolled down his arm, that too fascinated her – vampires still sweated, apparently.

As the darkness deepened even further, Reuben paused and picked up the white towel which was discarded by the tree. He wiped his face, then, as he lowered the towel, he glanced up. 'You can come closer, you know…'

'You knew I was here?'

'It's harder than that to sneak up on me.'

'I guess. Is that a martial art? It's very beautiful.'

'Sort of. Any reason you're skulking about in my garden?'

'No… I just… I just wanted to see you.' Bree paused and looked to the ground. The evergreen trees about the glade gave off the sweet scent of pine and for a moment she inhaled it, then exhaled and looked back at Reuben. 'I just wanted to be here,' she added. 'You left so abruptly and things are home are… are too normal…'

'How did you find us?'

'Google… on the maps bit, I knew roughly were we were so…'

Reuben chuckled. 'Ingenious,' he said, 'It must have taken some courage to just come over though?'

'Well, yes. Don't let me interrupt you, though?'

Reuben picked up his towel again and wiped his face, he shrugged, 'I was pretty much done.'

'Teach me, then?'

'Teach you?'

'Yeah – that…'

Reuben seemed uncertain. He wet his lips and glanced about him, 'I don't know how. I mean, I wouldn't know where to start...'

'Oh, ok.'

For a moment there was silence, but then Reuben moved to stand beside Bree. He paused a moment, but then stepped behind her into the shadows. 'I'm going to cover your eyes,' he said.

'Ok.'

He did so, his still slightly sweaty hands coming up to cup over her eyes, shutting out the light.

'Relax,' he ordered.

'Mmhmm.'

'No, really relax. Let your senses reshuffle without your vision and begin to sense what is around you.'

'Sense it?'

'Yeah, hear every sound, feel every sensation, smell every scent. Tell me now, at least four things you can hear.'

'Erm...'

'Don't think, just listen, and then tell me.'

Bree inhaled again, and then tried to obey.

'Ok, I Erm... I hear the sound of a bird – a corvid, I think, and the sound of the wind blowing through the fir of the evergreens. I can hear the sound of... of the cars out in the distance, just one every now and again, and I can hear... I can hear the sound of a dog barking, I think.'

'Good, now three things you can feel, physically?'

'I can feel your hands on my face,' she felt the sensations becoming more salient as she thought about it, 'I can feel the breeze on my neck, and I can feel the pressure of my shoes on my heels. More, I can feel the changes in temperature within me, the tickle of my hair as it moves...'

'That's it, now two things you can smell?'

'Your aftershave, and my perfume, I guess.'

'Just that? Try harder.'

'The trees, I can smell the trees, and… I can smell the scent of you… under the musk.'

'Good, finally one thing you can taste?'

'I can still taste the mint from the polo I ate in the taxi here.'

'Good, now, without opening your eyes, tell me what you feel, non-physically.'

'Like, emotionally?'

'No, more – what do you feel, all around you?'

'Energy?'

'If you like…'

'Well, it's… it's like a denseness, a crackling tingling on my skin – like when you're really tired and you can feel the whole world around you but you're like, cushioned from it.'

'Good description,' he said, and then released his cover of her eyes. Bree turned about, squinting at the evening air. Reuben was smiling, his eyes locked on her.

'That was your first lesson,' he said.

'I don't understand…'

'Peace, that comes first, then the rest. If I say ground yourself, that's what I mean.

'Ok.'

'Good. Now ground yourself.'

Bree nodded, then closed her eyes again, talking herself through the grounding. Reuben's hand on her arm caused her to jump slightly, but his touch was gentle.

'Now,' he whispered, his body moving behind hers, 'when you are grounded, I want you to move, let me put you into the poses first – it's a bit like a yoga-type thing to begin – the combat comes later.'

'Ok,' she whispered, again all of her senses momentarily filling up with him before dissipating back to concentrate on her surroundings again.

'Ok, move your feet so that they are parted,' he murmured into her ear.

Bree obeyed.

'Good, now put your arms here, and here, now breathe. Slow in, slow out. Feel yourself calming, feel your body relaxed but ready. Stay grounded, always, and if you begin to lose it go through the steps again.'

'I feel it.'

'I can tell, your posture is good. Now imagine your feet are rooted – in a good way. You can sway, move and all, but your feet are rooted to the ground.'

'Ok.'

'There, take a few moments…'

Bree felt the tension lifting from her shoulders, felt it all escaping. Reuben's hands took her wrists and gently he moved her form into a pose. Bree held it, stiffening.

'No, relax again, there, you shouldn't have to strain to hold your pose.'

Again, Bree forced herself to relax. For a few long moments, Reuben helped her to move from pose to pose, naming each one as she did so, talking generally about how to apply each one to a more combative style. By the end, despite the gentle movements, she was sweating too, and Reuben passed her his towel.

'You did really well.'

'Thank you – what style is it?'

'Mixture of a couple – most of what we did today was Tai-Chi – it's the gentlest of them all. I incorporated what works for me from several forms and I guess I made up a style of my own.'

'And you practice every day?'

'Yeah.'

Bree put out a hand to touch his vest, it was damp with sweat. Reuben looked down and then put his hand over hers.

'I will try to follow your example,' she said.

'I hope you never have cause to need to know how to fight again, Bree.'

'Me too, but I guess you can never be too prepared. Besides, I need something… something to do with myself…'

Reuben nodded. 'That I get,' he said, 'and thank you for this, tonight. It was nice to have the company.'

'Likewise.'

Reuben lifted her hand and kissed the back of it softly, then smiled, 'I'll drive you home,' he said, 'save you calling a cab.'

11

Bree sat typing at the little laptop that her mother had bought for her. She was sat at her desk, in her room where the warmth of the sun could spill in on her through the window. Her things were slowly reappearing too, most of her wardrobe, piles of ornaments, books – mainly her old vampire novels, something which made Bree smile. She'd forgotten how much she'd enjoyed that sort of literature! It just seemed funny to her now. Even as her fingers typed, though, boring everyday stuff – job applications and college enquiries mainly – she allowed her mind to linger back on the week before. Once again, she was struck by how different the two extremes of her life ran to. One minute to be training martial arts in a dark field with a non-human being, and then the next minute to be sat applying for college and jobs, back in her mother's world. It was a split that the seamy novels her mother had pulled out of the attic never fully encapsulated. There was something in each side which pulled, which beckoned, and Bree still didn't know which would win out in the end.

On her laptop, the little messenger icon pinged to show Angie checking in on her. Despite how they had both enjoyed a catch up a few weeks earlier, Bree and Angie were worlds apart now. Her friend was now a mother of two, married and grown-up – too grown-up. Bree answered the message in kind, then looked back at the application she was working on. This world was no longer her world, in some ways, on a lesser scale, she understood how Reuben and his friends must feel as what was once normal became archaic and modern tech took over. Every day, she sat for an hour reading the news of the past ten years, trying to catch up, to begin to recognise celebrities and politicians, but a lot of it wasn't sticking – maybe because she didn't really care anymore.

Bree looked down at her phone where it sat on the edge of the bed. Reuben had typed his number into it and hit save for her before she'd left, and then had called his own phone with hers to take her number too but so far he'd not used it and another week had passed in silence. He'd probably be lying low now, she realised, hiding from the beautiful day, but despite that she lifted the device and opened up the text messaging app.

"*Are you awake?*" she typed, then waited.

No reply. Well that answered that then. She laid the device back down again. She looked back to the computer, contemplating her next move but a shout from below for her to come and help her mother out with some chores interrupted the thoughts.

It was just past tea-time, later that evening, when finally Bree received a reply to her text message, just as she was washing dishes in her mother's wide basin sink, the smell of apple blossom permeating the entire room. As the little device vibrated in her pocket, Bree picked up a towel to dry her hands and opened up the message box.

"*Sorry, I wasn't but I am now.*"

Bree put down the tea towel and dried her hands on her jeans. "*Hey. Good morning – I guess*" she typed.

"*Thanks. U OK?*"

Bree smirked at the text speak – she certainly hadn't expected that from him! "*All good. Was just…*" she paused, what was she just? *"Just thinking about you,"* she typed, but then deleted it and wrote, *"Just wanting some company,"* instead.

"Sure. Can you get here?"

Bree's heart pounded, her lips pulling into a smile, *"Bit late for train but I can get a cab. If you like."*

Reuben's reply did not come in for ten long minutes, long enough for Bree to worry that he was having second thoughts, but finally it came in.

"I do like. C U soon."

Bree put down her phone and pulled off the little pinny she'd been wearing to protect her brand-new jeans from the dish soap. She paused by the mirror to check her reflection, then went upstairs to pack an overnight bag.

'Mama, I'm gonna go see Reuben again,' she said, running back down the stairs, bag in hand.

'Again?'

'Yeah. I'm gonna stay over there, so don't worry about me.'

'Stay over – with him?'

'No, well I mean yeah but not… it's just easier than trying to get home late… safer…'

Her mother's wrinkled brow creased even more so, her lips pressing so tight they were slightly whitened. 'Will you be back in time for your appointment tomorrow?'

Dammit, she'd forgotten the psychiatrist wanted to see her again.

'I can make sure I am…'

'Do. And there's nothing I can say to talk you out of this?'

'Nothing. Sorry Mama.'

'Well, I suppose… how are you getting there?'

'I was gonna call a cab, if you don't mind?'

'I'll drive you,' her mother said, standing up. 'That way at least I know where you are…'

Bree considered arguing but decided against it. Her mother was only looking out for her after all. Bree pulled on her coat and made her way out to her mother's brand-new Nissan GT-R and climbed in. The car smelled like false pine and the occasional cigarette her mother snuck whilst she was out with the girls. As her mother turned the key and a pop band Bree had never heard of started singing about how they were "Worth a gamble" Bree shut off, blanking out the bouncy music and the wanna-be sexy husk of the lead singer's voice. She didn't really know what music she liked anymore, but this wasn't it.

The drive took less than an hour, with Bree directing her mother as best she could, and only giving a wrong turn-off once. As her mother pulled up at the end of the drive, Bree unclipped her seatbelt.

'Be careful, love.'

'I know Mama.'

'Call me if you need anything.'

Bree nodded, grabbed her overnight bag, and exited the car to begin the quick walk up the driveway. When she arrived outside the house though, it was to find it dark, empty.

"*Hey. I'm here.*" She typed into her phone.

There were a few moments of silence which almost caused a panic, but then the light on her phone came on as the device began to buzz in her hand.

'Hi?' she whispered down the receiver.

'Hi. Bree. I'm in the glade.'

'Ah ok, shall I come down? The house is empty.'

'Not quite – Izzy's skulking somewhere but yeah, come down.'

As before, Bree paused to watch Reuben at the edge of the glade, rather than disturb his training until he saw her and beckoned her over.

'Heya, sorry I lost track of time, I meant to wait for you inside but didn't want to miss what I can get of the light.'

'Hey, I'm not your keeper…'

'I know, but it was impolite to worry you. Fancy a lesson?'

'I – yes… please…'

'Ok, good. Today I want to teach you something a little different from last time, if that's ok?'

'Oh?'

'Yeah, I've been pondering on what you said, and the reasons why you might want to learn this and I thought... I mean, I want... to teach you how to defend yourself if one of my kind attacks you again...'

Bree's heart thudded in her chest. 'I... I'm...'

'Bree, I know that what happened to you before was difficult to reconcile, and I wish I could take the fear away but sometimes foreknowledge and the ability for self-defence can help that.'

Bree glanced out into the thick inky darkness at the edge of the glade. The shadows were still but the thought that somebody or something could be out there watching was a sobering one. In the darkness, Bree's senses seemed to sharpen anyway though. She could barely see but her ears picked up every rustle of branches in the light breeze and her nose could sniff out the pine with a crispness normally known only in fear.

'Ok,' she said, 'yeah – let's do this.'

'I'll show you first, then I will try to attack you and aid your defence.'

'Ok.'

'First, you'll need this,' he added and rummaged in his pocket, he came up with a beaded rosary which held a silver cross, about the length of a cocktail stick He snapped the cord, scattering wooden beads, and slipped the cross off the string, hissing in pain as he did so. Bree put out her hand and looked down at the ornate adornment that he handed her.

'The cross? Bree said, 'I thought that was a myth?'

'It is, but this one is made of pure silver. Silver burns us – I don't know why, or how, but it's a good weapon.'

'Oh, I see.' Bree looked down onto the gilded silver, tracing her fingers over where it seemed to be tarnished.

'It looks old?'

'It is – it was mine... can't really wear it now...'

'I guess not. That was a rosary, wasn't it? You are Christian... Catholic?'

Reuben chuckled, 'Not anymore but I once was – a long time ago I guess. I'll fill you in more one day. Here, there's a chain in my pocket– that's silver too so can you grab it and save my fingers?'

Bree felt her lips pull into a grin as she stepped closer to him and slid her fingers into the pocket of his jeans. Her fingers touched rough silver links and she pulled it free. It was modern and longer than she would normally wear, with the cross falling between her breasts once worn. Bree paused, then unclasped the necklace Danny had given her and slipped it into her pocket to prevent them tangling together.

'There, suits you. I think this is a better home for it than my sock drawer!'

'You're giving this to me?' suddenly Bree was overwhelmed.

'I am. It's not just to look pretty though, it's for protection.'

'Ok, so I have a weapon. Am I allowed to inwardly smirk that it's a cross?'

At last, he smiled, 'go ahead… I see the irony.' Reuben stayed close a moment but then pulled back, business-like again. 'Now, of course there is always going to be variation on how one of us takes prey,' he said. 'I will show you how I personally do it…'

'You *take prey*, still?'

'I do. It's not forbidden but has rules now. We are not allowed to kill, and we have to cause minimal suffering and leave no memory of ourselves.'

'I see.'

Reuben moved to stand behind Bree, 'Now, you won't have time to ground yourself, the attack will be swift and unexpected. What you can do is to touch on the processes we worked through last time to keep yourself calm though.'

'Ok'

'Now,' his voice came from behind Bree, 'what I would do is this…' she heard the footfall, just a single one, and then his hand came over her mouth, pulling her head back. His spare arm encircled her chest, gripping both her arms in one hold. Bree froze, panic overcoming her even though she knew it was just Reuben, and her shoulders tensed as his lips came down to the side of her throat. He didn't bite in though, just stood holding her with his hot breath on her throat.

'Are you all right?' he whispered.

Bree nodded as best she could.

'Good, now, note how I have to use one hand to hold your mouth so you can't scream, that means I actually have quite a flimsy hold on the rest of you.'

Again, Bree nodded, hoping he hadn't noticed just how startled she was at his sudden attack.

'Good, now there's two things which are really important. Firstly, you've frozen tense…' so much for him not noticing then, '…that means when I bite you it's going to hurt like hell. Secondly, your eyes are open. Close them. Close your eyes, do that before you do anything else. Don't panic, don't struggle, relax first. There are two reasons for this, firstly, it's harder for me to exert influence over a person who can't see my eyes, and secondly, it gives you time to ground yourself.'

Bree struggled to do as he commanded, and finally her limbs fell into a more relaxed slump.

'Good, really good. Now I'm going to have bitten in by now, which means I'll be preoccupied. Stay relaxed, put up your hand to the chain around your neck and grip the silver. That will catch my attention so don't swing straight away, allow me another moment, and then bring it up into my face. You won't be able to turn so you will have to trust your other senses to guide you. The eye is a good target but any will be enough to make me step back at least one step.'

Bree did as commanded but was careful not to actually touch his skin. Reuben stepped back one pace, bringing his head up as he did so, in imitation of the silver touching him. With his body parted from Bree's, she felt the gap between them and realised her move; she rolled free of his hands, stepping so that she faced him.'

'Good, but now you are facing me and I can easily grab you again...'

'So spin 360?'

'Sort of, spin until you are free and able to run, feel the energy around you and allow it to guide you.'

Bree did so and found her body moved easier, but then his hand gripped her sleeve as she spun. Bree yanked and came free, almost tripping over her own feet to do so, but she was out of his grip.

'Ok, better,' he smiled. 'What you can do, though, is strike me again as you spin free. Don't drop that silver, it's a weapon, use it again if you need to! Try it mid spin as you free yourself from me.'

'Cool,' she muttered, then put herself back to try again, this time he kept his grip over her lips but a second strike did indeed force him to release her fully.

'Ok, now, with a human, if a human attacked you I mean, it's the same principle, essentially, only on a human go low, aim for the balls and squeeze...'

'Ouch!'

'Ouch indeed! I guarantee he'd release you though... doing that to one of us might have the same effect but we're more attuned to pain and might resist it, hence the silver. It's a more sure-fire guarantee.'

Bree nodded and found a small smile through her concentration. 'What sort of martial art is this, anyway?'

'More like street-fighting, actually, but effective. Ok, Bree – if you will allow it, this time I'm going to actually bite you...'

Bree's stomach clenched. 'What?'

'You need to know how it feels so you can counter it and whilst I'm loathe to hurt you, there's no use pussyfooting around... if you think you could stand it?'

'Ok,' Bree whispered. Reuben stepped closer, paused awkwardly, and then kissed her brow. 'I won't prolong it. If you can't get free I'll stop,' he said. 'Are you willing to try?'

'Yes.'

Reuben kissed her hairline again, then seemed to catch himself and stepped back. He indicated the shadows at the edge of the glade, 'go for a walk then,' he ordered.

Bree, still somewhat terrified, did as she was told. Her body was on alert though and his footfalls came easily to her troubled ears. Even as he came in, she was ready. The bite tore through her, causing her entire body to scream with panic induced by the agony, but she obeyed Reuben's teaching and relaxed, hand to silver, silver to face – and this time she made sure it landed. If he was playing for real, so would she! Reuben hissed and pulled back, giving her space to free herself from the hold and swing the chain at him again. It hit his face causing him to recoil again, and in that moment she was free. In the adrenaline fuelled haze, she actually got several meters before skidding to a stop. Reuben stood watching; the look on his face was obscured by the darkness, his silence a strange drought in Bree's emotions as her heart ceased its panicked fluttering.

'You're pretty damn lethal,' he said, at last.

Bree moved back to his side. Up close she could see a streak of redness across his face from the chain, and shock in his eyes. Reuben touched her throat where it was still bleeding from where he'd bitten her. He put his teeth to his own finger and again the silver gleamed in his eye as the teeth extended. Once punctured he pressed the finger to her throat.

'Wha…' Bree murmured as the wound healed.

'A little skill I have. My kind are all unique in our gifts, my blood seems to be a particularly potent healer.'

'I see. Was that…ok?' she asked.

'Very much so.'

'I wasn't sure if you actually wanted me to…' she touched the redness but it was already fading.

'I don't think I quite expected it,' he said, 'but more because I didn't expect your fear to take you so strongly, knowing it was just me. I'm sorry, I didn't mean to panic you.'

'I guess at least we know I can defend myself though.'

'I guess we do. Come on then, let's go again… less panic, more control. Panic responses will only get you so far…'

Much later, as the night had turned to the purple haze of the early hours of the morning, Reuben and Bree sat together in the long grass. They'd trained together for hours, different holds and how to escape them, and then some more of the dance-like fluid movements he favoured. At last though, Bree's legs had given out and she had allowed herself to fall down into the dewy grass.

'It's a beautiful night,' he said, 'are you warm enough?'

'Plenty, especially with you close.'

Reuben glanced over at Bree, but said nothing. He sat back on his elbows, back outstretched to look up at the stars. Bree followed his gaze, trying to find constellations in the clear night.

'It's easy to see how people were overwhelmed, isn't it?' he said at last, 'to think surely there must be a god up there somewhere.'

'I guess, yeah, sometimes I still wonder.'

'Do you? I didn't know you were religious?'

'I guess we're still brought up on it. I'm not overly so, but I believe there's something bigger than us out there. What about you?'

'Not anymore. I used to be a… well, I used to be very religious, but I have, over the centuries, come to understand my beliefs more as a metaphor and as a code. I no longer believe in a creator, but I believe in the energy all around us, and I believe that that transcends life, somehow. I believe too, in some of the moral codes of several religions but not all of them, especially when they discriminate against people for their lifestyle choices. I suppose I sample them all and turn them into some hybrid which gives me a set of principles to live by.'

'I guess so,' Bree murmured, then lapsed back to silence, looking up at the stars.

That visit was the first of several and as the weeks passed, Bree found that often she and Reuben fell into something of a pattern – training, then inside for food which often she provided after finding that Reuben's cupboards were generally pretty bare. After food, then it was time to talk and even once to play a game of chess together. Reuben didn't watch tv but he occasionally put on some music – fairly eclectic mixtures of genres. He didn't seem to drink much either, despite once or twice sharing a beer or a bottle of wine when she brought them. More than anything, he seemed more chill than most of the other people Bree knew. He didn't need anything to do to fill time, happy to just talk, train, listen to music, even just to go out walking in the darkness, showing Bree the gorgeous countryside around his home. In time she found herself making her way over to him more often even than she was at home, there was something comfortable about Reuben, something safe – despite the irony of that.

'I guess it's because I am the one who rescued you, in the end.' Reuben said, when she finally brought up the courage to mention her feelings. 'You know that more exists in the word than most humans could protect you from, but you know I can. That makes me and my home safer than a world which is still in ignorance.'

'Do you mind that? Do you mind me visiting you all the time?'

'If I minded, I'd say so.'

'Ok... ok yeah I guess but I…'

'I like your company ok, kid?' he smiled, 'I'm happy for your visits to continue.'

Bree bit down on asking if he then looked forward to them, not quite having the courage to ask it of him.

12

Reuben sat himself down in the kitchen at the little breakfast nook and cast his eyes over the girl sat opposite. Jessie was another of his family, although she was much more with it than the rest of them and was barely at home these days. Josh, stood by the table nearby, was making instant coffee – he seemed to live on the stuff – but was obviously listening in.

'Haverly will pay us too – if we take on the jobs for him,' Jessie was saying, 'and we're not exactly flushed with cash at the moment.' Her eyes shone as she spoke, pretty green eyes which had once been so filled with pain. Her blond hair was loose about her, her square shoulders set. Of all of his family, she was the most stubborn too. She'd been freelancing for Haverly for a while, and was trying to get Reuben to agree to work more closely with them.

'I never have and never will stop you from doing whatever you please, Jess, but I'm not joining forces with anybody. I like this little house, and I like my life just as it is.'

'I'm with Reu on this one,' Josh said, but then he would agree – he had been a loner even in life.

'They might be able to help Izzy…'

'Izzy doesn't need help, just understanding!'

'And what if anything happens to you, Reu? How do we get her to feed then? Who stays at home then and cares for her?'

'Well if anything happens to me, then you can take her to them – for now, I'm fine and nothing needs to change. Stop pushing this Jess.'

Jessie nodded, knowing when to back off, and pulled her hair into a ponytail. 'Haverly has donors too,' she said, 'Willing humans. Isn't that better than hunting?'

'You tell me.'

Jessie huffed but then stood and kissed his head. Most of his family, barring Josh, were pretty affectionate – more so than most of the kin were. He touched her hand.

'I promise I'll think about what you said,' he pandered. 'You have to remember, Jess, I was with them before and I chose to split. That was my choice and I stand by it, but if you want to join them, I won't stop you. We each have to...' he paused, interrupted by his phone pinging on the table.

'Bree,' he murmured, casting his eyes over the text.

'You're spending a lot of time with her lately?' Josh asked. 'Yeah...'

'I thought, after Lucy...'

'It's not like that...'

Two pairs of worried eyes took him in, but then Josh shrugged and muttered something about it not being his business, then picked up his mug and headed for the door. More World of Warcraft, Reuben suspected – that being the latest digital addiction. Jessie paused a moment longer, seemed to be about to speak, but then rethought it and patted his shoulder.

'Be careful, Reu,' she said, 'You got so badly burned last time you stoked that fire.'

'I know. I'm being careful.'

'I'll catch you later ok?'

'Ok, later...'

Once she was gone, Reuben picked up his phone and checked the message. Bree was coming over, did he want her to bring anything? He allowed a small smile. Caution was his middle name and yet there was something about Bree. She was a beautiful woman – despite his tendency to call her "kid" – but there was more than that. Jessie and Josh were right to be concerned though, after how badly things had gone at the end with Lucy. Reuben played with the phone a minute, then replied quickly and sat back to wait for her arrival.

That night, rather than training, Reuben took Bree over to the church. As he opened the old gate, a shiver took him but he repressed it. She didn't know about his past – what this place was to him, and she didn't need to, but still he wanted to show her it, to share it with her.

'It's eerie,' Bree commented, stepping through the old gate. She was dressed in black jeans and a knitted black sweater – they suited her. Her hair was still short, but it was growing out a little now, not so elfish. She looked happy, he thought, it was good to see her fleshing out a bit too, losing the gauntness. Women in his time had had curves, waifish-ness was a sign of hunger and suffering, not a goal to be attained as it was in this crazy modern era.

'Yeah – it's a graveyard in the dark – I guess that is always going to be eerie,' he said.

'Should we be here?'

'It's my land…'

'You own the graveyard? I didn't think people could…'

'Things were a bit different back in my day.'

'So you lived here back… back when…'

'When I was still alive? Yes. I didn't own the land until after… though, when I was turned my… my sire, Damien, helped to advance my… status. For his own gains, you understand, but when I left he took it all from me except this place. He left me here to rot just as I ordered him to. In the end, I guess I prospered but in a different way.'

Bree was very quiet – quiet enough for Reuben to turn and examine her features. Her face was serene though, her eyes vaguely thoughtful but more interested in what was about her. He smiled, glad he wasn't freaking her out.

The graveyard still smelled like old moss and dust – despite the showery rain they'd had earlier that day. The ground underfoot squelched a little, and some of the graves were slightly sunken, as old graves did when untended for hundreds of years. Not enough to disturb the dead, but enough to twist an ankle.

'Mind your footing,' he said to Bree, using it as an excuse to hold out a hand.

'I don't want to stand on them at all, is there a path round?'

Reuben led her away from the graves themselves and up onto the path. There he paused and looked over the overgrown resting places.

'You should come here in the daytime,' he said, 'Maybe tomorrow after I'm away. It makes more impact in the daytime when you can actually see the stones and such.'

'It's beautiful here though, calm…'

'Peaceful. I agree. There's a different type of energy here too, softer and… well… I guess I'm not sure – just different.'

Bree relaxed a little and Reuben glanced over to see her eyes closing. Good girl, she was tuning in. Within, his guides, the voices which spoke from inside, told him that this was right, was as it should be. As she stood, Reuben watched her, examined those pretty features. Yeah, she had potential, with a little training she too might be able to do what he did, feel the energies and subtleties of the universe like he did. He'd not give her his blood though, not the demon blood – that was something he was sworn never to do. Let her use her human magics, the parts of that vast brain which remained locked away for most as they passed on through lives of mundanity and boredom, let her be one of the humans who shone.

Bree opened her eyes and for a moment seemed to catch him watching her. She smiled. 'I can feel it.'

'It's strong here.

'Sad though, something here makes my heart ache…'

'Reuben caught his breath and his eyes moved almost involuntarily to the little unmarked grave right on the edge by the darkest corner. Elizabeth, his first wife, who had fallen here on this very land. Not dead by his hand but she might as well have been. There were others too, others he was less blameless in, around the edges. He pressed his lips together.

'Yeah, some pretty messed up stuff happened here, I guess. Some sad stuff too.'

Bree glanced out over the gravestones, 'What… no, I don't think I want to know!'

'You don't, but one day I will tell you anyway. Will you come back into the house now?'

Bree still looked confused, unsettled. He'd explain it all one day, but not yet.

Back inside it was warmer. The old boiler which worked the central heating was running, and so the old stones were nicely heated. Reuben led Bree inside and to the kitchen. The kettle was still hot so he just flicked it on to re-boil whilst Bree found the cups.

'Hungry?'

'Nah, not really,' she said, 'tea sounds good though.'

'Maybe with biscuits?'

'I swear you're trying to fatten me up!'

'I'm just concerned that you eat – especially around me. I don't need to and forget to half the time!'

'I've already had dinner but ok, tea and biscuits!'

Reuben nodded and grabbed the paper bag of sugar and the teabags. As his hand went for the tea though, he knocked the coffee jar, sending it shattering to the floor. He swore but grabbed for the dustpan and swept the shards up, into the bin.

'I'll grab some more tomorrow if you like,' Bree said, 'I'll probably stick around for a bit anyway, maybe go see that graveyard in the daytime, like you said then stay tomorrow night as well – I mean if you... if that's ok?'

'You're more than welcome to,' Reuben smiled, putting the tea down in front of her. 'Sorry, I'm not usually clumsy!' *I'm just shaken tonight* he nearly added, but resisted – that would require explaining why, what the old church was to him. Reuben and Bree drank tea at the breakfast nook, devouring almost half a pack of biscuits between them over tea as they talked. Finally Bree stretched herself out. 'I'm getting tired,' she admitted, 'but maybe a game of something before I sleep?'

'Sure? Chess again? Cards?'

'Whichever,' Bree said. She picked up the now empty biscuit packet as Reuben gathered the cups to rinse, and dropped them in the bin.

'Oh, it's pretty full,' she murmured from behind him, and then made a sound which was almost a squeal. Reuben almost dropped the cups into the sink as he spun around to see Bree holding her hand to her chest. She must have tried to push the rubbish down and caught herself on the broken glass. Then the smell hit him, the scent of the blood leaking through her soft skin.

'Oh... shit!' she muttered, 'Fuck... that's really bleeding!'

Something within him growled. He moved his gaze, his eyes glued to where the beads of blood dribbled loose, dripping into the still open bin. He'd been putting off feeding again and with a sudden jolt, he felt the demon stir. Bree didn't seem to notice, nursing the wound.

'Ouch, ouch, ouch!' she said again, uncapping her hand from where the glass had gone into her palm. The scent of the blood wafted by him again, and Reuben had to steel himself not to let go of his control. The blood was pumping fairly quickly too, she'd likely severed something inside for it to bleed that much.

'Bree, I... there's a... a dishtowel beside you – cover that up, would you?'

'I think it's ok, just sliced the palm.'

'Use the towel,' he said again, using everything he had to hold himself together.'

'Can't you... like... like when you bite? Can't you heal it?'

'I can but... but... use the fucking towel! Bree!'

At his tone Bree's eyes showed hurt but finally she picked up the tea towel. Even as she wrapped her hand though another droplet fell to the ground with a splash, staining the lino. Again the beast lurched within, hungry for that bright redness. How long since he'd fed? A week? Two? More?

'I don't understand. I mean, it's just the same, isn't it? You could even... you could...' she whispered, moving closer to him. Inside, the demon began to roar like a child having a tantrum over something it wasn't allowed but, using everything he had, Reuben repressed it.

'No sweetheart, stop it. Step back.'

'Why not? It won't make any difference to me if you do that and then heal me? Isn't that... that something you... Reuben, are you ok?'

Reuben steeled himself, holding back the want – almost need – to grip that wrist and lap away that blood, he already knew how she tasted, he'd bitten her twice already – once at the nest when he'd rescued her and once in training – but this... this was wrong. Haverly took in drinkers and they had donors but to Reuben somehow that was worse than what he did when he fed, more of a slave-relationship. Reuben had grown up in a time of slaves and he knew how wrong it was, even if half of the donors were in love with the old creatures.

'Reuben?' Bree thrust her bloody hand towards him again, the dilation of her pupils showed that adrenaline was doing its work too. Reuben's eye moved to her pulse where the blood was definitely flowing faster, pumping, he could almost hear the thudding of it, the rush as it moved around her veins.

'Bree – stop it. P...put that away... there's... there's... please! Stop!'

Bree's lips set, her brow creased. Dear God woman! Stop being so stubborn! But she didn't, instead she stepped closer.

'I don't understand why you won't take it,' she pushed. 'I… I am willing. I trust you and I want to feed you, since I can… since I'm already cut!'

Reuben's temper was fraying with the effort of holding the demon back as another drop of blood slid free, soaking through the towel to burst on the lino. His eyes moved to the bead, he could almost taste it and the demon roared again. Well, she was offering and he'd not fed in long enough that it was craving….

'Reuben, I… I want you to,' she whispered. 'I want…. I love…'

'What? No!' he snapped, before she could finish the words, and then suddenly control was gone and the demon began to shine through. Reuben pushed it back with a valiant effort but allowed the anger to enter his tone.

'Is this a fucking game to you? To you of *all* people? Some sort of Hollywood vampire romance? Do you think that feeding me will make me not need to feed anywhere else? Are you saving me? What?'

'I just…'

'You just what? This isn't a game, Bree! Don't you remember what it was like? I could… I could fucking kill you, if I mistimed anything, if I…' he gasped and pulled back the temper, trying to ground himself but within, the beast growled again, pulling to come to the surface. As any demon, it was strengthened by anger. He was struggling now, and in such a mindset, he was scared he'd hurt her. He forced coldness into himself. Another bead of blood dropped to the floor; that wasn't helping! He was losing control. He had to get her out before he hurt her.

'Leave, Bree… please… go… now!'

The girl dissolved into tears though, rather than leaving. He saw it happen, the pulling down of her lips, the tears in her eyes, the juddering as she tried to control the tears. Finally she pulled her damn wounded hand away, but rather than leave, she wrapped her arm about herself, the tears falling in little silver trails down her face and blood smearing all over her other arm, into the fibres of her jumper. She stood there for a moment, her chest juddering.

'Why?' she whined. 'Why are you being like this?'

Usually, the sight of a loved one so wrought would have set Reuben at once to comfort mode, but inside something snapped, control was lost and the demon came through. Reuben felt the subtle changes as his teeth lengthened, and his vison sharpened, a sure sign that his eyes would be shining too, as the demon took them over. Unable to maintain control, Reuben was overpowered by what was within, and what was within wanted to feed. He moved the three steps between Bree and himself in a half-second. She moved as though expecting an embrace, probably thinking he was sorry to have made her cry, but the demon only had one motive, one need. Even as Bree's arms opened to accept him, he grabbed her and sank his teeth deep into her throat. Bree made a sound which was almost a scream, stiffening so that she was rigid with her little hand gripping his hair, trying to pull him away. Reuben tore the flesh open, bathing his face in her hot blood. Fuck, it was like bathing in nectar.

'Is this what you wanted?' the demon's voice was a growl, nothing of his normal soft tone. He drank two more blissful mouthfuls of her hot blood, then added, 'is this your Mills and Boon vampire romance come true?'

Bree struggled, but Reuben had a good hold on her. He bit again, a second wound, and allowed the blood to run over his face, seeping into his skin, probing the wound with his tongue. Bree stopped struggling, her panting breathing slowing, calming. Her hand moved to clutch something at her breast and then he felt the burn of silver at his cheek. He grunted and pulled back, jerking away to see his own crucifix in her hand, the one he'd given her to protect herself just a few weeks before.

To protect herself from attack... fuck!

The thought was enough to make him reel, to make him pull back and begin to regain control. Bree was covered in blood, more of which was pulsating, seeping out from the wound between her neck and shoulder. Her face was a picture of horror and her skin was white as a sheet. For a moment they stood, face to face, eyes locked but then she bolted, knocking over one of the chairs in her panic, and slamming the door behind her. Reuben's whole form began to shake.

'Fuck!' he growled, then, as the demon retreated, satisfied, 'FUCK!' He lifted up the cup nearest to him and flung in at the wall, and then slammed his fist into the table hard enough to shatter his knuckles. Luckily, the old table was solid so held out and his injury instantly began to heal. Reuben panted a few times, allowing his legs to turn to jelly and deposit him down on the bench. What the fuck had he done? How the fuck had he lost control like that? He sucked in two juddering difficult breaths and used a hand to rub his face. He was dripping in Bree's blood. Another juddering breath, but then his eyes moved to the floor, to the bright red trail on the lino which led from where Bree had been standing, over to the door. Shit. That was a lot of blood. How deep had he bitten her?

For a few seconds, the gravity of the situation didn't hit as Reuben's mind recovered from the hostile takeover he'd just suffered, but then he moaned and jumped back to his feet. Wherever Bree was, she was bleeding out. If he didn't want her death on his conscience, he had to find her!

B

The driveway was difficult to traverse in the darkness, especially in a panic. Bree ran, one hand up over the wound in her throat and the other clutching her belly still in fear. The trees above the driveway rustled and whispered together, the wind causing them to sway and let loose the occasional leaf. Bree's breathing was laboured, her whole body seeming to be on fire. There was nobody else about, either. Izzy was usually around but she'd not come down and there were no lights on elsewhere in the house. Bree forced herself to pause halfway down the drive and rummage in her pocket for tissue – she'd dropped the tea-towel in his attack but it would have been useful now! There was some tissue in her pocket, not much but enough considering it was allergy season. She took the wad and held it to her throat but the blood soaked through in record time. Bree was feeling woozy too, light-headed. Her hand still ached from the cut and her neck was agony where he'd gone for her… Bree's brain locked down. She couldn't think about that, not yet. She staggered a few steps further, her boots thin enough to feel the rocky broken cobbles underfoot. She slipped, making her heart thud, but managed to keep her footing. The bottom of the driveway came clearer, but why were there two of it? Why was… Bree stumbled again, putting her hand up to her throat. She was still bleeding badly. Surely that couldn't be right? She staggered again, reaching out a hand for the gate which swayed before her.

And then there was the road. Bree knew the plan, flag down a car, get home to Mama. Mama would be so worried. There were no cars though, other than the occasional sound in the distance. Why would there be cars? There were never cars on this old road to nowhere. Bree sat down. Her head spun and she felt sick. She leaned herself against the gatepost, ready to stand if she needed to… if she *could*, a little voice within seemed to whisper. Bree's eyes began to close. A blink, then a long blink, then darkness.

The blackness was bliss, a calm inkiness where she could float, no body to pin her down, no worries to heavy her shoulders. Memories beckoned, memories repressed but so close they were almost on the surface – not quite, but almost. Bree moved away towards those, away from pain. Darkness washed over her again and she leaned into it, allowing the sensation of the gatepost behind her to vanish, the pain to recede. For a moment, there was just bliss, Reuben, vampires, kidnappings and ordeals all faded as she stepped back into the world of seventeen-year-old Bree. Drinks and laughter with Petey, teenage makeovers and giggles with Angie. Sitting around listening to Danny play his acoustic guitar – Danny, her contentious older boyfriend – he'd been twenty or so when she met him. Bree's mind replayed the music, showed her again their childish kisses and love-making in the basement room he rented in one of the tall city townhouses. Then something else, at the periphery of remembrance, but gone again. An almost memory.

But then something pulled, tugged her back. Bree struggled to maintain the feeling of lightness, struggled to hold on to the memories, but there was something, what? A voice. Calling her name. No, she didn't want to go, not back to the pain, not back to the fear. Bree scrunched up her eyes, but then the voice came again, insistent. Footsteps, running, and then a hand on her arm. No! Bree didn't want to have arms again!

'Bree, sweetheart?' the voice seemed to whisper, 'Bree?'

No! No mustn't wake up. Stay floaty now, let go, let it all go, but then the shaking again, and the feeling of her body being pulled about. Bree tried to let go again, but it was too late, already the bliss was fading.

'Here, poor baby, I'm so sorry! Here, drink this...' the voice spoke again, and then something touched her lips. If the place Bree was in was darkness and floating, then the taste of the nectar in her lips was rainbows and honey. It was thick, sweet. Bree moaned again and this time she knew her lips were working, pins and needles coming back into her body. Another droplet and another. The warmth of something soft against her lips. She gasped and opened her eyes. It was still dark. A cold wind rushing by made her shiver despite that somebody – Reuben – held her tightly in his arms. The softness was the flesh of his throat. Bree murmured, realising what the taste was, what he was feeding her.

'Bree?' his voice.

Bree pulled away abruptly, panting as clarity returned to her. She put her hand up to her torn throat but the wound was healing already, the blood no longer flowing as it had been.

'I don't...' she gasped, speech still difficult, 'I don't want...'

'It's ok,' he murmured, 'It won't turn you, just heal you.'

Bree's breathing turned difficult again, the fear returning with the memories of how he'd changed, how he'd hurt her. She made a little cry and pushed away completely, only his hold on her stopping her from tumbling onto the ground. Reuben's face was dim in the darkness, but his eyes still glowed a little.

'You're safe, it's gone,' he murmured.

'I... oh God!'

'Hush. I'll take you home, I just want to make sure you're ok.' Reuben's voice was dull, quiet and tired, not his usual voice at all. He sounded depressed, unhappy. And so he should be, she told herself, after what he'd done! Still… something wasn't sitting right. Bree pulled herself to kneeing, pulling away enough that his hands dropped free of her body. She knelt for a minute surveying him.

'What happened?' She finally asked. 'That… that wasn't…'

'That is what happens when the beast within me awakens,' he said, not moving to reclaim her, his hands falling into his lap and his face downcast.

'That wasn't… wasn't you at all…' she tried again, confusion battling with the fear now that Reuben was very obviously Reuben again.

'It is a part of me. We are fused together somewhat. I cannot deny it as part of myself, not after all these years.'

Bree stood and moved to the gate, she was covered in crimson stains drying to powder on her hands, her neck, and in places the stains were sticky still, but the few mouthfuls of his blood he'd fed her had at least stopped the pain, the bleeding. She stood by the gate and looked out at the dark road which led away from the house. If she left now, that was it, she knew that, she could never come back… but did she want to? Could she bear to stay now? Knowing what he was capable of?

She turned back around to where he sat quietly by the gate. Her eyesight seemed a little better than it should be, and she guessed that was for his blood he'd made her drink. Due to this, she could make out his features, downcast, and his face still covered in her blood. His hair was mussed, coming loose of its band. Suddenly her belly hurt, the fear giving way to pity she didn't want to feel – not for the creature which had just attacked her – and yet, despite what Reuben said, it was hard to reconcile that the beast within really was him too and not some imposter which stole his body.

'I…' she stuttered, trying to make sure she truly meant what she was about to say before she said it. She did, she thought. '…I forgive you, Reuben.'

He looked up at her, his eyes locking onto her face, he didn't speak.

'I forgive you and I… I am sorry for the part I played. I was playing a dangerous game and my only defence is that I didn't realise the beast I was poking.'

'And you should never have needed to,' he said, still in that dull monotone, 'I am disgusted with myself.'

Bree allowed the words to sit still in the air, then swallowed again, 'Can I come back inside?' she asked, 'I need to shower if nothing else. If I turn up back at home in the middle of the night covered in blood my mother is going to freak out.'

Reuben didn't move, still sat watching her. He seemed to take in a deep breath and then nodded. 'Yeah… yeah, of course… Bree – I'm so sorry… I can't… I can't control the demon when it hungers like that b…but… but it's fed now. I'm… it's safe again.'

Bree nodded and then wrapped her arms back around herself. Inside she felt hollow, fragile, but he looked the same way so she was determined to be the strong one.

Reuben clambered to his feet and then paused, he seemed to hesitate and then nodded and set off towards the house. Bree let out a long deep breath, and then started to walk back at his side. The door was open when they got there, Izzy and another girl – a stranger – standing in the dim light which escaped it. The stranger was blond too, but prettier than Izzy, more made up. Jessie, maybe, the other housemate? Reuben certainly didn't seem surprised to see her there.

'Reuben, what the fuck happened? There's blood all over the… oh!…' the stranger said, her eyes taking in both Reuben and Bree, her brow furrowed, but then she shook her head. 'I don't want to know, do I?'

Reuben shook his head.

'Are you ok?'

'Yeah. Yeah, I think so,' Bree said.

Izzy, silent until that point, looked at Bree for a long moment, then to Reuben. 'Reu, are *you* ok?' she asked.

'Yeah hun, yeah I'm ok,' he said, 'I… Bree cut herself and I…'

'You went feral?'

'Yeah.'

'Damn…' the girl murmured, but moved aside to let them both in. The other, the stranger, put a hand on Reuben's arm as he passed and Bree noticed he squeezed it gently before putting it aside.

Inside, in the harsh electrical light, Bree could see just how much blood she must have lost, both she and Reuben were covered in it. Her white shirt was ruined, although the black jumper she wore over the top and her jeans were probably salvageable. Reuben's face was red with it, the blood drying now into black and plum scaly patches. Bree took his hand and used it to draw him up the stairs to his room, ignoring the mess just for now. Behind them, Izzy whispered a goodnight and then wondered off into the kitchen but the other one had vanished already to god-knows where. Bree hoped one of them would clean up down there so she wouldn't have to in the morning.

Upstairs, Bree showered quickly and then wrapped herself up in a towel and moved back into the bedroom. Reuben was sitting on the floor. He'd lit candles and was sitting in an arc of them with his eyes closed, his hand rested on his knees with his thumb and middle finger pressed together. Meditating, she realised, regaining his control. He opened his eyes though, as she came back into the bedroom, and cast them over her. He looked calmer, more himself.

'Can you loan me a t-shirt?' she asked.

'Sure. Help yourself.' His voice was still a little flat, but stronger than it had been. Bree opened the drawer and pulled out a plain black shirt.

'Am I… am I getting dressed ready to leave… or…'

He inhaled, and then exhaled slowly and stood up. 'Let me wash my face,' he said, 'and then we'll talk. Ok?'

'Ok.'

Reuben slipped into the bathroom and, unsure of the situation, Bree pulled on his t-shirt and her pants. Her jeans she left off though, she wasn't planning on having to run again and she hated putting on jeans after a shower. She sat on the bed, but then moved to the edge so she was less comfortable, but more assertive. Reuben returned after a few moments, finally clear of her blood. He sat on the edge of the bed next to her and took her hand in his.

'Bree, now you have seen what I am,' he said. 'Not a romantic notion of it, but what it is in actuality.'

'Yeah…'

'That you are still here, and so calm, is a mystery to me. I nearly killed you. You were unconscious with blood loss when I found you…'

'I know, I felt myself drifting away.'

'Do you understand now, at least, why I seem to keep you at an arm's distance sometimes?'

'Yeah… yeah I guess so.'

'I'm… you can't see me as human, I'm not. I share this existence with a demon which is exactly the same as those who hurt you held within them – worse, maybe, but I can't explain that now. I work bloody hard, every single day, not to let it take control from me and for a little while I did have it under control too, but it comes and goes.'

'I see that now, but I… I do forgive you, what happened wasn't… I mean…'

'If I were a human man, and I struck you in anger – would you forgive me so easily?'

'I… well, no, of course not but this is different!'

'How so?'

'Intent.'

'Intent and control are the keys in both, it is the same, I think? Or similar?'

'I don't see it as such. You are driven by internal but alien forces which you cannot control, not that you choose not to.'

'Perhaps.'

'I meant what I said, downstairs, about how I feel.'

'I know, but that makes it even worse. Bree, I think it better to forgo human attachment – any attachment – for now. I see you look at me in a way which… which I am tempted to… but I can't. You see now, you *have* to see now, why I can't?'

'You are trying to protect me?'

'Yeah, I'm trying to protect you… but I'm also trying to protect me.'

Bree felt her lips press again, but pushed back the water in her eyes. She nodded, her belly hollow and filled with the same butterflies she'd once had reading a message on her mobile from Danny. She and Reuben were not even a couple – but she felt like she was being dumped again.

'Bree?' Reuben whispered, touching her hand.

'Yeah… ok, yeah…'

'I don't want to hurt you. I'm not asking you to… to go away and never come back, but I am asking you to just… just be my friend… can you do that? As cold as I must seem, I love your company – you… you make me laugh again, you make me smile, but I don't want anything more, anything deeper. I'm sorry, and I will never, ever take your blood as a means of feeding, ever again. Please don't ever offer it – because it breaks me.'

'You don't love me, then?' she could not help but ask.

'Bree, I don't love anybody. I can't. Oh, I have the right amount of family-type affection for Izzy and even for Josh and Andy, Jessie… I'm their protector, it'd be idiotic to say I don't have affection and an attachment to them. And it would be a lie to say I don't care for you, that you are not important to me now too – you are b-but… but I've sworn off all romantic attachments… I… I don't want to fall in love, or to have someone fall in love with me.'

Bree nodded. 'I understand,' she managed to whisper. 'Can I ask you something though?'

'Yeah, sure.'

'If you hadn't… sworn off…'

'Then yes, I think, things would be different between you and I.'

Bree allowed his words to permeate, to soothe and yet to worsen the feeling too. She wasn't sure which emotion was stronger. 'Ok,' she said. Thank you for... for telling me that.'

Reuben slid an arm around her and pulled her so that she was held close to him. 'Thank you,' he said, 'For your understanding and for your forgiveness... for what I did...'

'And... and thank you for your honesty,' she whispered.

'If nothing else, I promise you that I'll always be honest,' he murmured, kissing her forehead. 'Come on, get into bed, I'll take the sofa.'

14

Reuben always missed the scent of the sea air as he drove away from the coast and further up into the country, especially around Bristol where the factories poured clouds full of god-knows what into the air. As he drove, he tried to put the rest behind him too, the half-romance with Bree, his worries about her safety and the guilt of what he'd done to her. His own past, too, stirred within him, visions of his early days of being what he was, of how many just like her he'd done similar to, most of them never again opening their eyes. Those memories stung, they rattled about until he could barely breathe. Feeding tasted better after fucking, when the blood was pumped and filled with the release of hormones. How many corpses had he left naked in a bed? Women who had trusted him, given themselves over to him. Loved him, even. He couldn't bear the thought of it now. In an attempt to quell the troublesome thoughts, he thought instead of his redemption, of the work he'd been doing since. In doing so, he brought back those he'd helped, those he'd saved.

Isabelle was the first he'd rescued, back when his own mind had still been so fractured. For a time, after he'd left his creator, he'd wondered alone but a drinker like him, especially one with no training, no morals, had quickly caught the attention of a higher sphere. Sam Haverly had taken him in, and his brother, Hugh, had put him to work not long after. A chance of redemption they'd said, a slow transition from monster back to man. A journey he'd struggled with. The nest which had taken Izzy was the first he'd gone to alone, outside of Sam's influence. It was connected to Damien and the leader had been a blood brother, of sorts, to Reuben. Reuben guessed now, although he'd not seen it at the time, that this job had been his final test, in Hugh's eyes.

The group had chosen to nest in a house which was pretty stereotypical of the type such creatures used, middling in size but not big enough to be noticed, out on the edge of a fairly large town. Cities were better; more humans to pick from, but towns worked just as well if they were big enough. The house was fairly standard: brick walls, iron gate. It could just have easily belonged to a merchant or trader. The year was 1909, just three years before an unsinkable boat would sink, five before a conflict that nobody could even imagine – a loss of life which would change the face of society not just in England, but all over the world.

Reuben had entered the property through a small opening where the hedges had not yet grown over, and snuck up over the lawn. His initial thought was to simply burn the place to the ground. Sometimes, when he looked at Izzy's face even now, that thought still haunted him. Perhaps she'd have been better off that way and yet, no, she might be damaged from her time as a captive, but at least she'd survived it! In the end, though, it was the thought that the occupants of that isolated house might flee the flames which had stilled Reuben's hand and instead he'd broken a window and entered the property. Inside, the house was much like the one Bree had been held in; unkempt, dirty and neglected. The first two rooms he'd tried were empty, but in the third there was his first victim. In recusing Bree, Reuben had been training for many, many years and so his movements had been smooth and graceful – not so back then. A scuffle led to the two of them rolling on the floor. Reuben was strong – stronger than a drinker should be – but then all of his sire's children were. Damien's test subjects... not just turned, but tampered with, experimented on. The master race of the undead ranks. Reuben was triumphant though, in the end, and after wiping the then new blade clean on his jeans had moved to the next room, and then the next, taking out another three inhabitants in total, the last of which he drained well past saving despite that drinking from others of his kind was unusual and without the benefits of human blood.

Once the house was cleared, again Reuben paused with the intention of setting it alight, might have done but for his senses telling him there was another life somewhere out there in the darkness of those old mould-scented surroundings. Then instinct took over and he began to stomp his foot over the rickety floorboards. The trapdoor was under the frayed grey rug in the kitchen, just an old wooden door set with a ring to pull – most likely once a cold cellar – the house was certainly old enough to have had one. Below was one single room, dark and filled with cobwebs and dust. A human might have had to blink, to clear their vision and adjust to the darkness for a moment, but Reuben needed nothing of the kind. In the middle of the room were three pillars, a person bound to each. The two closest were still human – easy pickings and Reuben wasn't fussy then about who he ate. It ended their suffering at least although even then he felt a flutter of sympathy for the one who had to watch the other die – more painful memories stirred but he repressed them. The third figure, Izzy, was bound by her neck to the post in silver – that was Reuben's first clue as to what she was. Her hands were chained together and the silver chain which bound them was wrapped then about her legs. Her skin was protected at throat, hand and feet so that the silver didn't burn her. Reuben paused, again the memories of his own turning coming back to him – he'd once spent weeks upon weeks bound thus by Damien.

The girl before him hadn't stirred, didn't make a sound. Her eyes were glazed and her body trembled. She'd been starved, gnawing her own fingers and suddenly Reuben realised the game – how long she could last out against the hunger until she ripped free of the silver, despite the pain, and fed. More experiments – Damien's children were obviously carrying on his work. Compassion, a still unfamiliar emotion in those days, flooded through Reuben and before he'd even really registered what he was doing, he was pulling free the chains with his bare hands, despite how they burned.

Once free, Izzy merely stared at him through clouded eyes, her hair was one tangled mat and her body was thinly clad in petticoat and corset, the underwear of the time. She watched him like an animal surveys a threat for a long moment, but then those little fangs showed and she leapt. Reuben caught her but did not stop her from feeding, somewhat guilty that he'd just drained both the humans which could have sustained her. His blood would not soothe her fully, not end the ache, but it would at least help to settle the beast. She suckled for long minutes, but then broke free. Her body stiffened in his arms and then she began to cry. Reuben cradled her as a feeling of brotherly protectiveness grew within him, between them. Both, in some ways, children of the same blood, Damien's descendants.

Izzy was the reason he'd come home by himself, back to the church. For all their good intentions, Sam and Hugh Haverly could not have given the girl the care she needed, and in their service, he'd not have been able to either. It wasn't the easiest of splits, but with his vow to live by their rules, and to check in at least once a year, they'd let him go.

Reuben pulled himself back to the present and pulled the car off into a service station, not far now, but the more arduous part of the journey, into the Welsh countryside, away from motorways and cities, out into the wilds. His hands tightened on the wheel as he began to steel himself for what was to come. The job was another of Hugh Haverly's – he seemed to be taking on more and more of those these days – and involved a group of changers – werewolves – who had been rumoured to be acting out. Reuben was to politely ask them to stop… apparently… and then, if they declined, was to use "other means" to stop them. That was it, all he'd been told. He had no idea what he was walking into or why, but still he'd taken the job without much complaint, he needed some release, something to destroy – that was his own curse and at least this way he wasn't a risk to anyone who didn't deserve it.

As fate would have it, Reuben's destination: a house hidden away in a grassy hillock at the foot of the welsh mountains wasn't a far cry in appearance from the house where Reuben had found Isabelle all those years earlier. The same wrought iron gate, the same non-descript, middling-sized dwelling set into run-down grounds which held the shadows in the darkness. The only difference was the smell, even as he slipped through the gate, Reuben's stomach churned. Not just a case of over-keen senses, this, but pungent enough that even a human nose might have picked it up. Rotting flesh, blood, decay. Reuben's back straightened as his mind put Izzy here, and Bree, and already he knew there would be no conversation before the slaughter.

A sound in the darkness, a snuffle and then the pad of paws. Reuben was ready even as the beast hit him. Reuben fucking hated fighting changers. They were unpredictable, big and heavy, and they didn't follow human-esque, drinker patterns of defence or attack, but were much more feral and animalistic in movement. Reuben gripped the creature's hide in his hands and rolled it off him, its teeth ripped away a mouthful of flesh but that would heal. With a grunt, he pinned the creature and pulled free his knife from his belt. The squeal it made was something akin to a pig in the slaughterhouse and then Reuben was bathed in a spray of hot changer blood. Where drinker blood wasn't overly palatable, changer blood was a different matter, for Reuben at least, and so he put his lips down to drink. The feeding would help to keep him going.

Inside, the smell was worse. Reuben's spine prickled.

This was bad, really bad.

There was blood smeared everywhere, bits of flesh and, as he reached what was obviously one of the most used rooms, bones – so many bones, all gnawed and broken. Even his undead stomach lurched. Changers didn't do shit like this, as a rule, but sometimes, once in a generation or so, he'd faced similar. Just like the bloodlust the drinkers felt, the changers could go feral if they took to eating human flesh – especially if they ate the hearts although he wasn't sure why that should be a factor – dead flesh was dead flesh after-all.

Reuben stood for a minute and grounded himself, now wasn't a time to let the demon through, not a time to lose control! He pulled in a few deep putrid breaths and then made his way further in to where a staircase stood rickety and bare of any carpet over the wooden boards. There were more of them up there, Reuben could sense them. He allowed his body to relax, a stiffened body meant a heavier step, part of the key of stealth was to make his body like fluid. He crept up and pushed open the first door on his left. There he paused again.

The changer within was still in human form, applying a tourniquet to the leg of the human chained to the wall. The boy had already lost the other leg, part of one arm, and appeared to be missing an eye too. His hair was shaved close and there were teeth-marks in the flesh of his left arm which in turn was missing a hand. He was bleeding from the wound where his left hand had been removed and as he shuffled, Reuben could see another wound in his belly deep enough that his intestines showed through. Both the boy and the changer looked up as Reuben entered. The changer didn't have a chance to swap form though – that took long minutes of vulnerability – and in its human form was no match for Reuben. As the changer died, the boy tried to scrabble his way towards Reuben, perhaps seeking help. Reuben didn't have time for that though and turned about as another changer in human form came up behind him. This one gave him a bit more of a fight, probably older than the other two, but still fell to his blade quickly and cleanly. The rest of the house was empty of changers. Reuben moved from room to room quickly but if there were any others, they weren't in the house. As he scoped the upper floor, he pondered on the ones he'd taken out. At a guess, he'd reckon even the elder of them was no more than twenty-five years in the business, the others just cubs so he'd likely been the leader. At least this was a new nest, but God!

There were more dead humans in the other rooms as Reuben searched the place, some half-devoured, others just bones and one more, like the boy in the other room, taken apart whilst still alive – this one was in worse shape though, both legs and half his face gone, even his tongue had been removed. Perhaps Hugh Haverly, if he'd come himself, might have tried to save those left alive, might have been an angel of mercy for the dying, but Reuben wasn't good enough with the mind control stuff to take this away from them, nor was he willing to part with his own blood to heal them long enough to get them to hospital. Mercy killings, he told himself as he gently ended the lives of the two humans, there was a time and a place for them, and this was it. Besides, the blood would keep him going long enough to finish this business.

Back downstairs, Reuben paused. Ever since Izzy, he'd made a pact with himself to make sure he checked for basements in these old houses. He made his way to the kitchen and scrabbled about there, but there was nothing. He moved to the living area, the place where all the bones were, and tried again there. Aha! There it was. He pulled open the door and peered down. Yep, this was a storeroom all right! Reuben paused, unsure of what to do next. There must have been twenty bodies in the basement, all in various stages of decay but thankfully nothing living. Human, all, some so far gone that he couldn't tell what they'd once been, others very identifiable: a girl of about twenty-five, missing her arms and legs as well as her eyes, although that might just have been due to natural decomposition. At the side of the girl were two guys, early twenties probably, and then a woman perhaps closing on eighteen or nineteen when she'd died. Of all the bodies, hers was the least broken, least harassed.

'Who the hell are you?'

Reuben spun about to face another changer. How the hell had he missed the sound of a footstep? That wasn't like him! The changer was another newbie: about twenty years old in appearance, and most likely hadn't lived many more than those twenty years. His hair was cut into a buzzcut and he wore trainers and exercise trousers. Reuben rarely felt vulnerable, but for a moment a chill moved down his spine – he was still below ground level, easily trapped should the creature think to slam the door on him. Thankfully, it didn't, and instead came down into the darkness too. Once more on equal ground, Reuben pulled his knife and the creature fell. Reuben let out a shuddering breath and allowed his tightening limbs to loosen again. His eyes moved over the carnage before him again and suddenly he felt cold. He could burn the place down but the bones would still be found, better to leave this place to rot but that would mean a loss of closure for all the victims' families. Reuben's mind went then to Bree's mother, to her father's suicide. No, maybe before Bree he would have just walked away, but now he couldn't do that either. With a sigh he stood and made his way back up the stairs. He left the human remains, but lugged the bodies of the changers out into his car – he had no idea how anatomically different they were to humans, but he could guess allowing them to go into the police labs for testing wasn't a good idea.

With that done, Reuben slipped back behind the wheel and glanced into the back to ensure the bodies were covered enough for the half-hour drive to the coast. He hated this part, ditching bodies, but with a past like his it was hardly new to him. Let the sea have them, with the current pulling the right way, and they'd be gone long enough just to be bones when found. It was arduous and risky work but it'd be riskier to try to get them home to be buried in his own little graveyard, the one protected by his influence, hidden away from prying eyes.

Finally, once the ocean had claimed her gifts and the car was scrubbed clean with the kit kept in there for exactly that purpose, Reuben stepped into another rarity, a coin operated telephone box, and dialled 999. He didn't wait for the operator to connect him, just spoke clearly and plainly when she replied with the standard, 'Hello, what is your emergency?', stating that he smelled a funny rotting smell and gave directions to the house. Before the girl even had a chance to respond, he hung up. Then, undesirous of losing the last dregs of dusk slipped back into the car and began to drive. He'd grab a hotel or something somewhere to kip during the day, but now it was time to race the sunrise.

15

Bree sat quietly on the sofa in the family room of Reuben's house. Her guts were in knots and her heart skipped faster every time her phone made a beep or vibrated. The first night was hard, the daytime less so – Bree was used to Reuben not being about during the daytimes – but then the second night was hell, even despite the message she received about eleven saying he was rested up and coming home. It was just a job, he'd said, something he needed to take care of, like when he'd rescued her – but the timing was off enough to make her suspect he'd gone at least in part because of what had happened between them. Bree shivered and pulled the throw on the back of the sofa down around her shoulders, then went back to staring between her phone and the window, waiting for the lights of his car, or a text saying where he was, anything!

Bree waited up for most of the night, sitting quietly on the soft overstuffed sofa whilst Izzy sat close by, knitting. An odd hobby for a drinker, Bree thought, but whatever. Izzy barely spoke all night, and then, close on 2am, simply got up and walked out of the room, leaving Bree alone to her exhaustion. Miserable and stressed, she checked her blank phone screen again, and then laid her head down on the arm of the sofa. She had no memory of actually falling asleep, the tiredness taking her against her will. It seemed like only a blink, five minutes of dozing, but when she came around again she found that the room shadows had moved, and someone – likely Izzy, although Jess was still about – had covered her over with a silky blanket. Bree yawned and sat up, squinting at the brightness of the electric light overhead. Izzy was absent but her knitting bag and yarn were still beside Bree on the seat. Bree frowned for a moment and looked about her for what had woken her up. Then voices came to her ear from the hallway.

'Yeah, I know. Thanks...' Bree's heart pounded, that was Reuben's voice!

'Are you ok?' That was Jessie.

'I'm fine. I'm just tired…'

'Tired of body, or…' Izzy's soft tone.

'I'm all right Izz, you know how it goes sometimes. I'll get some sleep. Is… is Bree still here?'

'Yes. She worried for you,' that was Izzy again.

'She did?

'Ummhmm. She nodded off on the sofa in there, shall I wake her for you?'

'Nah, I'll go.'

Bree, not wanting to be caught obviously eavesdropping, put her head back down on the arm of the sofa. Reuben's footsteps came to her and then she felt a hand brushing her short hair behind her ear, the tickle as it fell free, not quite long enough to stay back but long enough to be in her eyes.

'Heya Sweetheart,' he whispered, 'are you awake?'

'Sort of,' she murmured, opening her eyes.

'I just wanted you to know I'm home safe. I'm going to go to bed, do you want to come upstairs?'

'I can do, if you want the company?'

'I am likely to just drift off to sleep, it's been a hell of a couple of days.'

'I'll come anyway,' she said, 'I'm obviously tired too if I drifted off here.'

Reuben didn't reply but took her hand and helped her to her feet. Bree folded up the silky throw and, with a final pat of the soft fabric, she left it and followed Reuben. True to his word, Reuben, once upstairs, merely stripped off to his t-shirt and boxers and climbed into the bed. Bree peeled off the hoodie and jeans she was wearing, then turned off the main light so that the room was bathed only in the soft glow of the lamp in the corner. She went to move to the bed, but Reuben remained there, comfy and wrapped in the covers.

'Shall I...' she indicated the sofa.

'No... there's room for two here...' he murmured, sleepy and depressed. Perhaps not quite so bad as he'd been before, on the night after he'd bitten her, but still pretty close.

Bree's hands trembled a little as she clambered onto the big bed beside him. Reuben rolled over to look into her face. His eyes were very dark. Bree noted inwardly how it always seemed to be easier to read him from his eyes. Even when his facial features did something other, it was his eyes to trust.

'Are you all right, Reu?'

'I was just thinking that it's nice to have somebody to come home to again,' he said. 'It's easy to lose the reasons for what we do, especially when it's tough...'

'Tough?'

'Yeah. Jobs like the one where I found you and Joe are rewarding because there are survivors. This one wasn't like that.'

'They were... changers, Jessie said...'

'Yeah, and they are normally less aggressive than my kind. These ones weren't. They were young, newly made I'd imagine. They had been killing people... eating them. They had stored... rooms full of kids barely old enough to be considered adults. Some dead, others maimed...'

'Oh... god! The changers eat flesh?' Bree sat up a little in shock.

'Not normally, no, but once they start, the beast starts to crave it,' Reuben took her hand and laid a kiss on the back of it. 'You can't imagine…' he said, '…it's hard to fight once it starts. In the thralls, they are dangerous as hell because it's like… like the worst addiction. It's… it's like the bloodlust… if ever I've been starved, don't let me near you. I'd likely kill you before I knew what I was doing.'

'Like the other day?'

'Worse. Then I was able to stop. That's not always the case.'

'Oh!'

'I'm sorry. It's better you know.'

'It is, and I still trust you, Reuben… despite it all. I meant every word I said the other night.'

'I know, but you shouldn't,' he murmured. 'You once said to me that of anywhere, here was where you felt safe but you shouldn't… not around me or any of my kind… we're monsters, Bree… fucking… monsters…'

Reuben broke off and Bree was shocked to see a tear in his eye. She clasped her fingers around his. Reuben didn't seem to notice. Even his skin looked a little grey, not so filled with life as usual.

'Days like today make it harder to remember that I have a noble cause…' He said. 'On days like this, it's hard to remember why I do what I do at all, why I didn't just end this whole fucking mess of an existence when I could have.'

'Was it really so bad, this job?'

'Yeah… yeah kid, it really was. What I do is thankless.'

Bree lifted his hand up in hers to touch her cheek. Reuben caressed the skin there with those soft fingers. His eyes moved over her face with what was almost a longing in them. Then they darkened again.

'I know… I know that you make no attachments now, to humans – to me.' Bree said, speaking quietly and choosing her words carefully, 'but I hope that even if you hold yourself distant, still you feel my life has value?'

'Of course!'

'My life, Reuben, my life that you saved.'

'I…'

'No,' she murmured, 'hear me out. Maybe you are correct when you say that what you do is thankless, if what you do, in your mind, is a crusade to wipe the stain of the kin from the earth. That probably is a thankless task… but if you look at the lives you have saved, the people you have managed to get free. Reu, if it wasn't for you, I might, no – probably – would never have stepped a foot outside of that house. I never would have seen my mother's face, never would have laughed again, would never have met my brother's wife, done dishes, sung in the shower, anything! You did that! What you do, did that!'

Reuben spilled another tear and then suddenly pulled her body closer to his, burying his face in her shoulder. Bree just held him tightly, her heart racing at the intimate touch which she'd never thought to feel from him. Her arms almost shook with the intensity of the emotions within her, and her heart thudded as a wetness dribbled on to her flesh. Her hand moved up to cup his head and she dropped a kiss onto his hair.

'Beatrice,' he whispered, using her full name as a rarity.

'Yeah?'

Reuben inhaled, seemed on the verge of saying something, but then seemed to rethink it and exhaled again.

'Reu?'

'I… it's nothing. I… I'm pushing my own boundaries here, aren't I? Last time I saw you I said I didn't want this but… but tonight I need it. I'm sorry to be confusing.'

'That's ok.'

'Do you mind holding me?'

'No, of course not,' she whispered, Pulling him tighter against her chest. Nothing had ever felt so intimate and Bree had never before felt such stirrings of protectiveness which gripped her in that moment. Reuben's lips dropped a stray kiss on her collarbone, then he settled in within her arms. Bree closed her eyes and allowed contentment to stir. It felt good to be needed like that, to be trusted with his vulnerability, even if it was just for one night.

16

Reuben lay quietly, holding onto Bree like a child held safe by its parent. He was the biggest asshole going, he knew that, holding her like this, confusing her and pushing the very boundaries he'd put in place himself, but still, it felt too safe to give up, too soft and cosy to leave. He moved a hand up to stoke her hair, knowing he shouldn't. He couldn't bear to hurt her; the thought of what he'd done to her previously still haunted him, still cut him deeply, but before that he had to confess, he'd been pondering giving in to the emotions bubbling under the surface. This was his compromise, one night of surrender. He hoped she'd understand.

As Bree drifted into sleep, Reuben's mind flit back to the pitiful creatures he'd found earlier, those two who had not already perished at the hands of the monsters he'd dispatched, those he'd had to end himself. This was another issue he had with the local changer packs, they tended to prize their own kind and demonise his – in truth a feral changer was even worse than a drinker. The word "feral" being so much more literal in those beasts, more animal than people – and yet human enough to still know better. His lip set and he pulled a little closer to Bree. Part of the reason he couldn't give in to his feelings was that he didn't want to expose her to any more of his world.

She'd suffered enough at the hands of the kin. Even having her here was more than he should be doing, he pondered. She needed to heal now, to go and continue her human life... a life he couldn't be a big part of... he'd tried that too before with disastrous results in the end. No matter what they said, humans didn't like to grow old around him whilst he stayed young; that led to resentment, and then to hate. He knew that well – too well. Lucy had grown to hate him. She'd even tried to kill him in the end.

Reuben awoke to the sound of Bree speaking in a hushed tone on her mobile phone. He was wrapped up well in the duvet on the bed but he could smell the scent of her body on him, still, if he closed his eyes, remember the closeness, the feeling of protection and love she'd radiated. It was enough to cause one of the worst waves of inner conflict he'd felt in years... since Lucy had died. Reuben kept his eyes closed despite that the day was already dimming behind the thick drapes, just for the moment, he didn't want to have to wake up, to be the bad guy again and pull away, break the closeness. But then, how could he do anything other? He'd come to her with literal blood on his hands, and she'd wrapped him up in her arms. That wasn't right! That was too much! She deserved better, and she wasn't safe, not with him and in some ways, not from him!

'Yeah, ok, I guess,' Bree was saying down the phone, then, 'Well, if I come home tomorrow afternoon we can catch up and then... mmhmm, yes I suppose... I have a dress that I... well, ok if you like...'

She sounded happy, he realised, and that broke his heart. If only he could fulfil the potential and give her what she obviously desired... and completely deserved!

'Yeah, yeah I'll get him to drive me over tonight then, ok sure Mum... yeah, bye.'

The room went silent and Bree sat down on the edge of the bed. She was very still for a long moment, very quiet, and then her soft hand came to touch his arm.

'Reu?' she whispered.

Reuben's whole body ached. This was the crossroads, the point of no return. He could either pull her in and kiss her, or pull away. He wished it were a true choice. He opened his eyes and for one last moment, imagined the alternative, then gently pulled away from her touch.

'Hey,' he said, knowing that his smile must look as forced as it felt.

Bree's happiness wobbled, it was almost tangible, but she held it together. 'Mum has this family wedding happening tomorrow and she thinks it's a good time to reintroduce me to all my cousins, aunts, uncles and whatnot.'

'Oh – sounds nice?'

'Sounds awful, but I suppose it needs to happen.'

'I guess.' He sat up, pulling himself further away from her, it wasn't easy to do. 'Are you heading home then?'

'Back to Mum's' she corrected, too quickly, 'just for tonight and tomorrow night. I don't suppose you could drive me? Or I could get a cab?'

'I'll drive you,' he said, 'let me get up.'

The drive was a quiet, sombre one. Reuben could tell Bree didn't want to go, but then she obviously also wanted to talk about the night before and he wasn't ready for that either. As he pulled up outside the house, she laid a hand down on his.

'Reu...'

'I... I'll see you in a couple of days, sweetheart.'

'I'll find my own way back, after the party, I...'

'Yeah.'

'And then we'll talk?'

Reuben pressed his lips together and gently pulled his hand away. He didn't want to part badly though, that'd just add pressure to what he guessed was already going to be a stressful weekend for her. 'Yeah... yeah, we'll talk then...' he said, well, they'd have to at some point. 'I mean, what I said before will still stand but...'

Bree shook her head, 'not now, later…' she whispered, then leaned over to kiss his cheek. Reuben allowed himself the luxury of slipping an arm around her and hugging her briefly, then released her.

'Go, have fun at the wedding,' he said.

When she was gone, the imprint of those worried sad eyes still burning a hole in him, Reuben slipped the car back into gear and pulled out onto the road. He couldn't face going home though, so pulled the wheels of the car back towards the city just as he had before. As before, the bright lights of Plymouth weren't exactly bright, but at least the city offered a grey embrace of anonymity. Reuben pulled into a parking space up on the seafront – a vast green park surrounded by coastline and grey concrete beaches. There he stepped out of the car and made his way down to the busier tourist area where the pubs and bars were still buzzing with people rather than to the seaside as he had before. The old roads down there were still cobbled, bringing a twang of nostalgia with them, just as some of the oldest buildings still stood, memorable from his younger years. Reuben moved to the snack bus which stood on the edge of the inlet of sea and bought a coffee – more to make himself mingle in better with the rest of the people milling about, than through any actual urge to drink it. Sometimes Reuben made sure to eat and drink every day, to help him to keep a hold on the tiny fragile thread of humanity which remained within, and sometimes he avoided it for the same reason.

The cup was warm in his hands, the scent appetising enough to encourage Reuben to take a sip – not bad, for coffee made in a bus. He moved to the very edge of the harbour and sat himself down on a bench there which overlooked the water. The bright lights came back and forth as the boats came in and out of the harbour. It was peaceful there and some of the knots in Reuben's back slowly began to ease. He closed his eyes briefly, taking in the smells of the water, seaweed and salt. Somewhere beneath that was the less savoury rotting fish and floating rubbish – it wasn't too bad here though; he'd smelled worse and in less urban areas. The wind on his face was chill, and the odd spitting rain icy-cold even against his dead skin. Reuben exhaled again, slowly, controlled, and then took another sip of the rich velvety coffee, revelling in the sharp undertone. His mouth salivated slightly and his stomach growled at the invasion.

Once calm, Reuben allowed his thoughts to wonder again, to Bree, and to himself. He knew he had to break things off, but it wasn't going to be easy – not for her, who didn't and wouldn't understand, and not for himself either now, he was in too deep for a clean extraction. It was going to hurt, and it'd be drawn out too – he imagined her heartbroken coming over to his house, tears and makeup all over her face, then he'd relent, he'd let her in and… yeah… back to square one He imagined too letting things revert to what they had been, that painful arm's distance. That wasn't going to work either, he'd shown them both the night before that he couldn't always keep himself together – perhaps less so than she could. Then the final choice, to let her in. Reuben had tried that path before, and whilst no person could ever really be compared to another, he knew how it felt to watch a loved one grow old and whilst the notion was romantic, the reality was not. His kind and humans could not "date" could not "marry", not whilst one aged and the other did not. Lucy was the firmest evidence of that.

Reuben sighed again, it was so bloody tempting though, and the more time he spent with her the worse that temptation got. He slipped his hand into his pocket and pulled out the old mobile phone. By the day's standards, it was old and outdated, but it was still modern enough to have a bright lit backdrop and touch-operated screen. His instinct was to call her, or to text, or something, but his attention was taken briefly by a message from Haverly. "*Anything to report in?*"

Reuben smiled a wry smile, then let out a sigh. "*Nest clear*," he typed, then with a sudden burst of cowardly inspiration, he added, "*Any more work further afield?*"

"*Tons if you want it*" the reply came quickly.

"*What you got?*"

Reuben waited a moment, but then jumped as the device rang in his hand. That was about right, he could go into a nightmare scene and take out a handful of cannibal werewolves without losing his calm, but his phone ringing was enough to make him jump out of his bloody skin! He answered the call to hear Haverly's fairly familiar tones coming through.

'Hugh?'

'You want work, you said?'

'Yeah…'

'Not like you to come looking for it?'

'I have a… a lot on my mind, I need a distraction.'

Haverly paused, obviously wary – the old bastard always was though. 'There's a job going on in London, if you want in?'

'A job?'

'Possibly a big one. There's been talk of a drinker club selling humans, we're not sure which yet as nobody's investigated. It's been mentioned several times though by informants and yet my brother has had no joy in finding out too much more using our methods.'

Reuben's mind sprang to Bree, of course it did, 'A club? Selling them? Like a feeding den?'

'We think so. You do undercover stuff, don't you?

'Well, yeah.'

'My lot don't, so your… hmmm… unique way of working might be useful. If we can discover which club it is and infiltrate, we might be able to get a better idea of what's going on there. I don't just want it cleared; I want to know who is running it.'

'I'll do it.'

'Just like that?'

'Yeah.'

'Do you need somewhere to stay? Money?'

'I'll take a place if you have somewhere already? Saves me the hassle of finding one. I have money enough for now.'

'What about contacts? Do you want me to put you back in touch with Sam or others from my clan who are up there?'

'No, just tell your guys who I am and tell Sam to stay away for now. I've got this.'

'Ok, thank you Reuben.'

Reuben muttered a goodbye and then hung up the phone. And so there it was, he thought grimly, the most cowardly thing he'd ever done in his life, putting himself in danger and risking it all again, rather than having "the relationship talk" with the girl who was in love with him. A thrill washed over him for the challenge though, at least this was something different to sink his teeth into.

Bree grabbed a flute of champagne from the tray held in the fingers of a penguin-clad waiter and then slipped outside. It was only ten o clock but she was exhausted already from socializing. This life, her parents' life, felt alien now and her smile had slipped, then cracked over dinner where suddenly, after the focus on the happy couple all day, she'd found herself the centre of attention. *How strange her ordeal had been*, people had said over shrimp pate, *did she really remember nothing? What about the doctors, could they not help?* was asked between mouthfuls of salmon and pork loin mains. *Did she remember being taken? Being released?* And so on… even when the meal was over and questions had died down, she'd felt the gazes of her distant relatives on her, the murmurs of gossip which were forming around her. Escape and intoxication were the best route to end the evening and so she headed out not to the beer gardens but to the plainer yard at the back. Cigarette ends littered about a plain door, leading Bree to believe that she'd strayed into some sort of staff smoking area. Despite that, she sat herself down at a small round table set in by a tall wall which was scattered with bright pink valerian flowers. The noise from within the stately house faded to a dull din and at last she felt relief. She put the glass to her lips, wincing slightly at the tart flavour. Why was it that the more expensive champagne was, the worse it tasted? She sipped again and then put the glass down with a slight clink in the table.

In her periphery vision, Bree saw a shadow at the far gate, by the wall. She started and tensed her body, ready to flee.

'Bree?' It was Reuben's voice, even as he stepped into the dull light.

'Reuben?'

'Hello sweetheart. How's the party?' he said, moving from the shadows into Bree's view. He was dressed in his customary black, a long-sleeved shirt over his normal jeans and black tee.

'Well, they're in there enjoying themselves whilst I'm sat out here drinking... alone' she said, trying a sardonic smile. 'Champagne?'

Reuben took the glass from her fingers and sat down opposite her. He wet his lips with the liquid, and then put it down on the table. His lips held a slight smile but his eyes looked very grave.

'What? What is it?'

'Bree, I need to talk to you.'

'I know, we need to...'

'No, I mean, now... I have to talk to you about... about something.' Reuben looked down at his hands, then back up to her face. 'Sweetheart, I have to go away for a while.'

'Away? Where?' Bree took back the wine glass and took a deep swallow, wincing again at the bitterness.

'I... I've had a... an order from Haverly... that is, the guy who gives me work... I have to go to London.'

'Oh.' The world lunged slightly but Bree blinked the dizziness away. 'Ok. How long will you be away?'

'I don't know.'

'But you are coming back, right?'

'I don't know, not in the near future.'

'Oh.' She paused, 'I guess I'll see you sometime though, and we can talk maybe? On the phone?'

'We might not be able to,' he said. 'If I have to go undercover, like I did when I rescued you, I might not be able to talk.'

'Ok.' Bree's heart sank further. She put a hand on his arm, determined to be strong. 'Look, I get it,' she said, 'I know you have to work and I know you don't... don't like to have attachments and last night was... was pretty intense but... I mean, if possible I'd like to stay in touch... not as your... your girlfriend but just...'

'Aren't you, though?'

'What?'

'My *girlfriend*? Kind of?'

Bree shook her head, remembering the time he'd spent sleeping in her arms with a pang so strong it almost physically hurt. Rather than get weepy again, she pulled on her annoyance. 'No,' she hissed, 'no, you made it very clear that I'm not.'

'And yet I know that you spend every moment you can with me. You are hurting now at the thought of me leaving. More so than you want me to see.'

'I am, but I can push my feelings aside, lock them away.'

'Can you? I know I can't.'

The words echoed out into the night, painful glorious agony. Bree took in a shuddering breath, tears brewing. 'What are you saying?'

'I am saying that even though I never meant for this to happen I am attached to you. I love... I... I care so deeply for you. I'm feeling stuff and I don't want to. I have to go, I have to stop this, whatever it is, it's not fair on either you or me! Leaving is already going to hurt like hell and nothing's happened between us yet!'

It was Bree's turn to take in a long inhale. The glass shook in her fingers and her mind seemed to suddenly blank. With real fear of spilling the dregs of the champagne, she put the cool glass flute down onto the table. Reuben was watching her like a hunter watches prey. His eyes showed the vulnerability he'd just laid before her, but anyone who knew him less well might have missed the trace of it on his features.

'I suppose you must know that I love you?' she said. 'I'll use the word if you can't!'

'Of course I know,' he murmured, picking up the glass again and taking another sip of Bree's almost depleted champagne. 'Of course I do.'

'So here it is, you love me but you don't want to, so now you have to go away you think a clean cut is better? Is that the gist of it?'

'I guess.'

'Well that's just… just fucking great…' she snapped, then put her hands up over her eyes. Her head was starting to pound again, fantastic! Another headache! She'd been having a few of them lately. She couldn't decide if she was devastated or furious but her heart thudded too loudly, her hands shook. 'Just fucking great…' she repeated.

Reuben moved closer and tried to take her into his arms but she pushed him off. 'No, get away from me Reu… leave me alone!'

'This is for the best…'

'No, it isn't, it's best for *you!*'

Reuben's eyes flashed again and his lips set. 'For both involved,' he snapped, 'What do you want? Me to take you with me? On a job? "*Hi guys, I'm looking for work in your ultra-dangerous feeding pen of a club… oh, and by the way, here's my human girlfriend…*" how do you suppose that would go down?'

'Don't be an asshole!' Bree hissed, standing to make herself feel stronger whilst fighting harder against the tears, 'and don't fucking snap at me…'

'I'm sorry, I didn't mean to snap.' At once Reuben was docile again, he shuffled from foot to foot, then laid a hand on her arm, 'I'm hurting too,' he murmured. At once Bree's anger collapsed. She stepped closer and physically lifted his arms, pulling them around her. He held himself stiff for a moment, but then gave in and pressed her to him.

'I'm tired of playing games of hot and cold with you Reuben,' she said against his chest. 'Could we not just give in to this now? I'll come up to London but find lodgings somewhere and... I guess see you when I can?'

'I can't. It's too dangerous. I'd move heaven and earth to protect you Bree. That fact alone could compromise everything if somebody with the motive to do harm discovered it. You become a weapon in the wrong hands, and I can't risk that.'

Bree pushed back against the tears again. She wasn't going to cry again! Her hands felt shaky though and her heart was racing hard enough to leave her feeling breathless. She stood for a moment in silence, her mind racing over the scenarios possible, eventually though, she stepped back so that she was facing Reuben, but no longer in his arms.

'So what then... when do you leave?'

'Now, tonight. The car is all packed up, I just came to find you before I left Devon. I had to say goodbye – I might seem it now, but I'm not cruel.'

'Now? Really? Now?'

'I'm sorry.'

Another tear fell, and then another. Bree pursed her lips, feeling somewhat unable to communicate properly. Reuben took up her hand in his and kissed it. 'I never, ever wanted to cause you – anyone really – any pain. I'm so sorry, I should not have allowed things to get this far.'

'No, you shouldn't! Neither of us should!' Bree's voice was harsh but she needed the harshness to hold back her churning emotions. Reuben kissed her cheek, taking up some of the water there on his lips. His hand slipped behind her head and pulled it to his chest again. Bree leaned in and inhaled the spicy scent of his aftershave.

'You're right,' he said, 'but on the same note I guess I'll never be able to genuinely apologise for the way I feel about you, I think that's probably the very best part of me.'

'Will you... will you do something for me then?'

'Anything in my power?'

'Leave tomorrow night.'

'Does it really make a difference when I go?'

'Yes!' Bree pulled away so that she could look into his eyes. 'It does! Until this very moment I had no idea that the way I was feeling was reciprocated. Tonight, you are laid bare – tonight I'm not just your friend, I'm more! Make this moment last just a little longer for me? I'll come with you now – I just need to get my coat… we'll go home, anywhere… and we can spend this one night together? I want to… I mean, I want you to…' Bree broke off, too embarrassed but Reuben was pondering it, she could see from the look in his eye. 'Please, Reu… it's all I've ever asked of you!'

'It will make it so very much harder to say goodbye.'

'Perhaps, but maybe it will make it easier to be apart.'

'I will still have to go, you realise?'

'I know.'

'This won't change my mind.'

'That's not why I'm saying it.'

Reuben nodded and ran a hand through his hair. His eyes lingered over her. 'All right then,' he said at last. His voice was almost a whisper, 'one night, one day. I'll leave tomorrow night.'

Bree's chest loosened a little. She picked up the champagne glass and finished the last mouthful, then stood. 'I'm going to say goodbye to my mother and grab my coat. Swear to me you'll still be here when I get back?'

'Of course.'

Bree all but ran back into the venue, a warm gust of air coming out through the door, accompanied by a wall of noise: cheesy pop music, people talking and laughing. A civilised party turned to more of a rabble for the litres of good champagne which had been consumed. Bree found her mother and whispered her apologies, then grabbed her coat from the stand and ran back out into the beer garden. Her heart thudded to see the space deserted, but then Reuben's voice from just beyond the gate.

'I'm over here, baby.'

Reuben drove not home to his house, but instead to a small hotel on the outskirts of Exeter. It was quite a drive but at Bree's murmured questioning Reuben merely muttered that he didn't want to share the night with others. Once at the little lodge-style hotel set into a backdrop of trees on the edge of the moors, Reuben unclipped his seatbelt and turned to her. 'Are you all right? You've very quiet...'

'I'm thinking, putting things to rights in my head. I'm sad too — obviously so sad but I'm not going to let that seep into this night...'

'I'm sad too but let's make a deal — no more weeping until tomorrow?'

'I think I can manage that,' Bree whispered, a lone tear calling out her lie but Reuben didn't seem to see it in the darkness. He took in a deep breath and then put on his half-smile.

'Let's go in,' he said.

Inside, the foyer was lit by an artificial orange glow. The guy behind the desk was smiling and adorned in the standard white shirt, black trousers. Reuben had taken Bree's hand as they got out of the car and held it tightly in his.

'Name of reservation please?'

'I don't have a reservation,' Reuben replied.

'Oh,' the guy's smile faltered, 'We're pretty much all booked up I think...'

'My name is Reuben Chamberlain. I work for Hugh Haverly.'

'Oh! Oh, absolutely, in that case, you will have something to tell me?'

Reuben nodded. 'That the day is colder than the night.' he said.

'Good, good. Follow me... will you be needing a dark room?'

'I will.'

Bree glanced up at Reuben, surprised.

'You might want to remember that phrase,' he said. 'It's nonsense but if the person who hears it is in our network, they'll ensure you are kept safe with a roof over your head.'

'I see...'

'I'm sure I'll get a phone call or two tomorrow demanding to know the meaning of this...' his lips moved into a wry smile. 'But for tonight, we are safe.'

The hotel porter led Reuben and Bree through several long corridors and then down a set of stairs at the back of the building. Down there was just one small corridor with three rooms off at each side. There were no windows and the air was cooler. Bree guessed they were down in the hotel's basement.

'Here,' the porter said, handing Reuben a key to the first of the rooms, '3a, all yours for as long as needed. If you need anything in daylight hours just use the intercom.'

'Thank you, very much appreciated. Is anyone else...'

'Nope, you have the floor to yourself.'

'Great, thank you. If anyone else checks in for a dark room will you let me know?'

'Of course.'

The porter departed, leaving Reuben and Bree alone. Reuben opened up the room and then took her hand again and led her inside. The room was well-laid out, more modern than she was expecting. There were no windows but the room was fitted with modern chrome features. The bed was on a metal frame, made up in a deep red duvet. The lighting was bright, but Bree spied a dimmer switch on the wall. There was a fridge, a kettle and two cups. A mini-bar stood in the corner.

'Wow!'

'Yeah, it's pretty nice. Remember this place if anything locally ever goes down.'

'Ok, I'll keep that in mind.'

'And Bree, if you're ever in a situation where you need that level of protection, call me too?'

'I will.'

'I mean it. Just because we're leaving this path we've walked together, doesn't mean I don't want to hear from you... not just when things are dire.'

The tears came close to the surface again at his words. Bree pushed them back with a 'don't...not tonight...'

'Ok, I'm sorry.'

For a moment they both stood in silence but as the moment thickened, Bree felt a giggle forming, mainly the product of nerves. Her hands felt a little clammy and the last dregs of the intoxicating wine seemed to leave her suddenly sober. Reuben's hand moved to the band in his hair, letting it loose, and slipping the little piece of elastic over his hand. Bree wet her lips, unable to coax her legs into making the two steps between them, crippled by an odd sort of shyness. Reuben caught her expression and smiled gently. He put out a hand, a bridge over the gap between them.

'Come here,' he murmured.

Bree obeyed, taking his hand and allowing him to pull her to him. He too seemed to take a deep breath as their bodies melded together. Not the most intimacy they'd ever shared, but made more so by the knowledge of where it was going to lead. Reuben slid a hand up the side of her face, catching her short locks and trying to banish them behind her ear. His eyes bored into her face which Bree just knew must be reddening for the heat she suddenly felt emanating from it.

'Beautiful girl,' Reuben murmured, 'I... thank you...'

'You thank me? For what?'

'Because in the feelings I'm feeling now, you've shown me I'm capable of more than just... I... never mind...'

Overwhelmed, Bree put her face down on to Reuben's collarbone, inhaling the scent of him with a deep lungful of air. Her fingers gripped the back of his thick cotton shirt whilst his slid around to cup the back of her head and for a moment he was silent, but then he spoke again.

'I hope I'm not making you regret coming here?'

'No,' Bree spoke against his flesh, then lay a small kiss just above where his shirt met his skin. 'Nothing could make me regret this – I feel a bit… wobbly though.'

'Ah, my giddy Bee,' he said, laughter in his tone, then gently used a finger to lift her chin so that she looked up into his face again. 'It's only normal to feel nervous,' he said, 'but there's no need – it's just me…'

Bree nodded and stood up a little on tiptoe. Reuben stooped slightly to meet her lips. The kiss was soft, gentle and sweet. Reuben's hand slid down her back to hold her about the waist whilst the other stayed up in her hair. Bree exhaled slowly against his lips and then found a small smile, biting her bottom lip. Reuben's eyes moved over her face again, he seemed almost to be mirroring her emotions. It was an odd expression to see in his old eyes; the newness and rawness of falling in love. With a gentle hand, Reuben unclipped the hooks at the back of Bree's dress and slid it down over her shoulders. She inhaled deeply but remained relaxed as the thin cloth pulled free. Reuben cast his eyes over her plain black cotton bra. His lips moved down just to touch, a tickle more than a kiss, in the swell of her breasts.

In the movies and books, passion always seemed to be such a violent explosion but with Reuben it wasn't: more controlled and self-aware, as ever he was. Bree stepped up to kiss his lips again, breathing in his breath, and then sliding her hand up under his shirt to feel the softness of his belly. She closed her eyes, allowing the mood to build. Reuben tugged the dress down over her hips and then released it to slide down to the ground, pooled at her feet. His hands caressed her skin, but his body was gently easing her to the bed. Bree acquiesced and allowed herself to be led, falling back onto soft duvet and pillows. Reuben pulled his own shirt off and then lifted Bree's hands to his chest.

'Touch me,' he whispered, 'Don't pull back, I want your skin on mine.'

Bree trembled but did as she was told, allowing her skin to feel his, allowing that all-encompassing sense of touch to overcome her. Reuben's hands finished uncovering her breasts, dropping the bra to the floor, and leaned down to touch his lips to her skin making her body push naturally towards him. Bree felt her hands moving almost unbidden to finish undressing, giving him access to all of her before moving to his zipper, wanting the same of him. Her hands trembled, but her heart juddered as he made a small murmur of pleasure too, pushing against her hand.

'Now,' she whispered, 'now? Reuben.'

'Are you really you sure you want this?' he asked, moving his body to meet hers.

'Yes!'

He exhaled, smiled and then moved his body so that they were one.

The physical act was over quickly, not unfamiliar to Bree but so distant from the teenage fumbling of her previous relationship. Together they moved, both lost in the sensations of it, but as the orgasm tore through Bree, Reuben sank his teeth into her shoulder. She moaned, gripping at the duvet with her hands at the heightened pleasure-pain reaction of her body. Reuben drank from the wound with a hunger she'd not known in him before, and Bree felt him come within her as he did so. Then he released her, pulled away and rolled over, hands going for the tissues on the side to stem the bleeding from her neck.

'Here,' he murmured, 'I'm sorry, I…'

'Hush, no apologies!'

'I was lost in the moment.'

'I know, I… I didn't mind it, I…' Bree blushed and glanced down at her fingers, 'kinda liked it actually…'

Reuben chuckled and held up his wrist. 'Let me heal you up at least?'

Bree nodded. She waited for him to puncture the vein in his wrist, and then put down her lips to drink. As ever, just a few trickles and then it was done. Reuben smiled again, that more-genuine of the two smiles he wore, the one that lit up his eyes. He pulled her naked body back into his arms and kissed her again. Bree allowed it, running her fingers through his soft hair, but then sat up.

'There's blood on the quilt…'

'It's ok, they're used to that here.'

'I still feel bad.'

Reuben slid a hand up her back, into her hair, caressing the back of her head. Bree closed her eyes, exhaling and leaning back a little. Her body still tingled but in the absence of activity, her mind was going back to the thoughts of the following evening.

'Reu…'

'Hmmm?'

'I…' she sighed, 'no, not until tomorrow…'

'If you need to be sad, be sad.'

'I'm trying not to be.'

Reuben kissed her cheek but then slipped out of bed and walked over to where his clothes were piled on the floor. He picked up his jeans and pulled them on.

'Where are you going?' she murmured.

'Just to get a bottle of something to drink. You must be thirsty? It's hot down here.'

'Yeah, I guess. Thank you for thinking of me, of my comfort.'

'Of course! I'm always thinking of it. You understand, sweetheart, that when I say I love you, I truly mean it?'

'You haven't… actually…'

'What?'

'Said it – you haven't said you love me.'

Reuben paused, then came back to the bed, shirt still in hand. He dropped the item of clothing though, to take her hand in his and kiss it. His eyes held hers, thoughtful, and then he spoke. 'I love you Beatrice Morgan.'

Bree sighed, the sound more wistful than sad, but enough so that it echoed in her chest.

'I know that my leaving must seem… hard… of me, but like I said before, I'd move heaven and earth if I could, to keep you safe. Of course I love you. I might not be a man to say it lightly, but you have to see it? Look further than what is said. I'd not have done this, tonight, with just anybody.'

Reality seemed somehow stretched, as though Bree had ingested something with mind-altering properties. Reuben slid an arm about her and pulled her back to him, his jeans felt strange against her naked legs, but she ignored the sensation, wrapping herself about him.

'I love you,' she said it again.

Reuben silenced her with a kiss and then stood up, 'What do you want? To drink?'

'Just a coke, and if there's a icy vending machine, ice-cream…'

'Ice-cream?' he chuckled.

'Yeah, like you said, it's hot in here!'

The morning seemed to come too quickly. There was little indication of it in the enclosed, boxed-in room in which Bree and Reuben lay, but for the clock hidden away on the corner by the en-suite bathroom. The room was very warm, made more so for their shared heat. On the dresser, Bree's half-eaten, melted, ice-cream sat amongst bloody tissues and the general clutter of keyrings and wallets. The silver crucifix necklace was coiled there too, to save Reuben's skin. Bree's senses tingled, her skin feeling a little like it was on fire. She lay with her head in the crook of Reuben's arm.

'Are you ok?' he finally asked.

'Yeah…'

'Really ok?'

'Yeah… I think so.'

'Ok. Sweetheart, I really should try to sleep, I'm sorry. It's gone nine and I am going to be driving for hours tonight.'

'Do you want me to stay?'

'Of course. You've been up all night too and need your sleep, besides, I want every moment of this stolen twenty-four hours, even if I am sleeping!'

Bree nodded and pulled aside the blanket to crawl under. The room was warm but it seemed cosier to snuggle in with Reuben. Bree was still nude, had been pretty much since they'd entered the room, but the state already felt natural around Reuben. He crawled in beside her and locked her to him.

Despite how she tried to remain awake, Bree too dropped off within twenty minutes and slept until jarred awake by the alarm on Reuben's phone, some seven hours later. Reuben was already up, absent from the bed at least, and she could hear the shower running. Her stomach growled, she'd not eaten anything but ice-cream since the wedding dinner the day before but she knew full-well if she tried to fill it now, she'd just make herself ill. All the sorrow she'd been bottling up suddenly seemed to rush to the fore as she realised their time was coming to a close.

The sound of the shower snapped off and Bree sat up in the warm sheets, drying her eyes with her hands. For a moment she simply sat and listened to the sounds of him clattering about in the bathroom, and then the door opened and he emerged. Even the sight of him, once more dressed, with his damp hair pulled back into a ponytail was enough to set her off again. Her hand went up to cover her lips, as though to hide the sobs which choked her. Reuben strode to her at once and put his arms about her.

'I guess this is the hard bit…' he whispered.

'Please, not yet! One more hour!'

'I can't… Bree, please…'

'Half an hour then! Ten minutes! God! You're talking about forever! Give me one more hour!'

Reuben squeezed her tightly, his body moulding to hers. He said nothing for the entirety of the embrace and when he pulled away she saw the pain on his own face.

'I can't...' he whispered, and the words were broken as though he too was struggling to hold himself together. 'If I don't go now, I never will... and I have to, Bree, I'm sorry!'

Bree let go of him entirely. She pulled away physically and forced an odd coldness upon herself. Her lips pulled down and her body hardened.

'Bree?'

'Go...'

'Don't let's part upset and angry?'

'I'm not angry but I can't prolong this! You have to go, so go!'

'Kiss me one last time?'

Bree did so, her resolve fading a little, but then pulled away. She pulled the duvet around her naked form like a shield and closed her eyes. Reuben paused, seeming unsure of himself but she closed herself up, holding the duvet close to her.

'Baby, please – I don't want to leave like this.'

'I know, but for the same reasons you need to go, I need to be cold now.'

'Ok darling, I get that. Bree...'

'Yes?'

'I... I... Goodbye, then.'

'Goodbye Reuben.'

18

Reuben threw himself into the car and exhaled heavily. His whole body felt ravaged and he did not even dare pry into his emotions. He'd not felt like this in so long, it was alien, choking and yet still somehow comforting too – to feel anything but the odd numbness of his existence. Reuben rummaged in the glove box and pulled out an old, tattered cigarette box. He rarely smoked but every now and then he indulged himself. The tobacco was old and stale, the smoke harsh, but Reuben welcomed it, pulling it down into his lungs almost painfully. For all his training, for all the care he gave his form, this one vice wasn't so bad. His mind moved back to Bree. How had she taken his leaving? She'd looked fit to burst, trying so hard to be strong. His heart hammered and his mind played the image of her over and over again. Reuben pulled on the cigarette and allowed himself one hot tear. Goddammit! How had she done this to him? He'd not felt so tied to another soul in so long, but then Bree did remind him so much of his first wife, of Elizabeth, in character at least. Poor Bess, half the reason why he couldn't give himself over fully again, between his experiences with her death, and Lucy's. Damn it all, and damn the kin too, all of them, but especially Damien for taking his life away and giving him this hollow existence in return.

Reuben had first encountered the kin in the autumn of 1786. The skies were darkening over the sweetly scented roses which lined the doors and hid away the sight of gravestones beyond in the yard of his little grey brick church. The church had, just before it, a large statue of an angel sat on a plinth which seemed to shy away from the gargoyles which hung over the roof. The tower was square, a Norman church, with a turret which leered over the tiny village on the edge of which it was situated. Inside, the candles burned in number enough to light up the cold stones with tiny flickering glows mingled together to create a fuzzy whiteness. Reuben stood by the altar watching as the last of his parishioners leave after the Sunday services. His eyes were soft and gentle despite that his lips were pressed. The Michaelmas service had been beautiful, but he was worried that his numbers were thinning again. There was a new, much larger church at the edge of the town of Wester which was pulling his parishioners that way. It was a shame and a worry for Reuben. His own church was a sight to see, too. Awe-inspiring architecture of the catholic church it had once been; before the reformation and the decline of Catholicism in England. Reuben had been drawn to this old church from the very beginning once he'd taken up orders – his own conversion to Catholicism as a boy, and then back to the Church of England as a grown-man, made it feel somewhat fitting and so when he'd been offered the parish, he'd taken it happily. He was young for such a position in the church, and felt the honour of such being bestowed on him. Perhaps it was the church's own history that the parishioners didn't like, he mused, an association with the now unpopular catholic faith.

Reuben sighed and then fell to his knees beneath the wooden beams which led up to the ornate stained-glass windows behind him. He had his rosary in his hands and worried the beads with his fingers as he prayed. Despite his conversion, he'd never given up his rosaries – if nothing else, they were something to fidget with, and as long as his parishioners didn't see, where was the harm? He always prayed alone anyway, once the townsfolk were gone; it was easier for him to do so, a direct and unfettered thanks to a god which was known only to him. It stilled the voices, unfurled the knots in his back. Still the empty church seemed to buzz with the echo of the bells, with the sound of the singing. The sweet smell of the Michealmas daisies which Elizabeth had placed about the church seemed suddenly more intoxicating too, and Reuben allowed some of his worries to settle. He sat back on his heels, breathing out and whispering his prayers. He'd been uneasy a lot lately, the instincts, the voices within, muttering and causing the worry to manifest more.

Reuben was mid-prayer when suddenly the outer door swung open, allowing a sharp blast of cold September air to enter the church. The gust extinguished several candles, as well as sending a prickle up Reuben's spine. Suddenly, the instincts came, not visions as such, but a sense of dread, the feeling of panic in his gut which gave him flashes of foresight, but not enough to really see what was about to happen, just enough to set his adrenaline pumping. He forced himself to be calm though, and stood, turning to face the newcomers.

Reuben's first thought was that the intruders were certainly not thugs or bandits. They were all well-dressed, if a little bedraggled. The first to enter was a man in his early-twenties or so. He was dressed in the height of fashion, French more so than the plainer English cut with his brocade frockcoat and white stockings. His wig was white, but short with curls at the sides. His cheekbones were high, almost girlish, but his eyes – there was something odd and ancient in his eyes. Reuben staggered to his feet as two other men entered behind. One fatter, with gleaming black eyes and a green silk coat, the other a little older, dressed all in black with longer hair and hard eyes.

'I... gentlemen... the service is over, I am afraid...' Reuben began.

The men looked about them as though he hadn't spoken.

'Yes, this will do nicely. Nobody in their right mind would suspect us of holing up in a church.' the fore-member of the group said, looking about.

'I... can I help you?'.

The men looked him over and then the fatter one grinned. 'Well, as it might be, I reckon you can, pastor,' he said, stepping forward.

'No, wait,' his young companion said, putting up a hand, 'he might serve other uses.'

Reuben's spine prickled and his instincts rose up as they had done since he was a child, more than a mere inclination, a vision of knowledge waving over him and giving him insight which could only be from god himself. He tensed and made to move, to run past, but the men were quicker than he, grappling him and wrestling him to the ground. They were strong too, stronger than any man Reuben had known before, and it took only moments for them to restrain him and use a thin rope they carried to bind his hands. Reuben struggled on, trying to pull his hands free but it was no good and in the end, a blow to his head stopped his struggles.

'Feed, but don't kill him,' the young man, obviously in charge, uttered.

'I'll try.'

'You will obey. I want this one, there's something about him.'

The fatter of the men moved closer to Reuben and leaned over where he lay prone. Before his eyes, the man's face began to change, the lips widening and demon's teeth pushing through. His eyes too changed, not in shape, but to emit a shining of silver. The man chuckled as Reuben pushed back against where he was bound, trying to free himself from Satan's minions even as the rope burned his wrists, and leaned in to loosen his shirt and pull it open, baring Reuben's soft pink flesh. The demon smelled of soap and expensive scent, and of something other, something unclean.

'Please!' Reuben gasped, 'please, pray God save me from this monster.'

God was not forthcoming, though, and the man pulled him up to sink his odd animal teeth into the flesh of Reuben's shoulder, making him howl in pain as the blood began to pump from the wound. The man drank until Reuben was woozy, and then pulled away. Leaving him weak and prone.

'That's enough,' the man-boy spoke. Reuben struggled to hold on to consciousness as this creature, with eyes glowing like the other, knelt at his side. He tensed for more pain but the stranger instead gently pulled the shirt back onto his shoulder and then broke the skin of his own wrist with his teeth.

'Here, just a little,' he murmured, he was kinder but Reuben could not shake the feeling of fear – this man frightened him more than either of the others, even the one who had bitten him. Reuben turned his head away, but the stranger simply pulled it back again and then pressed his jaw, just under his cheeks, the pain was too much and he opened his mouth. The stranger's blood was thick and sweet – like copper.

'There, good, nice and slowly, over a few weeks I think – don't want to change you all at once,' he said, his voice still soft, after Reuben had swallowed two or three mouthfuls of his blood, 'now, let us have a chat, hmm?'

'What?' Reuben murmured weakly, but already he could feel the cursed magic of the demon blood within him, 'what do you want with me?'

'With you? Nothing yet, nothing of import with you unless the blood takes you. Your church, however, and your position here as a leader of the faith, those are of much more interest to me.'

'You want my church?'

'For now. I'll take you with it, I am happy with that arrangement and should you cooperate, I see no reason to end your life.'

Reuben tried again to shuffle, feeling more alert. The headache of being struck passing with the pain at his shoulder. 'I don't understand.' he looked up at the two men behind, the fat one had sat himself down on a pew but the other merely stood in silence, observing.

'Tell me,' the stranger said, ignoring him, 'do you live alone, priest?

Elizabeth! The very thought of her cut through Reuben, pausing panic in his belly.

'Come, speak.'

'I… I live a…alone…'

'I can see your lies. Don't start this little arrangement by lying to me.'

'I…'

'A wife? Hmm?'

'Yes… I…Please, for the love of God, don't… don't hurt Bess. She is… she is with child! I beg you have mercy!'

The stranger looked up at the silent companion. 'Go and find the woman, bring her here,' he said. The other left at once on his command. Reuben's heart thudded and in a panic he tried again to move. He was definitely stronger than he had been a few moments earlier but still the well-dressed stranger restrained him easily, pushing him back down next to the font.

'Mind yourself,' he snapped, 'whilst it is convenient to keep you alive, don't become complacent, it is little enough more to end your life!'

Reuben's eyes flooded, blinding him with tears. He looked over to see the fat one was sniggering, sat lounged on the pew as though he were close on sleep.

It took only moments in the strange silence, before the other man came back with a wriggling and indignant Elizabeth grasped by the arm. Her long blond hair had broken loose in the struggle and so lay on her shoulders. Such pretty hair despite her plainness. When she saw his plight she began to murmur and struggle but, like Reuben, she was no match for her attacker. Poor Bess, with her dumpy frame and sharp nose.

Everybody had been shocked when he'd married her – so plain and poor, but Reuben had seen in her something others missed – the beauty of kindness and the glow of inner strength. He'd loved her almost at once and had married her despite that she'd brought no money for a dowry, no looks to be cooed over. She'd served him well too, her own love for him like life itself, burning through her.

'Ben…' she sobbed as she was thrown down by his side, 'What is happening?'

At once, he felt stronger and shuffled over to her, his eyes on the stranger still. 'It's well, Bess,' he murmured, 'These men just want something of us, and then they will leave.' How he kept his voice so calm, he didn't know.

'Not so, I'm afraid,' the stranger said, 'My good lady, my name is Damien, and these are my companions, Mr Farrow and Mr Gates… and I am afraid we're coming to stay, indefinitely.'

'Why? Why here, why us?' Reuben asked, pulling himself to sitting and holding onto Elizabeth as best he could where she clung to him.

'We need to lie low,' the silent one – Farrow or Gates, Reuben wasn't quite sure who was who – finally spoke. 'Who would think to look for men of our ilk in a church?'

'Men of your ilk?' Elizabeth asked.

'Hush,' Reuben murmured, not wanting them to show her the horror he was still digesting – that unholy face. 'Hush Bess…'

The stranger, Damien, nodded to Reuben and Elizabeth, his eyes skimming their faces impassively.

'You were a blessed man,' he said, 'I see that! I will give you five minutes to say your goodbyes.'

'My… what…' Reuben began to struggle again, almost making it to his feet before Damien knocked him back. Elizabeth took the opportunity to try to run, a protective hand over her belly where his unborn child lay still growing, but she got no further than halfway before she was accosted by the fat one. He grabbed her, lifting her from her feet and throwing her down with a thud. The fat one paused, looked up to where the leader was for a sign, and then lifted his foot and drove his boot into Elizabeth's skull. Reuben screamed, frantic, as she moaned and then lay still, obviously badly injured. He struggled with Damien and finally broke free, running with bound hands to where Elizabeth lay on the ground.

'Beth!' he moaned, falling to his knees beside her, 'Bessie! Oh god! Why? What have you done? Why? Oh… why?'

Damien walked up behind him, still calm, unflustered, 'Not how I planned this, but I'd say your farewells now, preacher!'

Reuben began to weep, using his bound hands as best he could to pull her head into his lap. There was blood in her hair, and a clear fluid too which seemed to be leaking from her ear and even as he pulled her to him, her nose began a light trickle too. Reuben roared, tears leaking his eyes as his chest felt like it was impacted in the shock and misery. Elizabeth opened her eyes, dulled as they were with pain, and looked up into his. She tried to speak but no words escaped her, and then closed her eyes again, never to reopen them.

She was dead. The man had murdered her.

Reuben stubbed out the cigarette on the old ashtray in the front of the car. The whole interior stank of tobacco-smoke, but he ignored it, the air-freshener would soon overpower it again anyway. Reuben glanced over at the hotel entrance and then sighed. Every molecule of him wanted to get out of the car and return to Bree, to whisper that he was sorry and hold her again, taste her again, but the rush of memories showed him, more than anything, the folly of doing so. His life was not one she could be a part of, not one she could ever understand. He closed his eyes for a long moment, swallowed the pain, and then switched on the ignition.

19

The taste of homemade alcoholic lemonade was tart on Bree's lips, drying out her tongue before the burst of sweetness followed, washing away the dryness. Bree took another sip, and then another, adjusting herself on the deckchair and watching her cousin's kids playing in the swimming pool in her mother's backyard. The three months since Reuben had gone had done something to ease the pain, despite that still every time her phone pinged, she jumped and her heart thudded. Every now and again it was him too, just checking in, making sure she was ok. Her replies of "*I'm fine!*" were almost true now.

One of the kids screamed and splashed about in the water and Bree sat up to watch. The littler one had something of a look of his mother about him, a cousin who had been a child herself when Bree had last seen her.

'Beatrice, can you come and man the grill?' her mother's voice drifted over from the barbeque. Bree sighed, knowing full well that the intent was to have her go over to socialise more – her mother was worried about her loner mannerisms: the only time she socialised was her monthly trek over to see Izzy and Josh – and even then she was never out long – the house holding too many memories and her relationships with the remaining occupants too flimsy now Reuben was gone.

Despite that, though, they were a good source of info on his wellbeing, and Bree didn't want to lose her last link to Reuben.

Still sighing, Bree stood and wondered over to the grill. Her mother had invited most of the neighbours and so the place was fairly busy. Her cousin, mother to the kids in the pool, was drinking a margarita and chatting away to her brother's wife and her mother whilst the next-door-neighbours from each side were deep in conversation. Probably bitching about her mother, Bree thought spitefully. The late afternoon sun made standing at the grill uncomfortable, hot and sticky with the scent of burger grease permeating her clothing. Bree stood and flipped burgers a while, but then handed the spatula over to Scott and gratefully tried a retreat back to the pool. Her mother was having none of that, though.

'Bree, darling, come and join us!' she said, patting the chair beside her. Bree sighed again, inwardly this time, and moved to take the seat. Her mother's dyed red hair was perfectly set and her nails glimmered with tiny rhinestones as she took Bree's hands and sat her down. Her cousin was not far off her own appearance, dark blond hair which was longer than Bree's, and similar features. She smiled and said hi, then turned back to Bree's mother.

'I don't know – in this climate, home ownership is risky…'

Great, a conversation about the housing market! Thrilling! Bree plastered on her "nod and smile" face, but then zoned out. Her eyes took in the kids by the pool again, well – somebody had to make sure the "little darlings" didn't drown themselves – and then moved to where a little white butterfly was flittering across the buddleia by the fence.

'…oh! Didn't your old boyfriend live there?' her mother suddenly asked.

'Eh? Sorry Mama, I drifted away…'

'Oh, my poor baby,' her mother said, squeezing her hand, then looking up at the cousin, Lesley, 'I'm sorry, this happens from time to time since the ordeal.'

Bree could have rolled her eyes but said nothing.

'We were just saying, sweet,' Cherie said, 'that the walled house down by the water is up for sale again. Wasn't that your old boyfriend... Danny, was it... wasn't that his house?'

Bree stared for a moment, her brow furrowed as she tried to remember. The memories were clouded, lost like so much of her past life but no, he'd had a city flat, hadn't he?

'I... I'm not sure... we... I mean he... he had a townhouse flat in the city but I don't recall another?'

Her mother pressed her lips in that way she had when Bree's memory hiccupped, but the look was gone quickly, 'I was sure it was his.' she mused, then turned to where the neighbour's kid had taken over the barbequing 'How are those steaks coming along, Henry?'

Later, Bree sat in her room. The French windows were open letting in a breeze which she enjoyed, it was still clammy enough that her hair felt greasy despite having been washed the night before. She was dressed just in nightie and her thin silk dressing gown – a gift from her mother on her 28th birthday, which had just passed – drinking another cocktail. As a rule Bree didn't drink very much since her return, but the sweet beverage was made with ice and was refreshing. In her hand she held her mobile phone. She'd spent the past couple of hours, since the barbeque, thinking about Danny, trying to remember him: for someone who had once meant so much to her, she realised she'd hardly considered him since her return, too lost in Reuben and this new world she'd discovered. Suddenly though, with her mother's bringing him up, she wanted to check in with him, see how life had treated him. He'd been questioned by the police after she'd vanished and she had an almost guilt-like feeling, remembering that, and remembering him.

"*Hardly ur fault babe*" Angie's reply had stated, when she'd texted asking for his contact details and explaining why she needed them. "*It's not like u asked to be kidnapped.*"

"*I just feel an apology would go over well?*"

"MayB. But he'll no it wsn't ur fault!"

Bree smiled nostalgically at Angie's terrible text speak, but still she pushed on, *"Do you have his number?'*

'Sry babe, I don't."

Would Pete know it?"

"Dnt no if I have Pete's No either. Leme check."

And that had been that.

Bree presumed no reply meant no, she didn't. A brief search online had shown that Danny seemed to shun social media. No manner of variations on his name had pulled him up, and nor did his old email address — if she was even remembering that right, which she wasn't sure she was. Bree put down the phone with a sigh, and leaned back in her chair. Her head ached, probably for the heat, a pain which throbbed through her temples and into her eyes. She glanced at the bed, pondering climbing in, maybe even texting Reuben, just for the chance of a short message back, but even as she considered, the phone buzzed, vibrating on the dresser.

A text message.

"Hello Bree. I hear tell you have been trying to contact me."

Bree's heart thudded in her chest, she curled up her feet under her on the chair and surveyed the message. *"Danny?"*

"Yes. You were looking for me?"

"I just wanted to apologise," Bree typed. *"I am home, safe, as I'm sure you know. The police questioned you when I was Kidnapped? I just want you to know I'm sorry for that."*

"Thank you" came the almost instant reply. *"I was, but we were all just concerned about you."*

"I'm sorry. I hope you weren't too worried."

"Of course I was. We all were."

Bree's eyes filled with tears, the past suddenly feeling closer than it had since her return. She sat for a long moment, then typed, *"Can I see you?"*

For quite some time the little screen was blank, but then his text came in. *"I'm sorry, I don't think us meeting is a good idea."*

Bree nodded and then, realising she'd been holding her breath, exhaled. Well, that was that then, he too had moved on, just like everyone else. She tried to think of a way of wording a text to explain that she didn't want anything from him, just to see him, to apologise in person and to chat, to see where the world had taken him but she couldn't find the words so instead she typed in a short "no worries" and put the phone back down.

The day was a bright and sunny Wednesday, about a week after the barbeque. Bree and her mother, along with the same cousin as before – minus the children – were lounging by the pool, basking in the sunshine and trying for tans. Bree moved her deckchair closer to the water and was dipping her fingers into the edge, enjoying the cold contrast of the water whilst she held her book in her other hand. Her mother was opposite, reading that week's "Cosmopolitan" whilst they waited for shopping to be delivered and her cousin was nearer the house, painting her toenails. The day was another warm one, but the light was fading away, shifting towards twilight and the breeze was light on Bree's skin, giving her gooseflesh where it touched. Despite the chill, Bree's mother was dressed in a one-piece swimming costume, but with a skirt over it to hide her modesty and a wrap about her arms. Bree had yet to see her actually get in the pool aside from her morning laps for exercise. Bree's cousin, Lesley, was fully dressed but for her shoes and socks.

'Here, have you seen what the Cunningham's are up to?' her mother asked, showing Bree a picture from her magazine of two B-level celebs who appeared to be sitting smiling with little to indicate why the magazine had singled them out for an article. Bree shook her head, and Lesley glanced over too to look at the article, but then froze.

'I… who's that?' she asked, staring into the space beyond, past the pool, where a few trees and shrubs grew wild. Bree was on her feet at once, despite that she could see nobody there, her book falling to the ground.

'What? What is it?' her mother asked.

'I… I thought I saw someone in the bushes…' her cousin replied.

At once, Bree's mother pressed her lips, anger and fear mingling in her eyes. 'Bree, Les, inside!' she snapped, 'Call the police!'

Bree didn't need to be told twice and all-but herded her cousin inside. Her mother brought up the rear, not brave enough to explore where the stranger was said to have been.

It took the police only ten minutes to get to the estate, but by the time they did, there was nobody to be found. In light of Bree's kidnapping though, they agreed to leave an officer to patrol the estate until morning.

Bree sat huddled in the armchair, a blanket around her swimming costume and shorts. Lesley had gone home and so it was just her and her mother.

'Do you think he's related?' Bree asked, 'To…'

'I don't know sweetheart, more likely just come to be morbid and get a look at you!'

'A reporter maybe?' Bree asked, hopeful.

'I suppose, yes, he might have been.'

Bree nodded and pulled out her phone. She knew she had to let Reuben know what had happened ASAP. She typed in a quick text and was shocked when almost at once her phone rang. Her mother jumped but Bree stood, 'It's Reu,' she whispered, then slipped into the next room to answer.

'Bree? Are you all right?' his voice was anxious.

'I'm… I'm a bit shaken but ok…'

'You said there was an intruder? In your house?'

'Outside, by the pool.'

'Was he one of us?'

'I don't know, I've not actually seen him…'

'But your cousin did? How did she describe him?'

'She only caught a glimpse… it was daylight though…'

'That wouldn't matter to a changer, or to an old one of my kind. Do you need me to come?'

Bree's heart thudded and she almost said yes, then her mind went back to the hotel, to how she'd clambered from the bed but collapsed in tears on the floor. How she'd sobbed in the shower, then laid foetal on the bed with the towel in her hands because it still smelled like him. In the months which had passed she'd done too much mending to let it all go again.

'N... no... the police are here and... and I think I'm safe. My mum thinks it's just a stalker or a reporter or something.'

'She could well be correct.'

'Or it could be...' Bree paused, but then pushed on, 'I spoke briefly via messages to Danny last week too...'

'Danny?'

'My old boyfriend... from... from before.'

Reuben's voice tightened, 'Oh?'

'Yeah... not... not like that, I just... just wanted to apologise to him, the police questioned him and stuff.'

'I see, and what did he say?'

'Very little, just that he didn't want to see me.'

Reuben was quiet for the longest moment.

'Reu?

'It's ok, I'm just digesting. Give me his last name and I'll have Josh run a background check on him.'

Bree paused, the confusion like that of her kidnapping rose again as she fumbled to recall. 'I... I don't know.'

'You don't know your ex-boyfriend's surname?'

'No, I... I'm not sure if I... if I ever... ever knew it.'

Reuben was quiet again, then sighed. 'Ok. I'll see if it was mentioned in the papers when the police took him in.'

'I... Reu, there's no need to be jealous, he's just... just a door I needed to close, that's all.'

Reuben said nothing, not confirming or denying the jealousy, but instead he was quiet again, then 'It's ok baby. As long as you're safe now?'

'I am. Thank you for calling.'

'Always... I said if you need me, call.'

'Ok.'

'Take care of yourself Bree.'

'And you.'

'I will. Keep me updated, ok?'

'Ok.'

'Goodbye then.'

'Goodbye Reuben.'

Bree hung up the phone with a press on the screen and then went back to her mother. She was drinking tea, a soap on the tv to distract her. Bree loitered a moment but then took herself upstairs, tv just didn't hold her attention anymore. She slipped into her room and sat down on the bed. Her phone was on the bedside table and for a moment Bree had to really fight to resist texting Reuben again. She lifted the handset and looked at her reflection in the dull glass, her eyes looked scared and her lips were pressed. Bree put the phone back down, stood and went to the window. For a moment, she froze, seeing a figure moving, but then he came into the light, a guy in a police uniform, obviously patrolling the grounds. Bree forced herself to be calm, them closed the curtains firmly and put out the light. She lifted her phone again and saw a text there, just Angie saying hi – she ignored it, then opened up a new message.

"*I really miss you tonight*", she typed, then added Reuben's number. For a full ten minutes she stared at the words, then deleted them and put down the phone, she couldn't reopen that wound, it wasn't fair on either of them to do so.

Reuben pulled his hair back into a ponytail and threw on a black vest. His little flat in London was bare of any ornamentation, white walls and plain pine furniture with just a rug on the wooden floorboards, a soft contrast as he walked over it in his bare feet. It was overly warm too, the neighbouring buildings trapping in the heat, but Reuben didn't mind that, he wasn't there much. Once his hair was tidy, he grabbed his phone, keys and wallet, and then glanced in the mirror. He looked worried, he realised, too tense in the cheeks, too dark of the eye. He'd been feeling on edge ever since he'd spoken to Bree. It wasn't easy being so far away from her when she might be in danger, but she'd said not to come home, and her explanations did seem fair enough. He'd given Josh the name too, via text, Danny something – to be looked up in the old newspaper articles online from Bree's abduction. If the kid was any threat, he'd know as soon as Josh finished playing whatever game he was playing and did some work.

Reuben loaded up his pockets, then sat to pull on his army boots, pre-worn and comfy despite being new to him. He felt the tiredness of his muscles, especially his shoulders and neck, and stretched his head from side to side in an attempt to loosen them. He'd need to train soon, and to feed – the latter being somewhat easier than the former in the vast city.

Outside, it was drizzling a little, despite the heat, and Reuben cursed himself for not thinking to put on a coat. He didn't need the protection really, not minding the rain, but he was always aware when he looked out of place, when people might be glancing at him. That was another trick old Sam had taught him *"Always wear a coat if it's raining, and a scarf if it's cold. You'll fit in better!"* It was the sort of thing Reuben had never thought of.

Reuben walked the entire distance to Chris's place, some three miles across the city, and then let himself in with his own key. The flat was a lot like his, non-descript and bare – plain walls and no ornaments, knickknacks. Just a base, somewhere to work. Reuben entered and closed the door behind him, he wiped his boots on the rug but didn't remove them and then moved into the main living area. Chris wasn't about but one of his associates, Virginia, sat quietly watching a black and white movie on the tv – her era. Ginny was elegant as hell, dark and mysterious but suffered what a modern world would describe as "resting bitch face". She was kind though, had a heart under her perfectly ironed black Dior minidress and cardigan which probably cost as much as a fairly decent second-hand car. He didn't ask about how she'd happened upon such attire – sometimes it was better not to know.

'Heya Ginny,' he said, 'Chris out?'

'Yeah, he's feeding.'

'Ah, ok.'

'Can I do anything for you?'

'Yeah, maybe. There's a club down underneath a warehouse in Soho, I think it might be our place. I was going to go check it out but wanted to let someone know where I was going in case I vanish.'

'There is a drinker club down there, yeah. Went to check it out a while back with Chris, back when we were fucking. Seemed legit and above board to us then.'

'Ok, noted,' he said, 'I shouldn't have any bother getting in and out then?'

'Shouldn't do, no.'

Reuben nodded, 'Great. Good news. Can I borrow a coat?'

'Yeah, there's a leather on the peg, that's my spare, you can use that. Take your hair down too when you get there – you'll look more in keeping with the club that way.'

Reuben smiled a half-smile and pulled on the leather bike jacket, it was a bit tight and he didn't like the restriction around his arms but it'd do. He left it unzipped and transferred his wallet into the breast pocket, then made his retreat.

Outside, the drizzle had turned more to proper rain. Reuben tucked his ponytail into the back of the jacket and quickened his pace. It wasn't too far now, past all the hookers and gambling dens, through the bright lights and billboards and then down a back street or tow. The club was underground, literally as well as figuratively. The entrance was down a flight of stone steps lined with metal railings, and through a door to a tiny black room. There was just a ticket box and a set of stairs.

'Help ya?' the guy in the box asked. He was long-haired, dark makeup around his eyes, about thirty when he was turned which hadn't been too many years previous if Reuben's hunch was correct. He turned to the box and, rather than speak, allowed the silver to glow in his eyes.

'Twenty quid,' the guy said, unimpressed. Reuben passed over the cash and then nodded at the stairs, 'Down there?'

'Yeah.'

'Any house rules?'

'Yeah, don't feed on the main floor, there's side rooms for that. Most of the kids suspect what we are, and some are feeders, but still, no need for a panic.'

'Noted.'

'And don't piss anybody off. Some feeders are owned, I don't want any fights over livestock.'

'Noted again,' Reuben said, then turned down the stairs.

'One last thing…'

Reuben half-turned and paused his step, to show he was listening.

'If you're a drainer, tell the barkeep and lock the door. Don't want any fuss if any of them see dead kids – causes too much hassle and that ain't pretty.'

'Fair enough,' Reuben kept his voice steady and headed down the stairs. So much for above board... unless it'd changed ownership since Ginny had visited last.

At the bottom of the stairs was a thick wooden door, obviously soundproof as when opened suddenly a din of heavy rock music roared out. There was a coat room at the foot of the stairs so Reuben deposited Ginny's jacket there and pulled the band out of his hair, letting it fall in a soft wave behind his still aching shoulders. Then he turned to the room. It was just like any standard rock or metal club, to the naked eye, anyway. Painted in purple and red, with a DJ booth at one end and a mirrored bar which spanned the whole length of the far side of the room. Reuben allowed his eyes to slowly take it all in. There were several corridors, and, just as the guy above had said, there were other rooms set in behind these, doors he suspected were locked with bolts on the other side. The club was pretty packed too, with most seats taken and the dancefloor filled with packed sweaty bodies. Ninety percent of the clientele were human, a handful of changers and a distinct presence of drinkers. It was a big place too, with two little comfy nooks made up of black leather sofas, a dancefloor, and plenty of chairs around the edge. In one offshoot nook there was a chaise longue too, occupied by a petite blond drinker in a black velvet gown. She'd obviously just fed and Reuben wondered if she realised that there was a dribble of blood over her breasts still. Probably, he thought grimly, so much for not feeding on the main floor.

In his pocket, his phone buzzed and so Reuben took it out and glanced at the screen. It was just Josh replying. Danny Smith was a loner, no family locally. He had been questioned once by police but had been cleared and then seemed to have vanished himself – moved out of town from what Josh could tell.

Reuben pressed his lips and tried to think. In some respects he couldn't blame the kid. First his girlfriend had vanished, and then he'd been questioned. Reuben might have made the quickest exit from town too, in those circumstances. He replied quickly with a thanks and a note to ask Jessie to keep an eye on Bree for a few days. This done he slid the phone back into his pocket and looked back up at the room. He was getting attention, he realised, not just from the other drinkers either. A young human lass, probably about twenty, was eyeing him up with doe-like brown eyes. She was pretty, dressed all in clinging black PVC and lace, trim of waist, dark of hair, and her throat already held scars. Ok, so they didn't bother to heal them up after, that was obvious. As he caught her eye, the girl smiled and put her drink down on the bar. She sauntered over to him and put a lace-gloved hand up to touch his chest.

'Now if you're not one of them, I'd be very surprised,' she shouted over the music.

Reuben lifted her hand and, holding her eye, ran his thumb over her pulse. She wasn't afraid, the blood was running quick enough to show excitement, but not quick enough for fear. The hunger within him pulled.

'Hungry?' she asked, almost seeming to catch the thought. Reuben pulled in a deep breath. He ran his eyes over that pretty face again, and then inclined his head. She was obviously a regular too, so she would be a good bet to teach him the protocol, where to go and so on.

The girl slipped her hand into his and then moved to the bar, there she leaned in and spoke to the bartender: a shorter, stouter guy about thirty, not a drinker – changer maybe. There for another twenty, a key was produced and handed to Reuben. It was a modern looking Yale lock key, with a number one printed on the plastic top. All this Reuben took in carefully, and then allowed the girl to lead him to a door marked with a tiny metal "1" on the front of it. She indicated the tiny keyhole and

Reuben used the key. The room inside made him pause another moment. It was better lit than the club, tiled in black and white, and despite that the tiles looked as though they'd just been scrubbed, they were still coppery at the edges. There were shackles at the wall, and a tattered, hard sofa opposite it. The girl pulled the door closed behind her, locking them in and the sound of the club out.

'Shackles?' he asked, eyeing them, 'I thought you guys were supposed to be willing?'

'Some of us like to be tied up…'

'Adds to the fantasy, huh?'

'Something like that.'

Reuben lifted her hand in his and kissed her pulse, 'And you?'

'I… am yours for the next however long you want me. Do as you like with me?' she purred.

'And how much is that going to cost me?'

The girl laughed, 'First one's on the house…'

'Not a great way to do business…'

'Most of my first-times come back at least once…'

Reuben put his lips to her throat, holding on to her hands, allowing his breath to tickle her throat but not biting in. He was still trying to play his role, stay in character even as the hunger took over him. The girl slipped a hand up into his hair, and pulled his lips up for a kiss. He allowed it, blanking it out, and then gently pushed her towards the shackles.

'Get back there then,' he growled, allowing the demon within some free range. Inside him, it felt triumphant and Reuben knew he'd have to work hard to get it back in its box after this. The girl stepped back, breathing heavily, and put up her little hands. Reuben shackled them into place and then ran a hand down over her body. She shuddered deliciously.

'You get to fuck me too,' she said, 'if you want? It's not all about feeding.'

At once, Bree's face swam before Reuben's mental eye. Before her, he might have taken the girl up on that to further his undercover identity, but not now. Sure, he was enjoying the moment, but for him feeding was just feeding, and a job was just a job… he was in character, but he hadn't entirely lost himself.

'I'll pass on that,' he said, inwardly wincing at how his voice took on an edge of cruelty, 'I'm really only here for this…'

He stepped forward and allowed the demon it's release. The girl, seemingly unperturbed, put back her head, trying to repress a smile as his newly sharpened teeth elongated and sank into the whiteness of her neck. Reuben was careful though, where he bit. Usually when he hunted, he went for a main artery and then caught them before they fell and healed them up. If this place didn't approve of healing, he'd have to be careful or risk falling back into murder, not a place to whence he wanted to return. The girl gave out a contented little sigh, her obvious masochism satiated and even as Reuben pulled away from the thick copper flow, her eyes began to flutter. She lost her footing a little and fell slack into the shackles. Reuben unbuckled the wrist cuffs at once and pulled the girl down, she was still conscious, just about, but floppy in his arms. He lay her down on the sofa and put a bloody kiss to her lips.

'Thank you,' he murmured, and then nicked his finger with his tooth so that a droplet of blood bubbled, Reuben rubbed it into the wound, not healing it, but at least stemming the flow. The girl looked up at him and half-grinned.

'Leave me here awhile until I recover,' she murmured huskily, 'Just tell Justin I'm here so he doesn't give the room out.'

'Sure…'

'I'm Kaleigh, by the way,' she murmured, 'What's your name?'

'Ben, my name is Ben… and you'll be seeing a lot more of me I think, Kaleigh.'

21

Yet another party, always parties, gatherings, soirees. Bree was getting somewhat tired of her mother's busy social schedule, especially in the wake of what had happened the month previous with the figure in the garden. Her mother had quickly got over the fright though, and had dismissed it as more PTSD on Bree's part. Bree wasn't so sure. The feelings it had stirred hadn't gone away, although they had lessoned somewhat since that day. Bree sat out on the balcony watching the sun set, whilst behind her the party was in full swing. Her mother had even hired a pianist and there were two men in black and white serving canapes... fucking canapes! Bree sucked in a mouthful of fresh air and tried to allow the gorgeous view over the grounds of the house in the fading sunset to soothe her. Still Reuben's teachings stayed with her, and she used them to keep herself calm, five things she could see, four she could hear, and so on.

As the year was pulling further to its close, the days were coming in closer, quicker. Already the orange light was turning purple as the sun dipped down behind the clouds. Behind her, Bree heard the door handle pull and sighed, likely her mother coming to find her and drag her back to normality again. The footstep wasn't her mother's though, and Bree turned to see a young guy in a well-pressed suit exiting the house to join her on the balcony. Ninety percent chance of him being sent out by her mother, she thought... but at least she wasn't being pulled back in by light-hearted nagging.

'Hi, sorry if I am disturbing you?' the guy said softly.

'Not at all. My mother send you out?'

'Your mother?'

'Mrs Morgan...'

'Oh... oh no she didn't. You must be Beatrice Morgan then?'

'That's me.'

'I've heard a little about you...' the man moved to the edge of the balcony to stand beside Bree and looked out over the view too.

'I'm sure.'

'Enough to know that all this must seem... very superficial to you now.'

Bree looked up, frowning. The guy was about six foot, or just under. He was well-groomed, just like any of her mother's guests, and had dark hair which was shot through with natural highlights. He didn't look anything outside of what might be expected at such a gathering.

'Superficial?'

'After your ordeal, I mean.'

'I... I guess.'

'I guess you don't like to talk about it either? I'm sorry, I'm being rude. Max, by the way...'

'Max?'

'My name.'

'Oh.'

Bree put out her hand and he took it. His skin was very hard and cool in the night air. Bree tensed slightly at the contact, and then looked up into his eyes. She started and stepped backwards, catching the gleam of silver most people didn't even know to look for.'

Max's eyes narrowed slightly at her response. 'Beatrice?'

'Oh… oh god! You're… you're…'

'I am.'

'What are you doing here?' he was between her and the door, Bree realised, blocking the path.

'I came to do exactly what one of my kind might do at a party such as this… rich pickings.'

'Just a coincidence then?' Bree almost whispered, not quite believing it.

'Not entirely, I was asked to come and introduce myself by somebody who would prefer to remain nameless, you understand…'

'Reuben?'

Max just smiled and then stepped aside, 'did you want to go back in? It's cold out here…'

'Don't feed here,' Bree said, false bravery, 'if you are a friend of Ben's, then you won't… won't do that…'

'As you wish, Miss Morgan…'

Inside it was warmer, but louder. Bree's eyes remained on the stranger, Max, for the entirety of his time out on the balcony, and then followed him as he moved through the house.

'Bree darling, there you are!' her mother's voice sailed over, interrupting her following of the drinker, 'I was just saying to Tammy here how you have been thinking about going to university! She works on the board and was saying, dependant on which course, she might be able to help you to get a place without A-levels…'

Bree groaned inwardly, she'd literally mentioned it once, but still turned her feet in the direction of her mother anyway and allowed the inane chatter to sooth her misgivings about the stranger. She didn't take her eyes off him though.

The night pulled in, the darkness blanketing the house and causing the lights to be lit, chasing shadows away into corners. Bree moved from one inane conversation to another, and then another, tired and bored, but making the effort for her mother. She'd once enjoyed all this – not quite so much as sneaking out with her friends and Danny, but still, she was sure she'd never hated it. She was dressed in the latest fashions, clothing which her mother insisted she needed, but still she wore Reuben's crucifix under her clothing. Bree put her hand on it. After seeing another of them here, in her own home, Bree was glad of it's burning reassurance.

'Here, take this and then go and speak to Cherie,' her mother said, dancing by with a glass of bubbly in her hands, 'she's with the Mathers – they just bought the old Hawthorn House and so are going to be our neighbours…'

'Let me guess, they have a bachelor son, about my age…'

Her mother giggled, enough of an answer for Bree. She sighed and headed to the edge of the room, but then caught sight of the drinker, Max again and turned her feet, hand on the crucifix under her dress.

'I thought I asked you to leave…'

'No, you asked me not to feed. I haven't!'

'Why are you here?'

'I told you…'

'Reuben would have told me if he was sending someone. I don't like this… reassure me, and go?'

The drinker's eyes moved over her face, but then he smirked, 'So be it…' he moved to the door, but then paused and waved. Bree didn't acknowledge the gesture, simply watched him leave. It wasn't until he was gone, that her heartrate began to drop to normal levels.

The following day was a dim rainy one. Bree stood by the kitchen sink looking out over the grey haze of rainclouds, spilling their loads down over the green of the gardens whilst she washed up a load of non-dishwasher friendly plates from the night before. Her mother was in the living room, picking up rubbish and bemoaning that she'd not thought to hire somebody to do that for her. The radio was on and Bree was enjoying its "classics" day, finally music which she knew rather than all the pop hits which she'd missed and couldn't ever seem to get properly caught up on! As she sang along, her eye caught the gate outside open. She frowned, then more so as she saw the man from the night before, Max, enter and begin to approach the house. Bree frowned, ok, it was dim but it was still daytime. Unless he was pretty old, like Reuben, and could stand the sunshine for longer.

Bree put down the soapy plate she had in her hand and, still watching outside, dried her hands on the rough tea-towel which hung on the drawer. Max walked all the way up to the door and rang the bell.

'Mama…. Don't…' Bree began but her mother was already at the door, having been right by it when the bell rang. Bree's stomach tied itself up in knots, somehow knowing something wasn't right. The sound of the door opening, and then her mother's voice. Bree's legs turned to jelly, her fight or flight response already kicking in as she walked towards the door. Her mother's voice rose, calling her she realised, and then Max appeared at the kitchen door, beating her to it. He smiled that sleezy smile and ushered Bree's mother in too.

'Max, I want you to leave…' Bree began.

'I'm afraid not. I've been sent to keep an eye on you and I intend to do so.'

'Bree, what's going on?'

'Mama, I want you to run away,' Bree said, 'Go! Now!'

'Oh, that's not a good idea…' Max said, smiling, 'Mrs Morgan, I really don't recommend making me chase you…'

'Who are you? What do you want?'

'My name is Max, just Max. I've been sent to keep your daughter company, Mrs Morgan, to… to keep an eye on her – for a friend.'

Bree's panic grew, there was no way this guy had come from Reuben! She moved towards the block with the kitchen knives inside but as she did, the creature let go of himself and let the demon shine through. Her mother screamed, the sound one of the desperate terror that was seeing such a sight for the first time. She staggered backwards, her hands over her mouth.

Max moved swiftly, not grabbing Bree, but moving to her mother, gripping her dress and pulling her to her knees. Her screams had stopped but her eyes were glazed over, shock and fear in their depths.

'Stop! Leave her alone!'

'Then stop being a silly girl and do as you are told!'

Bree's eyes filled with water but she obeyed, moving away from the knife block and stepping towards the man and her mother. Max smiled again, despite that his face did not revert, and then dipped his head to taste her mother's throat. Bree recognised the action before he made purchase and a strange squeal left her lips,

'Don't you dare! Not my mother!' She pulled the crucifix out from under her jumper and in one fluid movement, thrust it against his cheek.

Max screamed, flailing, his hands moving to claw at the broken skin. A few plates fell off the draining board where he knocked it as he fell backwards. Bree used his moment of distraction to drag her mother back to her feet and through the arch into the dining room. Max did not take long to recover, finding his footing and roaring, running after them into the dining room. Bree pushed her mother behind her, her breath coming out in little gasps. On the edge of the mantle was a silver candlestick, such a clichéd item, and inwardly Bree thanked her mother for her pretentious snobbery. Max came into the room still snarling. There was a cross-shaped welt on his face, and his eyes were brightest silver, shining out from dark sockets.

'You bitch!' she snarled, 'I'm gonna make sure you pay for that! Nobody said I had to be nice to you!' he moved closer again.

Bree desperately tried to ground herself, knowing she only had one chance. A wisp of Reuben's voice spoke into her ear, *"Just close yourself off to everything but your own bodily sensations... really feel everything, your hands, your feet, even your little toes..."*

Bree did so, her eyes flitting closed, she didn't need vision, she could feel Max coming closer by the ripples of energy he moved. Slowly she began to count the steps, her body relaxing despite the danger. As he came upon her, close enough to grab her, Bree allowed herself to fall into a fast ducking motion, and move past him. The aspect of surprise worked, leaving the man stood with no purchase on her arm where he'd gone to take it. She moved to the dresser and gripped the candlestick, drew it up into the air and then brought it down on the back of his head. Max screamed out again, just as he had before. Bree brought down the candlestick again, felling him, and then ran to a large oak dresser in the corner where she knew her mother kept the silverware, she pulled the drawer almost off its runner, and rummaged in the silver for a weapon. The best she could find was a dinner knife. Max was just standing again as she turned back to him, but his face was no longer smirking, no, now he looked afraid. And so he should! Bree didn't hesitate to stick him with the silver knife, aiming for his heart. The blade was blunt and so it was more force than anything which thrust it through his skin, and even then had he not been sensitive to the precious metal, it probably would not have had such an impact.

As before, back when Reuben had rescued her, the silver did its work quickly, destroying the heart which gave up the function of the body, making Max collapse in a heap. Bree turned back to her mother. Her greying hair was mussed and her eyes dark with panic. She'd fallen to her knees and her arms were crossed over her body. Bree moved straight to her and wrapped her arms about her mother.

'He was… was…'

'Shush Mama, I know. It's ok now, he's gone.'

Her mother clasped her tightly, holding on to her in her shock. For some time they stayed thus, and then Bree wet her lips and pulled away.

'Mama, is anyone due to come over today?'

Her mother shook her head. 'Maybe Scott. Probably not.'

'Good. We need to lock the gate.'

Her mother nodded, then stood on obviously wobbly legs and moved out of the dining room, stepping over the body to do so. Bree sat, panting, and then pulled her mobile out of her pocket. She dialled the number and waited, redialling when it ran out of rings, until finally, his voice.

'Reu?'

'Bree? Sorry, I was working. What's up?'

Bree opened her lips to explain, but then the tears came suddenly, choking her.

'Baby? What is it?'

Bree sobbed a moment longer, clutching the phone, then spoke, 'A... there was...was a drinker... here!'

'What?'

'In my house, last night and then today and he...' more tears spilled, the shock turning to normal fear. Bree's limbs started to shake, and her bladder felt suddenly full.

'A drinker! It's the middle of the day!'

'Yeah... I know but he... he came to the door and everything... he didn't seem to... to mind it...'

'He must be an old one... fuck... Where is he now? Are you safe?'

'I... I... he's... he's dead, Reu... I... I... killed him... he's on... on the fl-floor... in my dining room.'

'You... what...?' he muttered, then, 'Baby, I'm coming. Stay put and don't let anybody in. It's about a five-hour drive, but I'm coming.'

'It's the middle of the day!'

'I'll feed before I leave...' he said, and Bree heard the strain in his voice, 'just stay put!'

Never in Bree's life had time ever passed as slowly as it did in the hours which followed but finally the sound of the bell came to her ears. Her mother, sitting at the table in the kitchen, cowered but Bree kissed her head and moved to answer it, knowing at once that it must be him. She clicked on the CCTV screen just to be sure, yes – it was his car – and then hit "open" on the gate control. Reuben drove in and then came the sound of his engine slowing, footsteps, and a knock on the door.

Even as she answered, before she could even stop to take in his form, his arms were around her, holding tightly to her and bathing her in his musk once again. He was trembling, tense.

'Bree,' he whispered, 'Baby, are you alright?'

Bree managed to nod against him, overwhelmed by the feel of his arms around her, his aftershave and the scent of his soap in her nostrils. Her eyes leaked tears and her body suddenly felt weak.

'Bree,' he murmured, pulling away slightly to look at her face, 'Talk to me! Are you ok?'

'I think so.'

'Was he one of the ones from... from before? Did I miss one?'

'I don't know? He tried to make me believe you'd sent him...'

'I didn't!' Reuben said, 'he didn't hurt you?'

'No... no just gave us a scare.' Bree wiped away the tears and resisted the urge to grab him and pull him in tight again. 'What about you? Are you...ok?'

'I'm fine. It's fairly overcast out and I fed before I left, I'll need to again later – soon – but that's no issue here. How is your mother?'

'In shock.'

'I can well imagine...' he paused and swallowed. 'Thank God you are both safe.'

'I'm fine.' Bree said, trying to sound reassuring, 'honestly... but now we have a... a dead vampire in our dining room and... and...' she exhaled, letting go of some of the stresses.

Reuben's eyes searched her face one last time, then he stepped away, 'can I come in?' he asked softly, 'I'm ok but staying here stood in the sunlight isn't ideal.'

'You need permission to come in?'

'No, not like you're thinking – I just have manners…' Reuben managed a small smile, making Bree smile with him. A tired smile, but a smile none-the-less.

'Come in then…'

Once inside, Bree led Reuben to the dining room, passing the kitchen where her mother sat in silence without a word – she'd explain Reuben in a minute. The body lay as she had left it, slumped by the dining table, her silver dinner knife lost in the mess of his blood and gore. Reuben knelt and turned the man's head, then paled.

'What? What is it?' Bree asked.

Reuben looked up at her with shining eyes. 'This is Maximillian Farrow,' he said quietly, 'He's my… my blood brother.'

22

Reuben stared in shock and horror at the face of the man who had killed Elizabeth. His heart thudded too quickly. Farrow was one of Damien's cronies – what the fuck did Damien want with Bree? Mentally he did the maths. His offering to Damien was due, but not overdue, not enough for his sire to have come looking for him. Unless he'd stumbled on Bree somehow and realised Reuben's attachment to her – Damien was both possessive and jealous! His eyes met Bree's again and he wet his lips, whatever, she wasn't safe here – not if Damien knew about her. This was exactly what he'd feared and here it was salient before him.

'Your blood brother?' Bree asked.

'Yeah, made by the same sire as me.'

'So your sire is… is involved in my… in my kidnapping?'

'In your kidnapping? No, this was aimed at me, Bree, not you. It was a warning, a message. I'm so sorry.'

Bree nodded, 'Can we get rid of… of the body…'

'Yeah, I'll put him in my graveyard – fitting really…' he paused, not wanting to get into all of that, not yet. The panic was receding though, and his mind was becoming less clouded.

'Let's go and talk, and then I'll sort this,' he said.

Bree seemed to take in a deep breath and then led him back down the corridor to a fancy chrome and glass kitchen. An older woman with grey hair sat at the kitchen table and was smoking a cigarette, using a saucer for an ashtray. The kettle was on too, such weird normality in the oddest of circumstances, even to Reuben. Bree pulled the blinds down, cutting out the last of the afternoon sunshine, thoughtful as ever. Reuben paused at the doorway, then pushed on and sat down opposite Bree's mother. Bree took the seat between them.

'Mrs Morgan?' he asked.

Bree's mother looked up at him, really examining him. 'I think I need... I need to know everything,' she said. Her voice was surprisingly strong considering she'd spent the entire time since the attack in silence. 'You have something to do with the monster which broke into my house? And that had something to do with my baby disappearing all those years ago?'

'Mama...' Bree began.

'No, your mother has a right to her questions,' Reuben said. 'Mrs Morgan, my name is Reuben Chamberlain, I'm the one who rescued your daughter from where she was held captive, and I am a creature like the one your daughter killed today, just as were the ones who took her before... although I don't think that her kidnapping was related to this, today. I know the creature in there. I'm sorry but I think this was... was aimed at me, by one who would do me harm.'

'How are you involved?' Mrs Morgan asked.

'I spend my life trying to... to rescue those who are... who are taken or hurt by others of my kind. Mrs Morgan. There is more to this world than what you know, even begin to suspect...'

'I saw a little of it today. You are like that creature, you say? A...' Mrs Morgan gave out a small uncomfortable laugh, '...a vampire?'

'I am not like him as in I do not prey on innocent people but yes, we are kin. I, like he, am a drinker... what you would call vampire, although, forgive me, but your popular culture is very inaccurate about what that word means.'

Bree's mother pulled on her cigarette again. She stood and went to the side where the kettle was boiling but rather than making tea she returned with a bottle of amaretto and three glasses which she proceeded to fill. Reuben took his and took a cautious sip, it tasted like alcoholic marzipan. Bree's mother drank one straight down and then poured another and lit another cigarette. She offered the pack and whilst Bree shook her head, Reuben took one and lit it up. Bree's eyes examined him in surprise and he managed a slight smile.

'Vampire,' her mother said, after the second smoke was nearly gone. The kitchen was starting to smell a bit now, pungent smoke and the sweetness of the liquor which Bree's mother seemed to be putting down her at some rate.

'Yes,' Reuben was watching her carefully, much as he'd been around Bree when he'd first rescued her. Humans either accepted easily, or they didn't, he wasn't yet sure which way this encounter was going to go.

'And they took my… they took you, Bree…'

'Yes, from the club,' Bree said.

'To… to…'

'To feed from me,' Bree whispered.

Reuben put his hand over hers, relishing the feel of her fingers under his. Waves of guilt and protectiveness washed over him. She'd already suffered so much, and now he'd put her right back into the path of danger. But how could he have known Damien would show up again, he'd not bothered Reuben in over a hundred years other than to take what he was owed!

'And you found Bree?' Mrs Morgan asked him, Reuben forced his racing thoughts to focus.

'Yes.'

'And you brought her home.'

'… yes…'

Bree's mother reached over to take his other hand, making a strange triad of linked hands. 'Thank you,' she whispered. 'You gave me a gift I was past dreaming of!'

Reuben's lips twisted with emotion but he held it together. 'It was my pleasure,' he said, then gently but firmly removed his hand from her mother's. He couldn't bear the gratitude in her eyes, it was too much.

Bree's mother lit a third cigarette and Reuben took another from the offered packet too.

'And what about... about now?' Bree asked, 'Are we safe?

'Probably not.' Reuben admitted, then glanced at her face. He couldn't leave her here, that much was certain. Chris would have to tolerate a houseguest for a time! But what about the mother?

'Mrs Morgan, do you have any family you could go to?'

'I... erm, yes, my sister?'

'Ok, you go there and I'll have somebody keep an eye on you until my work in London is finished.'

'Do you have to go back?' Bree's mother beat her to the question but Reuben could see she'd been about to ask the same. His heart ached but he couldn't abandon his job now.

'I do, I'm sorry. I've stumbled into something big, some sort of operation up there, and I'm investigating.'

'Rescuing more children?' the old woman's eyes shone as she asked him the question. He felt humbled.

'Trying to.'

'Then yes, you have to go back!'

Reuben took a deep breath. So here it was. He wet his lips and then suddenly he was committing, 'Bree, will you come to London with me?' he asked.

23

Bree's family home had a large enough garden for a city residence, a patio first with the pool, then a sweet-smelling flower garden before the open lawn at the back, lined with old oak trees. Bree had led Reuben outside, after his shocking question, and together they sat in the peace of the dying light in the garden. Reuben took her fingers in his, holding her tightly enough that his worry was still apparent.

'I've missed you so much,' he said. He was so much more relaxed than he had been in the kitchen, Bree could see the loss of tension in his shoulders.

'Same.'

'I'm sorry I left... the way I did. I needed some headspace I guess.'

Bree nodded, remembering the hotel, the cutting agony of his departure. She wasn't going to let him know how much that hurt. Instead, she smiled a small smile, 'you are forgiven. Thank you for coming – today.'

Reuben's eyes burned but he simply nodded.

'So...' she said, her voice low, not wanting to spoil a moment, but needing clarity, 'If I come to London, what then?'

'You will be safer there, I think.'

'With you?'

'With my friends. I am working, I guess you'd say undercover, but there you would be close to me, protected — more so than if I left you with Izzy and Josh!'

Bree managed a half-smile at the idea of Izzy or Josh trying to protect anyone. 'Yeah, I guess,' she said. 'You are sure this… this assault was aimed at you?'

'Yeah, Farrow… Farrow was one of my… of my blood-father's favourite lackeys. He and I have a history too, but I think this was a message from Damien.'

'And this Damien, he's your blood-father?'

'Yes. He won't get to you again, I promise.'

Bree stroked his hand softly, allowing her fingers to skim over his skin. 'And what of… of us?' she asked. 'If I come to London? Do we go back to being friends or… or…?'

Reuben shuffled slightly, then sighed. 'Bree, you don't realise how much you ask of me, to ask me that,' he whispered. 'I'm… Bree I'm afraid and yet, today my worst fear was realised even despite the distance. I want you to come with me, I want you close.' Reuben moved both hands to her hairline, cupping her face. His eyes seemed very bright in the darkness, deep and unreadable. His hands trembled slightly and then a smile lit his lips. 'I love you,' he said it as though he was almost in wonder of the statement. 'I want you to be safe but it's more too. I don't want to be apart from you anymore.'

Bree shuffled forward, pulling away from his hands to lay her head down on his chest, 'You know it was hell when you left…' she whispered.

'One of the hardest things I've ever done was to drive away.'

'We can't keep doing that. I don't want you less than committed.'

Reuben exhaled slowly, his hands pulling her closer. 'I've never wanted anything more,' he whispered, 'Fuck it. Let's give this a try.'

'I want to.'

Reuben kissed her, his lips soft on hers. He lingered a moment longer, then, 'I need to get rid of that body, and I need to feed after all that time in the sun. Be ready and packed in a couple of hours for me?'

Bree wet her lips, then nodded, suddenly life seemed to have purpose again. Reuben looked out over the city from where the sun was setting, bathing the world in its orange and pink glow. He seemed faraway for a moment, but then smiled.

'Come on then,' he said, 'let's get going.'

24

Reuben paused at the door to the club, his hand on the old wooden boards of the door like a man walking to the gallows. It was harder to go back to work knowing that Bree was now only a stone's throw away. So much harder, especially when he was leaving a warm bed, with a naked and enticing Bree there pining for him. Still her image was burned on his retina, eyes content with satiated lust and lips red from kissing. Her hair was mussed, in his visual memory, and her breasts just peeking from the duvet she had pulled around them both just an hour earlier, causing the heat of love-making to rise and to make them both dizzy as together they'd moaned aloud in orgasm.

Reuben made his way down the same old stairs, through the same old door, and into the club. Bree's image moved with him, but he repressed it. He had to leave that behind him now, not turn soft and stupid. He'd have to earn this now, he'd abandoned the job that only just given to him, as a barman in the club, to go and find Bree, so he wasn't likely to easily walk back into it. Before opening, the club was eerily quiet. The strong electric lights felt wrong as they cast away the shadows, allowing Kim – a young drinker from America – to get the place as clean as possible. Important even in a normal human club where the worst you had to remove was beer and semen and worse in a drinker club where the blood had to be scrubbed away too, lest you attract rats and flies... the flies were the worst.

'You're in for it...' Kim muttered as he walked towards the bar. Her voice still held the husk of having smoked most of her days as a human. She'd been turned in the 80s and you could tell. Her hair was still frizzy, and her clothing dated.

'I am?'

'Fucking off like that...'

'Had to feed.'

'Coulda fed here.'

'I like to hunt, not shoot fish in a barrel,' he snapped, then, 'Boss man about?

'Out back.'

'Ta...'

Reuben sucked in a deep breath and prepared himself to meet with Barnes. Barnes wasn't the big boss – as in the one running the operation, but he ran the club side of it and so it was to him Reuben would have to go for his job back.

The corridor beyond was fairly dark but that was no issue for Reuben, his senses were keener than even some of the others of his kind. He made his way to the room out the back, and then tapped on the door.

'What is it?' Not the most hopeful response.

'It's Reuben.'

The door opened. The guy stood beyond was a bigger set drinker, blond of hair and with small piggy eyes and tight lips. He was dressed in a black shirt and jeans. His gaze moved slowly over Reuben's face.

'Thought you'd fucked off?' he said, not giving up entry into the room.

'I went to feed.'

'Plenty to eat here.'

'Yeah, and no hunt. I wanted to hunt.'

Barnes ran his eyes over Reuben again. 'Didn't take you for one of them.'

'Of them?'

'A hunter – a bleeder.'

Reuben shrugged, not dropping the man's gaze.

Barnes stood stationary for another long minute, then moved to let Reuben in. Reuben didn't pause – appearances were too important – and took himself into the room. Dark, windowless box that it was, the room was at least pleasantly decorated with an old mahogany desk and two bookshelves which were both full to bursting, if dusty and unused. Reuben had never seen the use of ornamental books, to him they were sustenance to be devoured, tools to be used, not dusty old relics to be looked at. In front of the desk was an old wooden chair and Reuben allowed his body to relax into it. Barnes moved back behind the desk.

'Lucky for you, the big boss has noticed you and so I have orders to bring you back in,' Barnes said, 'If it was down to me I'd garotte you and hang you from the rafters. I don't like jumped up little pricks like you thinking you can do as you please.'

Reuben, actually several hundred years older than Barnes, said nothing but maintained eye-contact.

'If we do take you back, though, it'd be full-time. No more fucking off when you get the urge! If you want to "hunt" then grab yourself a punter here and set him or her lose in the building. Have your fun that way, but you don't leave here, ok?'

'Noted,' Reuben said. Poor Bree, but she'd understand.

'You carry a mobile?'

'Yeah…'

'Crunch it, or hand it over…'

Reuben's gut churned again, he actually had two – one for "work" and one for Bree and Hugh. He pulled out the work one, tossed it on the floor, and put the heel of his boot through the screen.

'Good man,' Barnes said, 'It seems we are on the same page after all. Welcome back. You're on bar duty and clean-up.'

'Cheers,' Reuben said, then stood.

'Don't fuck this up, nobody gets more than two chances.'
'You can count on me, boss.'

Back in his own room in the old warehouse above the club, Reuben lay in quiet contemplation. So, here it was, again. The avenging angel on a mission to save the innocent at risk of his own life. Had he ever really been such? He didn't know. He still didn't even really know why he did this, why this was his crusade. Perhaps a lingering trauma from his own time as a slave, as a captive of one of the worst of his kind. The thought took him back to Max's body, now buried close by the woman he'd murdered, Reuben's wife, Elizabeth. Then of course, those thoughts led again to him, to Damien. Once the thought came, it was unavoidable, uncontainable. Tiredness didn't help at all, either... and he really was so tired.

Damien had started what he called "his experiments" on Reuben only weeks after taking over the house and church. In those weeks, Reuben had been little more than a blood-slave, bound and locked away to be fed from by Damien or his cronies. Then, suddenly, something had changed. Damien had brought him out of his captivity and had put him before his congregation again, albeit with the firm warning that should he mention an inkling of what was happening, they'd lock the doors and kill them all. Reuben hadn't realized in time what they were doing – building an army of blood-slaves. Take the person away from the flock, into the old confessional booth that he'd never removed. Feed from them. Make them forget. Rinse. Repeat. And Reuben was so grateful for freedom that even when he did realise what was happening, he'd gone along with it. Maybe that's why Damien had chosen him the way he did to be turned – or maybe it was the voices – maybe Damien somehow *knew*. Either way, at the turn of six months, Damien had come into the chamber where he was chained to the wall by one lone shackle – normal procedure when he was not out in the church – with a communal goblet filled with thick, cold blood.

'The blood of Christ, in a way. Drink,' he'd said.

'I can't drink that!'

'Do not mistake in believing you have a choice, preacher.'

And so he'd drunk.

Usually, when a drinker was made, the process was done in one night. A person, rendered helpless, would be drained of all blood and then fed the demon blood. The process didn't work unless the carrier – the drinker – was firmly within the grasp of the demon element, with humanity pushed aside. A bond was created, the body died, and then was reborn. For Reuben, it wasn't done this way. Instead, over the course of a year, Damien brought him goblet after glass of cold, thick, blood once a week like clockwork, and Reuben drank them. He had no other choice. Tainted blood, more so even than he'd realised then.

'You were one of my first experiments,' Damien told him, much later, 1830s or 1840s. 'I wanted to see what turning you like this would do to you.'

Damien's experiments. Never before or since had Reuben known a drinker with such a passion for discovering the ins and outs of the kin, how they worked, why they worked. Reuben, sitting across from Damien then, in a skanky old lodging in Bristol, had looked down at his hands. He sighed. He had no idea what he was, not anymore. Not a true drinker, not the other either, no – he was something worse.

'I wish you'd just killed me,' he said.

'No, you don't.'

'I do,' he whispered, but it wasn't true, he didn't really wish that at all. Despite it all, he was glad for his life if nothing else.

'I wish…'

'You want for nothing, so there is no point in wishing, preacher.' Damien always still called him that, and it still grated. It was true though, the two of them spent much time alone together, and in that time Damien had made sure they lacked for nothing. Still not equals, but not master and slave anymore, either. Still Farrow and Gates were around, but they didn't share Damien's favouritism with Reuben. As far as Reuben knew, he was the prize, the one person Damien actually opened up to.

Damien sighed and stood, 'I need to feed… and to satisfy other urges whilst I'm at it. It's like an itch I can't scratch at times, will you join me?'

Reuben shook his head. Damien gorged himself on a regular basis, raping, torturing, feeding, rejoicing in the devil that tainted his soul, but Reuben at least now was able to decline to join him. If nothing else, that was a positive to their ill-born friendship.

Damien stood, and Reuben with him, intending to go past to his own chamber and sit with a book for a while. Damien took his arm though, as he tried to pass.

'Can I… I mean, I need to take some more of your blood, tomorrow…'

'Another experiment?'

'I need to know why you were the only one who survived what I did, the only one it worked on.'

'I don't think the key to that is in my blood.'

'And I am sure it is.'

For a long moment they stood thus, and then Damien's face changed, became something Reuben had never seen there before, tenderness, 'Do you really wish I had killed you?' he asked.

Reuben shook his head.

'Good. Because I have never been gladder to have let a man live.'

The atmosphere in the room was suddenly thick and cloying. Reuben tried to push through, in his mind, to make his escape but instead, somehow, he was leaning in, allowing his lips to meet those of his sire.

Reuben sighed and pressed his head into the pillows behind him. The love he'd once had for Damien was his biggest shame. Not for the fact that his sire was a man, he didn't care about that, but because of the kind of man he was. At least his other loves had been sweet, pure – even if Lucy had tried to kill him in the end! That had not been an example of her impurity, but of his own. But Damien, God! He was a monster, he'd killed Bess in cold blood, kept him hostage and destroyed everything he'd once held dear… and yet in those early days, Reuben had loved him perhaps more than any other love he'd yet known.

25

The night-times seemed longer, now that Reuben was away undercover. Bree had settled in fairly well at Chris's place under the care of he and Ginny, despite that she was pretty sure neither of them were thrilled at her presence, but she was restless, worried. Several nights that first week, she'd been hit with headaches too, blinders that had made her almost bedridden – most likely the change in air, Ginny said, but then Ginny didn't really know much about headaches! This was normal though, that's what she took from her new companions, for Reuben to vanish.

'These places are like secret clubs,' Ginny said, 'Once you're in, you cut off ties outside. Him vanishing like that means he's in.'

'Or dead for deserting to come rescue me…' Bree said, determined to be gloomy.

'Well, maybe I guess…' that was Chris. Bree was sat at the edge of a modern leather sofa for this conversation, in the living room of the flat by an open window which at least let in a breeze. Bree wasn't thrilled at living so high off the ground; the flat was on the sixteenth floor, and the lack of air in the block was stifling – it probably was causing her headaches, just as Ginny had said. At least it was a nicer area though, a luxury apartment rather than a tower block with scary run-down corridors and graffiti. She couldn't imagine Ginny ever living anywhere else though, her wardrobe probably cost its original owner thousands of pounds, and her jewellery could probably feed a family for a year. Bree was pretty sure somebody had died for those jewels.

Bree allowed her eyes to fall on Chris. Of all the drinkers she'd met he was the most stereotypical of what she'd expect a vampire to be like, tall, gaunt, short dark hair, well-dressed. He was older-looking than the others, in his forties when he was turned by the look of it. He was secretive too, unwelcoming and quiet. Reuben said he was to be trusted though, and Bree trusted Reuben's judgement.

'Can somebody go and… I don't know, check in on him?'

'It's safer we stay out now, Reu won't want us there,' Ginny said, 'These types get cranky if too many new drinkers turn up in one place.'

'Besides, I don't fancy the ear-bashing we'd get from him if we were to waltz in there whilst he's undercover,' Chris added.

Bree wet her lips and held his eye. 'I'll go.'

'Don't be ridiculous!'

The dismissal in Chris's tone set Bree's nerves on edge, she pressed her lips and glared at him, 'and why not? I love Reuben and so am probably the most trustworthy person you have! I'm not kin and nobody knows my face… I can pose as one of those confused kids who fall into that place, but I know how to defend myself if things get ugly. I need to do something…'

Chris's grey eyes darkened a little for her tone, but he nodded abruptly. 'Fine, have it your way. Don't take stupid risks though and I will be personally keeping close tabs on you!'

'Deal!'

Chris sighed, probably remembering a time when young ladies did as they were told without arguing, but then nodded, 'Fine. Ginny'll dress you and school you in how to behave, and you will carry your mobile at all times so I can track you.'

'Thank you,' she said.

'Don't thank me, just don't get yourself killed!'

Bree nodded, relief to finally be able to do something useful flooding her form.

The night was never really dark in London, that was one thing Bree had come to realise even in the short time she'd been there, there were never any stars either, just the slightly glowing smog. She sat alone in the back of Ginny's car whilst she drove on in silence, weaving through traffic just like her human counterparts, until they arrived at the edge of the area called Soho where Reuben was working. Ginny pulled the car in on double yellows, prompting a loud beep from the car behind them, and turned around to face Bree.

'I won't come any closer than this, we need to keep some of us unknown...'

'Ok.'

'You have your directions?'

'Yeah.'

'Let me see your neck!'

Bree pulled aside her shirt to show Ginny the fairly fresh bite mark Chris had put there the night before. To make it more likely they'd give her admittance, he'd said. The wound was small but raised up and sore.

'Good enough,' Ginny murmured, then dug in her pocket and handed Bree a fist full of twenties, 'I have no idea how much they'll charge you for entry but this should cover it,' she said. 'Be careful, and keep your mobile on you at all times, we'll be tracking your GPS through it.'

Bree nodded again, already she was shaking with nerves. Ginny ran an eye over her once more then half-smiled – the closest to a smile she had ever seen on the girl's features at least.

'I am appropriately grateful for the risk you are taking,' she said, 'thank you.'

'I'm doing it for Reu,' Bree whispered, but smiled back and unclipped her seatbelt, 'Wish me luck.'

'I pray you don't need luck. Goodbye Bree, I'll be waiting for you at the address you have written down as agreed just before dawn.

Outside of the car the night seemed busy. As with everywhere in London, Friday night was always going to be a busy one, especially as the clubs were beginning to open. All around was suddenly a bustle of noise and activity. Bree paused outside of the car a moment to catch her breath but then pushed on. Soho was so brightly lit that it seemed hardly believable that such a club could exist there right under the eye of the busy city. Neon lights, brightly lit shop-faces despite the late hour, and so many people milling about. Off the main drag though, and away from the lights and noise, things began to become clearer: little side-roads led to basements surrounded by fences, some with lights above, others with just music pumping out. One little alley seemed to have nothing but adult shops lining its walkway, and then a little kebab shop spilling out the scent of spiced meats into the air. Bree moved quickly up this road but then back out onto another wide and normal-looking thoroughfare.

Bree paused, then crossed and slipped down another alley, trying to remember the directions she'd written for herself and hoping beyond hope that she'd not get herself mugged walking through dodgy streets alone at night with a pocket full of cash. At the midpoint of the alley Bree discovered steps going up too here and there, to doors set into the sides of dilapidated old buildings. Sometimes the word "Models" indicated that there was the comfort of a paid embrace to be had at the top. Another smaller road led off away from the main streets again. Here were less people about, and those there were looked at her with speculation. Doors stood open, invitations, some with bouncers, others without. There were illegal brothels here still, Chris had warned her, as well as the exclusive clubs and hidden basements – an underground playground for both the rich elite and the petty criminals of London, all hidden away down wrought-iron lined steps or up dark corridors. Bree clutched at the paper in her fingers, making her way past a couple of homeless guys sat in a doorway, then past a wide arch to cross over to another small alleyway. This one seemed almost inconspicuous compared to the garish city behind her. Bree glanced up to the side of a tall building to check the road name – she was in the right place – and then began to count. At the third door along was another of those sets of steep stone steps leading down to a door. Bree paused. There was no music leaking out, no light, no nothing and she was almost convinced she had the wrong place. She glanced about her but there was no indication of anything nearby which could be the club she was looking for.

'I guess this is it,' she murmured, glancing down into the darkness and for the first time, a seed of fear started up. It didn't seem right, not at all but she couldn't back out now. She took in a deep breath, feeling her lungs expand, and then stepped off of the path, onto the steps.

The steps down were steep and wet from the rain, about twenty or so, to end abruptly with an old wooden door. Bree paused again but then, before she could lose her nerve, she knocked. For a few minutes, long enough that Bree almost started back up the steps, nothing happened, but then a bolt sounded and the door opened. At last Bree heard the feeble strains of music, heavy music, and her heart leapt. Maybe this was the right place after all.

'Yes?' the guy who opened the door was about thirty, or at least looked it. He was very goth with dark hair to his shoulders, dressed in a shirt, a waistcoat with chains on it, and black trousers. His eyes were suspicious but ran over Bree with interest too. He was a drinker, she knew enough of the tell-tale signs to see it.

'I was told that a girl with my… interests… might come here.' Bree said, then pulled down the neck of her top to show him the fang marks there.

'Hmm. Who sent you?'

'I don't know his name, I simply call him…' the last word choked, seeming too cliché but she managed to whisper it just as Chris had ordered, '… Master.'

The guy on the door chuckled, 'Oh, one of them, eh?' he laughed and then moved to give her access. Inside the door was a plain room, red walls and a set of stairs descending even further down to what must have been a sub-basement.

'Down there?' she asked,

'Yeah, afraid?'

Bree sucked in her breath but she knew her reaction was at least not unjustified. 'No…' she muttered and then started down.

'Wait!' the guy behind her snapped, causing her to almost slip on the stairs, heart thudding again.

'I… what?'

'That's twenty quid, love.' He smirked, 'nothing for free these days…'

Bree's breathing eased again as she pulled out a scrumpled purple note and handed it to the guy.

'Thanks…' she managed, then descended down into the depths of the house. At the bottom there was another wooden door and this she pushed and then almost stepped back at the wall of music which had been repressed by the sound-proofing. Bree paused, steeled herself, and then entered the club

Inside, the room was very dark and all about was the crashing of heavy metal music, the raised voices of people trying to shout over said music, as well as the chaos of people dancing, socialising and generally having a good time. Bree paused for a moment, the wall of smoke, sound and the stench of beer crashing over her like a wave. Her gut tightened; the very last time she had set foot into a nightclub had been the night of her abduction. Somehow, that hadn't occurred to her until then but once it did, it was almost enough to freeze her in place. This was a drinker club too, so she could guess how easily people vanished from here, hell, they were probably accepted on the basis of how easily they'd be missed. Two blinks and then her vision cleared to give her a view of the place. There were people everywhere and, in the dim room, she could not tell the drinkers from the humans as they danced, drank and generally partied. A multitude of people too, all dressed in dark colours: the goths in jet black, hints of red and purple here and there alongside their more colourful punk counterparts. Metallers in baggy jeans and tees, dark-clad steampunks and steamgoths too, lots of them – she supposed the fall-back to Victorian styles was appealing to a group like this. Bree drank them all in, not sure where to go, how to conduct herself. Her palms were suddenly sweaty, her heart thudding, but then she saw him.

Reuben was behind the bar. He hadn't noticed her yet.

In some ways, despite how he looked just the same, Reuben was so different. He was dressed much like the others in the place with his long hair loose to his shoulders rather than his normal ponytail, his standard black vest, over-shirt and black jeans. He was polishing a glass – a movement so much a stereotype it was almost laughable – whilst talking to another guy behind the bar. He seemed at home there, comfortable, as though he belonged. It was strange to see him like that where she was so very much the opposite, but she supposed he was used to this, doing the job he did.

Bree pulled her handbag up over her shoulder and fidgeted with it. She looked as out of place as she felt. She'd dressed herself in the end and her naivety showed in the choices she'd made; plain black jeans, an embroidered t-shirt and with her blond hair clean and brushed. Perhaps for a rock pub, even maybe a standard club, she'd have been ok but the order of the day here seemed to be over-the-top, leaving her looking a bit like a lost uni student. She'd need at least to get her ears pierced before next time, maybe some colour in her hair and definitely some new clothes… that was, if she survived for there to be a next time! She moved forward a few more paces and willed him to look up. At last he did. Reuben's eye travelled over the room and there stopped on her. Shock registered; a slight widening of his eye and a catching of breath, and then he put down the glass and stepped around the bar, coming towards her.

'You look lost, love?' he said, over the music. The words were casual, stranger's words but his eyes asked a million questions.

'I... first time...' she said.

'It shows.'

Reuben's fingers grasped Bree's wrist and she put up no resistance as he pulled her from the doorway to the bar and there sat her down. His eyes were searching but he remained in character, pouring her a drink and putting it down on the bar before her. JD and coke, although not overly strong. Bree took a sip and looked about her again. Reuben served two customers and then came back and refilled her glass. People were looking at her, she realised, or maybe that was just paranoia. Panic tried to flutter up and for just an instant, she felt uncomfortable enough that she almost wanted to get up and flee, might have done if not Reuben's keeping half an eye on her.

'You look ready to be eaten up,' he said as he wondered past for a glass to serve up a beer, his words obviously chosen carefully, 'what's a nice girl like you doing in a joint like this?'

'Looking for a bit of excitement I guess?'

'You've picked the right place for that at least...' He pulled the sweet-smelling beer and handed it to the guy stood waiting, then after a quick glance to check for more customers, came back to her.

'You have a name?'

'Bea... a... I mean... Trixie?'

'You don't know your name?'

'My name is Beatrix, but most people call me Trixie...'

'Well Trixie, I'm Ben.'

'Nice to meet you, Ben...'

Bree sipped her drink again, then glanced about her, no, nobody was paying her any attention now. Reuben went to speak again but then caught the eye of somebody behind her.

His eyes flashed, but he swallowed and moved back to serve another customer. Despite how with every fibre of her being, she wanted to turn, Bree managed to remain facing the bar. The music changed, and then a stranger came to her side and sat down. He was fairly young and fairly obviously human. He had short spiked hair which was shot through with a blue wash and was wearing a sleeveless work-shirt and jeans. He grinned at her and rocked a bit on the bar stool.

'You're new!' he slurred.

'I am.'

'Vamp?'

'No.'

'Ah, pity! Thought only one of them would dare to dress so low key…'

'Maybe I'm just brave?'

Reuben's attention was caught by her words and he served up a pint of Guinness which was mainly head to a longhaired greasy drinker in record time and then came back to stand in his previous spot.

'So, what're…' the boy began but Reuben caught his eye and almost growled the words: "Get lost, kid."

The lad didn't even reply but scarpered back into the room, fear in his eyes. That the humans there knew what they were facing was obvious and she supposed she'd be a bit scared if a strange drinker had spoken to her like that. Reuben's expression changed back to its neutral state and he poured her another drink, putting it on the bar before her.

'You don't have to keep giving me drinks,' she said, shifting on the uncomfortable barstool, 'I have money…'

'Don't want your money.'

'Maybe I don't want your drinks?'

'Perhaps I'm hoping that you'll return the favour?'

Her spine tingled. Despite that it was all a rouse, she was quite enjoying the flirting. It was a phase they'd skipped.

'I guess…' she said, and leaned forward so that she could whisper, albeit loudly enough that a few people around her could hear, 'Like I said, I guess that's why I came… a bit of excitement?'

Reuben smirked, he dithered a moment, and then called over to one of the other drinkers, an older woman with long hair and bangs who stood at the edge of the bar.

'Taking a break,' he said, 'mind this for me?'

The woman cast an eye over her and then chuckled, 'Not even you can resist a good girl, eh?' she said.

'Well, it's been a while…'

'Go on, then, don't take forever with it…'

Reuben skulked out from behind the door and took her wrist in his hand. Unsure of protocol, she froze and tried to look scared.

'Come on, you wanted to get a bit of excitement. Come with me, love…'

Reuben pulled again and Bree gave in, allowing her feet to move but glancing about herself as though still nervous. It was a hard act to keep up, but one she knew was important with eyes upon them. Bree continued thus until they came to a door which led out of the main hall. Reuben produced a key and pulled open the door, dragging her inside by her wrist. Bree let out a whimper which turned to a moan of pleasure as the door was shut and his lips came down on hers.

'What the fuck are you doing here you crazy girl?' he whispered against her lips between kisses.

'I had to come, you just vanished!'

'You could have got yourself into so much trouble if I hadn't been here tonight!'

'I know but I had to come… I was worried sick!'

'Baby,' he murmured, nuzzling her face.

Bree accepted the kiss, then glanced around her. The room was fairly dark but as her eyes adjusted, a bead of disgust formed in her belly. The room was lined like a wet-room, with tiles which were probably once white but were now stained with a rusty pigment. Blood. There were shackles at the walls and two on the floor too. Bree physically stepped back and pulled in a mouthful of oxygen.

'What…'

'Sorry to bring you in here,' he whispered, 'I didn't know what else to do. You threw me a bit coming like that.'

'What is this?'

'It's a feeding room…'

'People die in here?'

'Sometimes but not often. There's enough people vanishing from here without adding nightly kills to that list so it is… discouraged.'

'What?'

Reuben went to reply but something caught his attention and he spun around, his ear obviously catching something she did not hear.

'Shit!' he murmured, then indicated the shackles. Do you trust me, baby?'

'With my life.'

'Good,' he said, then gently pushed her body so that she was against the wall and lifted the shackle nearest her right arm. Bree nodded, she understood; if anyone came in it was better if she looked as though she were being fed from. Bree swallowed again, exhaled and then put up her hands for him. Reuben eyed her for a long moment, then clicked the shackles about her wrists. He paused and then kissed her again.

'There at least that looks less suspicious… catch me up,' he whispered. 'Quietly, I don't want to be overheard and my kind hear better than yours.'

'There's not much to say. Chris was worried and I was half-mad with anxiety. Chris thought it was too dangerous to send in another drinker so he was wary of who to trust as well as anything else. So I came instead. I'm just a harmless human, we didn't think anyone would suspect me.'

'I…' Reuben began, but then tensed. Even without his extra sensory hearing, Bree heard what he heard, footsteps coming to the door.

'Cry,' he hissed, and then put down his face to her neck, the sharpness of the bite removed the need to fake tears, and Bree added in an extra moan for effect. The door opened letting in a rush of music and light, as well as the stench of the bar. Bree struggled a bit, still crying, and Reuben's teeth left her throat.

'Taken,' he said, not looking around.

'Was looking for you, actually, Ben.' A male voice.

Reuben sighed and turned about, not wiping her blood from his lips. 'I'm taking my break,' he said.

'I know, but there's a queue forming outside – all humans. Seems we're trendy at the moment.'

'Just send them away.'

'There's probably a few too many in here too – thirty-seven…'

Reuben sighed and turned away completely, he wiped the blood from his lips leaving a smear across the back of his hand. Bree's mind raced, trying to take it all in, but then she remembered she was supposed to be frightened and began to pull on the shackles. Her wrists screamed and the new pain made more tears easier to fake.

'Throw them out then.'

'I'll get someone to sort it,' the stranger said, retreating.

'Do it yourself, please…'

'I… me?'

'Yeah, I'll be out in five minutes or so, if you have any problems,' Reuben promised.

The other guy nodded and then closed the door, leaving them back in darkness. Reuben turned to her and ran a now bloody hand down her face.

'Sorry, did I hurt you?'

'Yeah but it's ok.'

'See… it's too dangerous for you to come here! You look like bloody dinner on a plate, you're…'

'I'm the only one who can keep an eye on you, that's what I am!'

'I don't want your face becoming known.'

'I'll only come once a month, and I'll make sure I fit in better next time,' she said. 'Anything to report in for Chris now?'

Reuben broke open the skin of his thumb with a tooth and smeared the blood onto the wound at her throat, then nodded, 'tell him that it's as I suspected.'

'Just that?'

'Yeah.'

'And he'll understand?'

'Yeah.'

Bree nodded, she hadn't really expected confidences, she was just a foot-soldier yet. Reuben sighed again and then slid his hands around her waist, his eyes were filled with concern. Bree leaned forward against the bonds which held her hands to kiss him and with a sudden movement, Reuben lifted her up. Bree wrapped her legs about him around the waist, knowing that he'd be able to hold her weight, and kissed him again, her hands gripping tight about the chains above her head to stop her weight falling onto her wrists. Reuben ran his fingers over the back of her jeans and made a murmur in his throat.

'Maybe next time, I'll wear a skirt,' she whispered, flirting again, and was finally rewarded with a real smile, albeit brief.

'Just don't look like a church camp runaway next time, yeah?' he asked.

'I promise. I'll see you in a few weeks.'

'I love you, baby.'

'I love you too,' she whispered and kissed him one more time. Reuben released her and then unclasped the shackles at her wrists. The skin was sore and bruised but she didn't care. Reuben kissed her once more time, almost greedily and then used a sleeve to wipe away most of the blood around her throat. Bree closed her eyes, memorising the touch, and then steeled herself for the door to open.

'Act dazed and confused,' Reuben whispered, 'I'll see you safely out and vouch for you to come back. They have

"Feeders" here – regulars – so you can just become one of those as far as anyone knows.'

'Ok.'

'I can't be kind though, not out there.'

'I know that too.'

'Ok,' he said, then sucked in a deep breath, 'ok, come on then,' he said, gripping her by the arm and pulling her so that she stumbled. At once the pounding music returned, the harshly bright lights of the club and the bustle and scent of hot sweaty bodies. Bree stumbled again and again, almost tripping over her own feet as Reuben pulled her through the club to the door. She tried to murmur, gripping his sleeve but he was immobile as he marched her to the entrance. The door opening brought in a blast of cold air, enough to make her shiver, and then she was deposited outside.

'Ben,' the guy on the door said.

'Give this one a blue pass,' Reuben said, 'and stamp it as taken – she's mine.'

The other's eyes took in her frame, and Bree made a point of looking dazed.

'All right,' he said and moved into the small room beside the door. When he returned, he held out a blue laminated card with the stamp of a black bird on it. Bree took it and then turned to Reuben.

'Go home, and tell nobody about this place,' he said, 'if anybody comes here at your say-so, or looking for you, I'll kill them and then I'll kill you, do you understand?'

Bree nodded, forcing her eyes to widen, and then turned about and all but ran up the stairs which led to the road level. Behind her, Bree heard laughter and then Reuben's tone,

'Anyone wanna put money on that one coming back for seconds?' then more laughter.

26

Bree was more prepared for the trip the following month. At Chris's agreement, she bought herself a load of new clothes and washed a red dye through her hair. Despite her shyness at doing so, she asked Ginny to help her to dress and then stood and looked into the mirror at the almost stranger standing there. She was garbed from head to toe in dark colours but for the red in the skirt. Black stockings, boots, too short tartan skirt, black PVC corset and all. Her hair, currently chin length, she wore tied away into two little tufts behind her head. Her eyes were dark with eyeliner and her lips blood-red with a hint of black at the centre.

'Hmmm,' Ginny murmured, and then rummaged in her jewellery box, coming back up with a black leather dog-collar set with silver spikes and what looked like miniature diamonds – knowing Ginny, they probably were. This she buckled around her throat.

'Should I not keep my neck clear for…'

'He can remove it if he wants to. Makes the outfit! Look.'

Bree did so and she had to agree, the rough leather collar made her look badass, despite the sparkly bits. She smiled tentatively, then looked back to Ginny. 'I guess I'm ready.'

Bree was more nervous than the time before as Chris's car pulled away, leaving her stood alone outside of the club; this time she knew what she was walking into. She had on her a cheap mobile phone, fifty in cash and the card Reuben had given her last time, with the crow stamp on the back. She swallowed a couple of times and forced a calm on herself, then approached the steps going down. Like last time, the club was completely hidden, the stairway seeming to lead only to a darkened residential place. Bree walked down the steps and then found the door. Here the music could be heard but still, only mildly. The guy at the door, not the same as last time, eyed her with interest but shook his bald head.

'Full.'

'Oh…' she said, but then her fingers found the card and she lifted it. Her hand was shaking but she didn't try to control it – in normal circumstances, she probably should be a bit scared. 'I have this.'

A hand came forward and she deposited the card into it. He glanced over it, then handed it back and pushed open the door. It seemed that Reuben had some sway then.

Inside the room was much as before, lively and packed out. Sweaty bodies, pounding music, blood. Bree paused a long moment to allow the change in volume to register, and then looked about for Reuben. As before, he was behind the bar. His hair was loose about him, and he wore a back vest and jeans. Out of all of them, her Reuben was probably the least extravagant, but still the most striking. He seemed to share a joke with the other guy serving, then picked up a glass and drank. Bree's heart swelled painfully. She stepped a step closer, but found herself jostled by a drunk chick, probably her age, definitely human. Her lips opened to apologise despite that the other girl had bumped her, but then she remembered she was supposed to be Trixie, and so made herself rigid instead, pushing the girl off her. The girl muttered something she didn't catch, but then stumbled away. The commotion was enough to have caught Reuben's attention though, he turned and looked at Bree, and then, very obviously, did a double take. Bree inwardly repressed a smile, although the colour must have climbed in her cheeks as his eyes moved over her body. Bree held his gaze, channelling her inner Trixie, and then walked slowly to the bar.

'Trix...'

'Is this better?' she asked, shouting a little over the music, 'No more church camp?'

'That works. I have a break in an hour,' he said, and then turned away and continued to talk with the other guy there. Bree waited a few moments, surprised but not downhearted at his neglect; she was supposed to be his toy, not his girlfriend. Finally, she waved him back over and asked for a drink. He served her with a bored air, but his finger touched hers as he passed her the drink, just for a second, and again she had to repress a smile.

Eventually the hour passed and Reuben moved out from behind the bar. He put up a hand for Bree and she took it, remembering to look a little nervous as he led her back behind the bar and through to a little room behind, not the same one as before, with the shackles, but more of a homely room with a sofa and an old clock in the corner. Once inside, Reuben turned a key in the lock and then turned to her and opened his arms. Bree flew to him, gripping him tightly. His chest was slightly damp with sweat but she didn't care, it was bliss to hold him again properly.

'Is it safe here?' she whispered.

'As safe as anywhere here, we'll still have to be quiet...' he murmured back, then, 'God... look at you...'

'You approve?'

Reuben didn't answer but placed one finger on the dip in her cleavage. 'Do you think Trixie is the type of girl who would...'

'Oh, I think so.'

'So, I don't need to tie you up again then?'

'Only if you want to…' the words were out before she could help them, a level of flirtation she never would have believed she possessed. Bree expected laughter from Reuben, but if "Bree" was locked away to some hidden place within, to give her over to Trixie, so was Reuben for "Ben". His body moved closer, his hand moving behind her to find the knot in the lace of her corset. Bree said nothing, didn't move as he loosened the hefty item and pulled it free, popping the clasps like a pro. Bree didn't move, didn't touch him but her eyes must have burned as his hands came up to cup her breasts. She inhaled deeply, then moved away from him, to the sofa. He caught her as she had her back to him, and there his hands caressed her flesh, his arms coming from behind her. Bree allowed him to push her forwards so that she essentially fell over the arm of the sofa. His hand slid up over her shoulder, the other sliding under her skirt. He leaned in and whispered into her ear, 'Is this ok?'

'Yes,' she barely gasped out, and then moaned, lost in feelings of lustful passion she'd never experienced before. Reuben's lips caressed her shoulder again, and then, as he fumbled his zipper and pushed inside of her, his teeth too broke the skin, causing a massive contrast of pleasure and pain which rocked her whole form. Bree cried out, her voice echoing loudly enough that they must have heard it on the other side of the door, but then stifled the sounds so that moan was almost a growl. Reuben's body moved as he drank, and by the time he moved away, her form was already slumped in pleasure. Reuben lifted her gently and pulled her into his arms. His lips caressed her face, kissing her cheek, her nose, her throat. He inhaled a few long breaths, and then put his lips so close to her ear that they were almost on it.

'I love you, Beatrice Morgan' he said, so lightly spoken that the words were almost just a breath.

'I adore you,' she murmured back, a tad too loud probably, but he didn't reproach her for her words. A lot of the humans in the club probably spoke the same to those they fed. Reuben's arms clutched her to him for a long moment, his face buried in her hair where it had come loose from its bunches, but then he sighed and released her.

'I've gotta get back to work,' he said, but as he spoke, he pulled a small notebook from the pocket of his jeans. The book was one of those tiny ones, like a novelty, which were often found attached to a keyring or suchlike. This he placed into her hand. Bree nodded and clutched it tight. Reuben picked up her discarded corset and gently placed it back against her skin. His hands moved to do the clasps but she stopped him briefly and placed the book underneath, the way that corset laced, it was the safest place to hide the item. Reuben nodded and did up the rest of the clasps, then turned her around and pulled on the laces. Bree pondered that this was a man of a different age, as the strings pulled tight around her, laced like somebody who definitely knew what they were doing. A twinge of jealousy took her for his now long-dead lovers, but she repressed that too. If she wasn't going to see him again for weeks, she didn't want to end on irrational jealousy.

Once Bree was laced into the corset, Reuben moved to kneel in front of her and his long delicate fingers put her stockings to rights, tugging and clipping until she looked almost normal again. Finally he stood up. At once her eyes filled with tears; he saw them but did not speak, just ran a gentle finger under her eye. Bree put up a hand and slid it under his vest so she was touching his stomach. There she traced the shape of a love-heart on his skin with her fingertip. Reuben smiled, pressing her again briefly, but then stepping back.

'I can't heal you,' he murmured, very low, 'they don't really do that here…'

'It's ok.'

He pressed one last kiss to her lips and then opened the door and led her back out into the club.

Bree's next few visits went as smoothly as the first and so it wasn't until several weeks later that she encountered her first problem at the club. This problem appeared in the form of a handsome redhead dressed in a nine-inch nails t-shirt and black combats. He looked about eighteen but Bree could already see he wasn't quite as young as he seemed – drinker, not human.

'Come here,' the redhead said, a cajole as she entered, following her to a set of sofas at the back of the room she'd started to frequent, 'come and let me taste you, pretty thing!' as he spoke, Bree realised he wasn't alone, he had a buddy – also giving her the eye. This one was shorter, looked more to be in his twenties. His eyes were darker too, less playful. Bree cast her eyes over to the bar. Reuben was out the back, and the bar was being kept by one of the others, a tall handsome guy with skin of chocolate and tattoos on pretty much every piece of uncovered skin. Not human.

'I'm here for Ben… I feed Ben!' Bree's heart took up a hammering in her chest, and she could feel her chest starting to restrict as at the same time adrenaline began to flow.

'Ben won't mind, sweetie – we all share nice here…' that was the buddy, his voice was rich and deep, and in other circumstances might have been gentle.

'I don't… I mean, I am for Ben… I love Ben…' that wasn't too dangerous, a lot of the humans claimed to love their drinker friends.

'I said, Ben won't mind,' the redhead said, his voice growing harder. His buddy moved around so that he stood behind Bree and she flinched as his hands came about her waist from behind her, pulling her in tight to his body. Bree forced stillness even though she felt as though she were close to a swoon. *Come on Bree* she thought to herself, *you knew this might happen!!* With another long breath, she allowed herself to murmur an assent, and closed her eyes. The darker guy, behind her put his fangs into her neck, right there in the main room of the club, whilst the redhead lifted her arm and broke the vein in her wrist. The feeling of being so vulnerable was horrendous. Her bladder wanted to release, her body shied from not just the pain, but the hot breath too, the stray hand on her breast from the attacker behind her. The redhead was gentler than his friend but still her wrist throbbed with a hot searing agony, and the blood trickled free where he spilled it. Bree moaned in pain and fear, her whole body trembling as they began to feed.

'Not... not too much,' she whispered, 'I have to feed Ben tonight.'

The pressure on her wrist abated a little. 'Hush little girl...' the redhead began, but then an agony shot through her shoulder as the guy behind her was suddenly ripped away. The redhead looked up and, in an instant, his face returned to its human counterpart. He didn't seem scared though, just smiled a cheeky grin.

'Ello Ben.'

'Alfie,' Reuben's voice behind her. Bree could have passed out with relief. 'Any reason you and your goon are chewing on one of my pets? You know that's against the rules – unless given permission.'

Bree sank to her knees as he spoke, the tears which spilled not contrived.

'The lady herself gave permission.'

Reuben knelt before her and lifted her chin in his hand. 'Did you?'

Bree wanted no more trouble – the whole point was not to be noticed – and so she nodded. 'In a fashion,' she whispered.

Reuben's eyes searched hers and she could see he was repressing his temper. Bree hoped he could see the true answer in her eyes. He examined her for a long minute, then stood up and pulled her back to her feet by an arm.

'Don't do it again,' he said to Alfie, 'this is one of mine, she's off limits. I don't like other people playing with my pets. Understood?'

'Sorry boss.'

Boss? Well, that was new!

Reuben nodded and looked at where Red's companion was still on the floor, her blood spilled about his lips, 'that goes for you too.'

The other guy nodded.

'Good, and you – Trixie – have a care you don't become more trouble than you're worth. There's a whole club full of potential pets here, remember you're privileged to be mine.'

'Yes, Ben. I'm sorry.' she whispered.

Reuben parted his lips to speak, and she saw the apology in his eyes. 'Good, go home. I'll feed elsewhere tonight!'

'Please…' she murmured.

'No, go home!'

Bree broke into a flood of tears, somewhat feigned although not entirely – she well understood the game they played; Reuben couldn't be seen to be soft for Bree, and she certainly couldn't lose too much more blood without passing out. Bree stumbled to her feet but he gripped her arm in his hand and pulled her towards the door.

'Come back in a couple of days, Trix,' he said, 'And think really, really hard before you let anyone else taste you! I do not share!' his voice rose enough that they were noticed by others, especially as they passed from the rowdy club to the quieter cloakroom. Enough ears met, enough people reached that Reuben's claim on her was complete. Bree doubted anyone would ever try to touch her again after that. As Reuben and she arrived at the door, he spun her about.

'Do you understand?' he said, the question two-fold.

'I do.'

'I hope so…'

'I promise, I get it,' she said, and then turned and left the club.

27

Kaleigh's throat was soft and gave easily under Reuben's teeth. He pulled the blood into himself with a hunger, an anger, which must have hurt like hell. The pro was quiet though, not really struggling. She was probably really getting off on it, he realised. The demon within pulled him to finish, to leave her drained and broken on the floor. He was senior enough to get away with that now, probably enjoy a few laughs from his colleagues as they took the pool for which of the working girls would go down next, or maybe even a bonus, if somebody had named him as the killer – gambling was big amongst the staff, their own death-pool. Reuben paused at the thought. Undercover was one thing, but kills led to cravings, and that to more – to a life he'd abandoned long ago. Almost abandoned, at least. The boon he still sent, once every twenty years, was a small price to pay for his freedom, despite what it cost him to hand it over. Nobody knew about the literal blood-money Damien still exacted from him, not even his family.

Reuben pulled away and rubbed the blood away from Kay's neck. Whilst the demon was still burning underneath, he knew well that he would not fully have control of the situation, but killing another innocent, that wouldn't help. Reuben closed his eyes and allowed a light to start within, the swooshing of energy building, and then used that to force calmness.

'Thanks, Kay,' he whispered.

She looked very pale, her lips grey and her eyes dazed. Reuben doubted many took this much from her at one time.

'Kay?'

Nothing. Reuben knelt and checked for a pulse. Yeah, she was still going, just. He tapped gently on her cheek, rousing her from that almost unnatural sleep. The girl moaned and rolled over, her hand at her throat.

'Come on, time to wake up,' he said, trying to sound kind without breaking character.

'I… yeah… no worries…'

'What do I owe ya?'

'Two…' she said, still dazed. Reuben pulled out his wallet and counted out two hundred pounds. He paused, then, a plan formulating, added another fifty. Any of these drinkers that would force themselves on somebody – Bree or otherwise – deserved what they got. She'd said she'd consented, but he doubted that was the truth, he'd felt her terror radiating across the room. That was the problem with these younger drinkers, they didn't flinch at just taking what they liked. A lesson needed to be learned.

'Here and an extra fifty to send that redhead in…'

'I can't do no more…'

'No, you go, I stay.'

Kay put a hand to her throat, she was still bleeding. Reuben's compassion pulled again and, despite knowing the risk, he used a fang to split his thumb and offered it to her. Kay eyed him suspiciously.

'Go on, a few drops and you'll be back to rights.'

'I drink it?'

'Yeah or rub it on the wound, whichever. Nobody ever healed you up before?'

Her expression gave enough answer that she didn't need to speak, but she rubbed her fingers over his bloody thumb and put them to her lips. Reuben waited a few moments, watching the blood work its usual magic, and then nodded at the door.

'The redhead...' he said.

'What shall I say?'

'Say the bar-tender he spoke with earlier has bought him a drink...'

The redhead came almost at once, Reuben wasn't surprised. The kid was fairly new, less than a decade, and was probably made in the basements of this very club – Reuben was pretty sure that that was a thing. The kid can't have been very old when he was taken, either, and certainly wouldn't be missed. As he entered the room, and there found Reuben, a glimmer of panic started in his eye.

'What the fuck dude?' he began, but Reuben ushered him in, and then closed the door behind him.

'Nah, mate – not...'

'Shut up,' Reuben said, allowing the demon to show. Somewhere within, sympathy for the kid tried to pull free but he quashed it. The demon wanted more, it wanted a kill and a kill of this nature would allow for rules to be respected, and Reuben to be feared. He needed that – wanted the fear. It'd keep Bree safe if nothing else. The lad tried to push past, to get out but Reuben gripped him by that mane of red silk on his head and forced his head back.

'You touched what was mine...' he said, 'did you really think to break rules and get away with it?'

'What? The fucking *human?* This is over that?'

'My human, yes. Whisper a prayer to any god you still worship.'

The kid began to really struggle, really wriggle. Reuben hardened himself, then allowed his demons to show. He took a deep breath, and then used all the strength awarded to him by his supernatural body-share to rip the kid's head clean off his shoulders.

Reuben washed the blood from his hands and tried to steady himself. He glanced down at the body. He'd have one of the young nestlings clean that up. Night was winding down now, most of the drinkers going to ground and just a handful of humans loitering. Reuben slipped out and closed the door behind him. The guy behind the bar, Logan, was loading up the dishwasher, a strangely mundane job for a drinker – enough to almost make Reuben smile.

'Logan, can you send someone out the back for me to clear up a mess I seem to have made?'

'Not like you to drain a victim.'

'Wasn't my feed – Kay's over there.'

Logan eyed him carefully, then moved to the room behind the bar and glanced in. 'Awwh, fuck… Ben!'

Reuben said nothing, but held Logan's eye for a long moment, then, 'People need to learn not to touch my shit,' he said with a shrug.

'Yeah – these younger ones can be disrespectful I guess.' Logan finally said, but still he seemed uneasy, just as Reuben wanted. He held Logan's gaze just a minute longer, then smiled. 'Anyway, dawn's coming in, I'm going to bed.'

'Sure thing man, catch ya later.'

The club was quiet for a Friday. Most of the regs, as they called their regular customers, were all about of course, and a handful of hungry drinkers, but there weren't the crowds that had been gathering recently. Logan was talking, disgust in his tones which was aimed at a young couple who were all over each other on the dancefloor. Both male, which seemed to be most of the basis for the other drinker's consternation.

Reuben pulled the dishwasher drawer out and started to load the glasses in, ignoring anything beyond the bar for a moment. Logan, however, continued to speak.

'It still flummoxes me,' he confessed, 'two lads getting it on, right in the middle of a club. I know society has "moved on" or whatever since our day but...'

'When was "your day", Logan?' Reuben asked, putting the last glass in and then standing up.

'I was born in 1890, you?'

Reuben smiled, '1700s.'

'No shit?'

'No shit!'

'That's older than most than come in here.'

'Yeah, some of us can move with the times.'

Logan nodded then moved off to serve a drink before coming back to Reuben's side. He indicated where one of the vamps had come up to the young gay couple and was obviously flirting, he shook his head.

'You'd think that our kind at least would be cautious,' he said but his voice wasn't accusing, just curious.

'Maybe, but then even in my day this existed, it was just better hidden then.'

'Yeah?' Logan asked.

'Yeah, if you didn't see it maybe you were pretty sheltered,' *says the parson* he thought grimly.

'Maybe. What about you, ever fuck a dude?'

Reuben sucked in a deep breath. He'd been expecting the question in the way the conversation was headed but still it took him off-balance. He could lie, that was an option, but in the end what was the point of that? Lying wouldn't change his past.

'Yeah,' he said, 'yeah, I *fucked a dude*. My sire.'

'That why he changed you? He loved you?'

'No,' Reuben said with a small depreciative laugh, 'not at all.' *but he did, later.* Again, he added the thought silently. 'No, he took me into this because I was convenient, he fucked me because I was there. My sire was one of those drinkers who seek a thrill, pleasure above all.'

'Aye, know the type,' Logan said, somewhat absent, and then moved to serve another customer. Reuben though, was lost in the memories again. Damien was due soon, he always seemed to be able to find Reuben, and Reuben owed him – a bargain struck in the heat of anger which had haunted him his whole life.

The year had been about 1870 or thereabouts and Reuben had been with Damien for eighty years by that point. The night he'd left had been a cold November evening, an evening which would never quit his memory, but one which started much like any other.

Reuben lay naked in the crisp white sheets of a hotel bed. his hair was loose about him and his body aching from the passion Damien had just spent on him. His throat ached too, despite that it had healed – Damien tended to bite as he fucked, a habit Reuben had picked up from him – and there was still blood on his skin, on the pillow. This type of activity wasn't a common one, not anymore, in fact the frequency of it had reduced dramatically after the first two or three years that he'd been Damien's lover. His sire got bored quickly. Still, one thing had led to another, and so for the first time in a while, Reuben had allowed Damien to take him to his bed.

The hotel room was one of the more luxurious ones London in the 1870s had to offer, with a four-poster bed, lush thick carpets and a fireplace set into the far wall, before which was a chaise longue dressed in soft fabrics. On the chaise longue was a young man. He was young, perhaps 18 or 19, and beautiful. Not a lost beggar but a rich playboy plucked from the garden of a grand house near Southwark. There'd be an outcry for him on the morrow – if he wasn't already missed. He was bound, half-crying and half in shock. Blood covered his white shirt already. Damien had already had his fun with him, had already fed too, several times. Reuben couldn't look at the boy. Damien's tastes were wild and brutal, they always had been, and despite that he loved him, Reuben knew he was an evil son of a bitch. Damien himself sat, dressed in his trousers and untucked white shirt, in a hard-wooden chair where he watched the girl cry silently. His hair was short and he'd grown the fashionable mutton chops and moustache of the era. Handsome, but evil through and through. Reuben hated him.

He loved him too though.

'I think this one's nearly done now,' Damien observed looking at Reuben. 'Shall I kill it?'

The young man murmured but his spirit was broken and he didn't even attempt to fight his bondage, to flee.

'Do you have to frighten him so? Just feed and have done with it!'

'Aren't you ever tempted to let your dark side out? We're all going to your hell anyway. You kill readily enough, why not enjoy it?'

'Rape? Torture? No. You push even my limits with your depravity.'

'I should have known better than to turn a man of the cloth!' Damien laughed and then turned back to the young man, making him whine. 'I could *make* you lose control,' he said. 'I am your sire after all.'

'If you do, you will lose me, even if I have to put a shard of silver in my own eye.'

'So dramatic,' Damien sighed, then stood and moved to sit down beside the boy. He put an arm about him and whispered something into his ear. The boy gave out a low moan and began to sob again, depleted as Damien showed him the demon face.

'Or maybe I should turn him instead,' he mused, 'I've not indulged in any experimentation for a while and he is such a handsome young man…' Damien's hand slid down the young man's chest, reaching below, between his legs as he squirmed. 'Why so much struggle?' Damien cooed, 'you were willing enough to spend your depraved urges on me in your father's garden… is this too much adventure for you, hmm?'

Reuben's chest hurt suddenly and he stood. 'Desist, Damien! Stop this!'

And then there it was, just like a switch was flipped, Damien sprang back to his feet, grabbing the boy by his throat and slamming his forehead into the heavy bedframe, killing him instantly. He spun about to look at Reuben and triggered the demon again so that it would look more menacing as he glared onto Reuben's face, furious.

'Do you really think you can tell me what to do, eh? Didn't you learn last time?' His lips pulled into a sneer and his hands moved to grip Reuben's hair.

Reuben's temper flared too, and then also abruptly, snapped. He roared and allowed his own tainted soul to show,

'Get your damn hands off me man!' he growled, pulling away so abruptly that Damien was left with a handful of his hair. Adrenaline pulsed. He'd never, not once, allowed his temper to go with Damien, a fact fuelled by both reverence and fear. Now it was gone, it felt good. He struck Damien across the face and, much to his shock, Damien went sprawling. Reuben hit him again, clumsily as one not used to it, but Damien grunted and did not try to stand. He was staring at Reuben's face, his breath panting.

Reuben stood for a moment in shock at what he'd done, then, almost painfully, he pulled his humanity back. Damien remained sprawled for a moment, then stood again, his eyes burning. He moved to try to kiss Reuben, turned on by the interaction – or so it seemed – but Reuben threw him off.

'Don't,' he warned.

Damien all but growled, but he didn't come towards Reuben again, still seeming somewhat shaken. Reuben took his moment to grab for his trousers and put them on, and then his shirt, waistcoat and jacket.

'What are you doing? Come… come back to bed… We'll feast on this young man and then we'll sleep, this tension will be gone soon enough. Come, I am sorry.'

'No. No more. I… I'm leaving,' Reuben said. It sounded so easy, so obvious once spoken aloud.

'No!'

'It is not to you to stop me, unless you wish to make me your prisoner again.'

'Reuben, don't do this.'

'I have to… I have to go.'

'I won't let you!' Damien almost whined. Reuben's temper frayed again, his shoulders tensing. He stepped backwards but then recoiled as his still bare foot crushed the arm of the dead boy on the floor. Sickness churned in his stomach, unsteadying his whole form as he pushed the corpse under the bed with his foot.

'Please…' Damien seemed calm again now, but Reuben was far from it. 'Please, calm down, here, come back to bed. I need you, Ben, I need you.'

'You don't need me,' Reuben growled, then picked up the knife from the dresser and thrust it into his own shoulder, making the blood flow, 'you need *this*! This was never about me! You don't even know me and you have spent years trying to crush me into your own creature. Tell me I am wrong, if you can?'

'Reuben…' Damien whispered, subdued.

'No! Here, if this is what you want, you may have it!' Reuben lifted the glass he'd drunk wine from the night before off the dresser and put it to the cut on his arm. Due to the way his skin knit back together, he had to reopen the wound twice before the glass was full.

'Take it!' he snapped, 'Take it! You say my blood is the key, that I am the only one of your experiments which ever worked – so fine, here, take it! You won't get another drop from my living body!'

Damien watched with eyes like a snake, and then held out his hand for the glass. 'This isn't enough,' he said, his eyes dangerous.

'It's all I offer.'

Damien shook his head, 'I don't want to enslave you again, Reuben, but I will.'

'You can certainly try!'

Damien paused again, then moved forward towards Reuben and gripped his arm, 'Where will you go? You have nothing without me!'

'Home. My house is still there, my church… I can make it so that nobody comes close and I can live there alone. I don't need you, Damien.'

Damien did not release Reuben's arm but he looked thoughtful, 'And what if I were to ask a boon of you, in exchange for your freedom?'

'What boon?'

Damien dipped his finger into the blood in the glass he held and tasted it, 'That.' He said, 'Once every ten years or so, I'll come to you and you'll give me a tankard-full.'

'Every twenty-five, and a phial.'

'Twenty, and a mug.'

Reuben suddenly reeled, was this really all his freedom would cost? 'T-twenty, and a mug…' he agreed.

And thus he was free, free but lost and broken by what he'd endured. That very night, the night of his escape was the night he'd wondered under the eye of another ancient one, one who would show him what a real sire's love felt like, and how the beast within could be tamed. Sam Haverly had been his saviour, but more so, he'd fast become Reuben's only real friend.

…'Pint of Otter, and the cause of whatever put that look in your eye,' a voice pulled Reuben out of his ruminations. He blinked and laid an eye on the young man at the bar. He was young, attractive, and maybe it was just the lingering memory, but he looked a little like the boy that had died the night he'd left Damien. Reuben eyed him a moment, but then snapped back to normality.

'Sure, Otter, yeah,' he said, pulling the pint of real ale and handing it over. The guy put a fiver down on the bar and Reuben picked it up. He paused thoughtfully, and then glanced at the back rooms. Bree would come again soon, he knew, but as ever his anguish was making him want to feed. The guy was watching him too, with big innocent eyes and parted lips. Horny as fuck for a drinker's kiss.

'I wonder...' he said, then glanced over at Logan, 'Dude, can you man the bar or me for five minutes?'

Logan glanced back, then his eyes roamed to the guy at the bar, he pondered but then shook his head, 'Nah,' he said, 'Not for that one.'

The young man looked intrigued, but said nothing. Something about the whole situation didn't feel right to Reuben, he shooed the lad off and then moved back to his work-mate.

'What was all that about?' he asked.

'He's on the list.'

'What list?'

Logan shushed him and indicated that they go out the back. Mystified, Reuben followed him, leaving the bar completely untended. They walked down a short corridor and into one of the offices out the back.

'What's going on?' Reuben asked but Logan ignored him and rummaged in a filing cabinet.

'Been meaning to go into this, boss man says you can know, now.'

'Know what?' Finally! A breakthrough! Reuben had been beginning to despair of ever being trusted again!

Logan opened a paper file and showed it to Reuben, there was a list of about twenty names on it, mainly female but a few male. At the top was the month and year and the name of the club.

'I don't get it.'

'Punters. They've been marked… sold…'

'Sold?'

'Yeah, you think this place is just a feeding ground? No. There's something bigger underneath, the boss man labels out the regs and puts them online to bid on. These are the ones that have been sold this month. When they come in, they get taken downstairs and that's that, gone. Your cutie at the bar is probably on her way out already, so I thought I'd best stop you.'

Reuben's blood ran cold. He'd known it was something like that but still, didn't mean he liked having it proven. He glanced down at the list and then back at Logan.

'Noted,' he managed.

'Good. Boss'll want to talk to you now. I have to go back out, refile that for me, will you?'

Reuben nodded and waited for Logan to leave, then reopened the file. None of the names sprang out at him but then most of the punters he'd associate with had been those for hire. At the bottom of the page, though, there in sharp black letters, was a name he certainly did know, one he'd scratch his eyes out not to see on such a document. "Trixie Morris".

He stopped dead, the file shaking in his hand. Oh God, no! He had to contact her, stop her coming – she was due any time! He dropped the file into the cabinet and then made his way to the bar, trying to hide the panic.

'Logan, mind the bar for me?' he said, then without even a reply he left the main floor, almost running by the time he got up to his chamber. The phone he'd not crushed – his personal one – was hidden in a rip in the mattress. He pulled it out with a shaky hand and began to type onto the screen. He couldn't risk being overheard on a call but a text would convey enough.

A shadow at the door was his first indication that he was caught. He looked up to see Logan stood there, arms crossed.

'Dude...' he began, but then his eyes widened as he saw the figure stood behind Logan. The phone dropped from his fingers as the trap closed.

28

When the attack came, it was swift and without warning. Bree had waited the full week, until the following Sunday, and then put on her "Trixie" outfit again and headed out, getting Ginny to drop her on the outskirts of Soho as usual, and then heading down the steps, rapping on the door and showing her card, the blue one with the crow stamp. She turned to descend the staircase, when suddenly the door below opened and a man came through. Oh, that familiar face, that long black hair, broad shoulders, vampire-stereotype realised. Bree froze. After Reuben had cleared out the nest which had taken her, she'd never expected to see that face again, the face of her previous kidnapper. He didn't see her at first, and as he lifted his head, Bree dropped hers, hiding behind her bangs and hoping he'd not notice her. The guy ran up the stairs two at a time, but as he reached her he paused, then stopped. Bree's stomach clenched.

'Hello lovely,' he said, that smile she'd once upon a time found charming spread over his lips, 'well, I'll be damned...'

The man's hand came to grip her arm but Bree went into cat-mode, scratching and fighting as the drinker grappled her. Seeing the struggle, the doorman came out of his little booth and stood in her path too, also smirking. Bree felt panic brewing, she opened up her lungs and screamed, hoping that the sound would carry to Reuben, but then a hand came over her mouth from behind, and those fangs which had once tasted her in the back of an old BMW sank once more into the flesh of her throat.

Bree's next memory was of darkness. Just like before, when she had been abducted. A strange haze, like the memory loss of her previous ordeal, and then a hard awakening laid down on a concrete floor. She rolled over, half in a dream-state, and then let loose a little mutter of panic as the situation seemed suddenly to crash down on her. Confusion, and then a sense of dread settled in. The concrete floor on which she was laid was rough, hard and cold, her vision obscured by almost impenetrable darkness.

Bree managed to sit up and still her trembling somewhat, but inwardly her guts felt as though somebody was twisting them. She blinked twice and fought to keep her lips from letting out a cry. She could not show weakness, she didn't dare. Last time he'd taken her, she'd been a frightened victim, and she was determined not to be such again! The cold seemed to seep into every limb, especially since she was so scantily clad. Her skirt was short, her abdomen bare and then a scrap of leather about her breasts in the form of a halter-neck top. Her body begged to be allowed to shiver but she repressed that too, rubbing her bare arm above the leather wristbands she wore. She stood, as well as she could on shaky legs, but then stopped dead. Somebody was sitting at the edge of the room, watching her. She did not need to be able to see his face to know who it was.

'Hello again, Beatrice,' he spoke. 'It's been a long time…'

The figure stood and moved closer and when Bree saw what he had in his hand, she did let out a murmur. It was a shackle, attached to a chain on the wall to his side, it was about the right size to go around her wrist or ankle. He approached her slowly – slowly enough that she could possibly have bolted, had fear not held her in its thrall – and slid the cold bracelet over her hand, tightening it so that it pinched slightly.

'Please… please, who are you, what is happening?' Bree asked, 'how are you… how are you here?'

The man looked down on her briefly, then smiled. 'It'll all become clear soon,' he said. 'You're lost property, my girl, and I've been sanctioned to bring you back to your master.'

'Please… I did ten years of this! Let me go? Find somebody else?'

The man chuckled again, and ran a gentle hand over her cheek. He didn't bite her though, simply caressed her face and then departed the room, leaving Bree in the darkness alone.

It seemed like hours then, that she was left alone to her own devices. For most of it she simply sat repeating a mantra to keep herself calm. Ok, so she could see nothing, but four things she could hear, three she could touch, and so on – just as Reuben had taught her. She'd been through this before, had been taken before, and so none of this was new. She bit her lip and draped calmness around her like a cape. She could survive this. This was not the end of her world.

Eventually, a good few hours later, the sound of footsteps returned, moving down the stairs and then towards her. Bree struggled to her feet, not wanting to wait on her knees like a cow awaiting slaughter. Her feet were numb, but she bore it, pressing the weight into her toes to bring them back to life quicker. A light shone briefly in her face, blinding her, and then went back out again.

'Don't let her see me yet…' a voice spoke. Bree's head shot about, she knew that voice, a distant echoing memory that was on the tip of her tongue, but could not be placed.

'This is her?'

'Thank you, Mr Gates, yes this is her.'

Bree stiffened, her ears feeding her brain that familiar tone and begging for an explanation. Bree strained to see, but it was just her kidnapper, and in his hands he held a piece of cloth, a blindfold! Bree considered struggling but decided to pick her battle instead.

'Good, there,' the familiar voice spoke. 'Now, let's go and reintroduce her to the preacher.'

'Sure thing...'

'He gone over yet?'

'Close, he's been in the sun since Friday morning and we've starved him like you said.

'Good man. I suspect that the scent of her blood will send him over. Bree felt the presence of somebody close. She murmured and tried to shuffle away, but then felt hands on hers, a shackle released.

'Who... who are you?' she whispered, shuffling on her knees as she tried to stand on numb feet.

'You'll know soon enough, Beatrice, just do as you are told now, and all will become clear.' The voice was gentle, soft, and still far too familiar. A hand came to touch her arm, to half-lift her. Bree had no choice but to obey. The touch somehow felt familiar too, the energies of her captor not a stranger. Bree was walked blindly down what seemed to be a long corridor and then pushed through a door. There she paused.

'As you leave this room, you'll feel the sun on your face,' the voice said to her. 'When that happens, you can remove the blindfold.'

Bree was half-tempted to fight, now that her hands were free, after all Reuben had trained her blind too, but in the heat of it all, fear held her back.

'Sorry for this, just a nick,' the voice spoke again, then a sharp cut to her arm made her gasp but with her eyes covered there was little she could do but tolerate it. She allowed herself to be led to another door, a bolt sounded, and then she was outside. With the heat of the sun, she put up her hands and lifted the blindfold. She was in a courtyard, bricked in below the level of the road, but with the hot sun beaming down on the slabs. Bree's eyes took it all in quickly, then fell on the figure in the corner. Out in the broad daylight – with the rays falling on his inhuman skin, was Reuben. He was curled into a ball in the corner, his hands over his face and his body prone. Behind her, the bolts closed.

'Reu…' Bree whispered, somewhat fearful.

Reuben's eyes swung to her. He stared for a moment, and then staggered to his feet. His head snapped about, showing no recognition, and his lips pulled into a snarl. Bree whimpered and pulled herself up against the door.

'Reu… Reuben… it's me…'

He said nothing, but then something started to happen, something abrupt and terrifying – more so even than a blood-starved Reuben. His eyes turned not silver, but an odd yellow. He grunted, then moaned. For half a moment there seemed to be a glimmer of understanding, of remorse, but then he fell to the ground, pulling loose his clothing – first jeans, and then t-shirt – scratching at his skin with his nails. Bree pressed herself up against the door, watching, as Reuben's hands came to rip at his clothing, throwing it down before him. His skin was turning black, his nails growing out, and then his skin was changing again – the outer layer of dermis flaking away to… to… not… it couldn't be? Fur? As Bree watched the change begin, realisation began to dawn.

Reuben wasn't a drinker – at least not *just* a drinker!

Reuben whimpered again, his form juddering as his limbs began to pop, grinding together and moving, actually moving to their new positions. Bree's heart was racing, her stomach in knots but she was petrified to the spot, unable to move, to speak. Reuben let out one more cry, one more painful whimper, and then he was gone, his body twisted and shackled into its new form. Bree felt water on her face, although she had no concept that she was crying. The door under her hands felt splintery and rough, the concrete under her bare feet cold and grainy. Bree started forward, unsure of how to approach, but then the monster looked up at her. It was a wolf, of a kind, black furred and with eyes that glowed unearthly silver. It was larger than a normal wolf, and deadlier. It showed no glimmer of recognition.

'Reuben...' she whispered, awed.

The creature sunk down, ready to pounce.

'Oh no.... oh God, Reuben...' suddenly Bree realised the danger, why they'd locked her in. The first thud as the animal hit her knocked her backwards, and it was at her throat almost at once. Bree wriggled free, kicking, and managed to get away for half a moment before a pain like she'd never known shot through her leg, her knee cracking open like an chocolate egg, cartilage tearing free in the maw of the beast. Bree screamed, really screamed. She pulled her body away, making the injury worse, and then slumped herself against the door. The creature leapt again going for her face, but Bree was quicker and drew out Reuben's silver crucifix. This she slammed into the eye of the wolf. It screamed and retreated, sticky goo and blood gushing from its face. It growled but almost at once the damage began to heal, much like Reuben's human body did.

'Please, Reuben...' she sobbed, cupping the crucifix in her hands, 'Please!' but he showed no recognition, didn't even pause as once more he came at her. Bree screamed again, and closed her eyes, fearing the end but even as she did so, trying to ground herself as he'd taught her. The heaviness came, and then agony.

29

Prey. That was what it registered first. Food. A hunt. Not much of a hunt, locked away with him. Can't escape. Still prey. The bloodlust was strong still, demon within fighting demon within. Reuben wanted to maul the prey, to rip it to shreds, but at the same time he wanted the blood, thick copper satisfaction. Either way, ripping it apart would release blood. The prey was screaming, bleeding already! He wanted to lap it up, cover his snout in it but he couldn't whilst it flailed and screamed. Reuben-wolf moved forward again, tear out the throat, easy kill, less screaming, but then something hit his face, something burny. The wolf snarled and leapt backwards. For a moment, its vision clouded, but then the itching of repair. Reuben-wolf resisted the urge to sit and scratch at it with his paws, knowing it would heal fast enough without.

The prey was sobbing now, saying a name – Reuben – the host's name. Did she think he could hear her? Perhaps he could, somewhere within the unholy trinity of this form's ownership. Perhaps somewhere, deep down, Reuben looked out through wolf eyes and he screamed and cried too. If so, Reuben-wolf couldn't hear him. The prey was annoying him too, now, so much noise, burny things, fighting. End it quickly and snuff it out... and then lap the blood, came the other one, drink it all down into the host's body.

Reuben-wolf, his sight easily recovered, shuffled back to his feet again, the prey had almost given up the fight, it was sobbing, wet and slimy face with tears and snot – yes, almost done in now – and so he tested his form with a slight shake, and allowed the muscles to tense, then leap onto the prey. His weight knocked it back against the door, his jaws snapped and then the soft flesh of its belly tore, ripping open the lining to reveal the rich intestines there. Victory seemed nigh indeed, but then the wolf sensed something else, the other! Master.

He paused over the prey which now no longer seemed the ultimate goal. The prey still moved, albeit feebly, and as he paused, it struggled away towards the door. Wolf-Reuben paused still, hackles raising as the master's voice sounded on the other side of the door, and then a click, the grinding of a door being pushed open. Wolf-Reuben tensed again, ready to leap, ready to finally have his final revenge on the man who had spliced them all together into this agonising existence. If it could have smiled, it would have. The blood of the prey was forgotten, the kill delayed, as the door opened and master stood there. Reuben-wolf made the lunge, leaping, but then in mid-jump, he was stilled by a pair of old silver eyes resting on him, by firm, snapped words – a command which was undeniable.

'That's enough, I think. Change back.'

30

For a long moment, Bree could barely register what had just happened. The floor was rough under her hands where she'd been pulled free, something cold and hard to hold onto. Her breath came in short pants, and her blood still dripped to the floor from where Reuben had attacked her. Still clutched in her fist was the weapon – Rueben's silver crucifix – still somewhat wet with his blood. The pain was almost absolute and overwhelming but adrenaline gave her consciousness. She lay blinking for a few moments, but then a voice spoke her name.

'Beatrice, here, drink…' and then a droplet of blood hit her lips. Bree moaned in appreciation, she'd drunk enough of Reuben's blood to know to accept the nectar of kin blood when offered, even if it wasn't his. The blood was thick and sweet, different to Reuben's, but much the way as any blood tasted, coppery, sweet, bitter – all in one. Bree felt a body shift behind her, and then her torso and head lifted into something of a clumsy embrace from behind, that wrist still at her lips. She drank more, and then laid back – still unsure of her rescuer but knowing that she needed to close her eyes and allow her body to heal.

'And now you know… let it all start to come back now, begin to remember, my sweet,' the voice came again. As her body healed, so Bree's mind began to return to her from the adrenaline and pain-soaked haze. As soon as she should, she turned and looked up into the eyes of her teenage boyfriend, Danny.

'Hello my little Bee,' he smiled, 'long time no see, eh?'

And then, suddenly, it all came back and Bree had no idea how she could have forgotten so much.

The memories were blurred at first, a rushing, whirr of frenzied images. Bree, Beatrice, as she was then. First as a girl – a child – holding on to a teddy-bear by its ears and listening in to the voices of those about her, not the mouth voices, the mind voices. Even before she was able to properly understand the adult themes in them, Bree had been able to hear them. Gone-people, no-more people, passed-people. A storm of voice which, as a youngster, she'd not even really understood that she needed to block out. There was more too, a feel for the stuff of the ether, a warm, yellow swirling which, if you pinged it with your mind, could make objects move, and make them bend or break. That's what had happened the day her father had found all his screwdrivers folded neatly in half, the day her mother's collection of china pigs all flew off a suddenly broken shelfing unit.

'It just... exploded...' her mother had explained to the bemused handyman, 'I think it must have been poorly installed!' but even her mother hadn't sounded sure.

'I did it Mummy, with my brain!' she'd tried, but had been rewarded only with a chuckle and a rough hand mussing her hair from the handyman, alongside his "Sure kid, sure you did".

From here, the memories went on, a dulling her abilities with age, a psychic damper which allowed for the obscuring of her gifts in the mundanity of everyday life. Still they loitered though, with the whispers at night, the figures seen only in the corner of her eye. Bree ignored them, mostly, sensible enough even as a child to give in when her mother had insisted

"They're only imaginary!" and "There are no monsters under the bed, babe."

Enter Danny.

'Damien Danvers,' he'd purred, 'but you can call me Danny.' Him - the creature before her, the man she loved. He'd clocked her at once, another psychic to play with. The memories of him were the most powerful. The crushing, overwhelming love as he'd held her in his arms and kissed her that first night. The confusion and fear of seeing his true face, and then the pain as he bit, fed. Thick cloying blood dripping from red lips, seeped in the eroticism of Hollywood's vampires who she had already borderline worshiped. Bree had felt she was living in a dream, one of hot passion and old-timey love. As he'd undressed her, caressed her, and then taken her virginity, all had seemed little less than euphoria.

'Turn me,' she'd whispered, hungry, 'make me like you…'

'No, I'd not waste you on such vulgar blood.'

'I don't understand.'

Danny pulled the covers tighter about her naked form, kissing her again and again until she was dizzy, then rubbed a smear of blood from her lips, her own blood.

'I have bigger plans for you, my love,' he'd whispered.

Bree gasped, sucking in oxygen and putting both her hands around her head. Pains shot through, seeming to start at her eyes, her temples. Her bladder felt weak but she held it, just about. Her vision swam, moved to double and then refocussed into place. The other man, Gates, who had brought her downstairs was coming out of the hell-pen where Reuben had nearly killed her with another – the guy from the door of the club. Between them, Reuben was held fast, half-dragged out of the cell. They'd at least helped him back into his jeans, although his chest was bare. Bree's eyes ran over him, taking him in. Now she knew, now she realised it all.

'The preacher is the only one who ever took the blood of both myself *and* of a changer and survived,' Danny had said to her, back in that bedroom of her youth, with her blood still drying on his lips. He'd put his jeans and t-shirt back on, ready to leave before her parents returned from whatever party or soiree they were out at. Bree, still naked, sat enraptured by him, watching him with the devotion he enjoyed.

'Why him?'

'I think it was his innate psychic abilities, they helped to mingle the two different types of blood, my own and the wolf-changer we held captive and drained. I mixed the two and fed him the blood over many months.'

'And so he is both?' she'd asked.

'Both and neither – more powerful than any I have known. He is wild though, stronger even than me and unpredictable enough to make me wary in the end. Violent, angry and dangerous.'

'And you want to give me the same?' Bree asked. 'Because of my own psychic abilities? You think I could take it?'

'I want to give you *his* blood! That is the key. Even you, with your abilities, are not as strong as he was. I don't want to risk you with such a pure mixture as I gave him. I don't want to kill you outright, my little Bee.'

'But he will not part with his blood? To turn me?'

'He hates me, he's sworn that if I trouble him again it'll be my death or his… and of everyone I've ever known, he might just be capable of killing us both. On his release, I persuaded him to give me, every twenty years, a jar of his blood. This I have used and experimented with but with poor results. Mainly it does nothing. No, you need it from the source, freshly birthed from his demon – or demons. You need it from the source and so we need to trick him into giving it to you.'

Bree's eyes examined Reuben's face, running over those familiar features. The very idea of her betrayal, of her perfidy, it was almost too much to bear. His eyes ran over her too – concern, anguish and shame. He didn't know yet! How could he? He was ashamed of himself, ashamed of what he'd done, not realising yet that Danny – Damien – had orchestrated it all. Bree wanted to reach out to him, to communicate that it was all right, he'd not known, but then her own voice echoed again in her memory, the ultimate lie, the thing which would drive him away, for good.

'You can take it all away,' she'd said to Danny. 'If I remember my gifts, I'll never be able to not use them and your preacher will suspect! If you want him to buy into this, to love me, then you need to make me forget!'

'You'd forget me too, forget it all, and this could take years to perfect, to set up.'

'I still have some years yet, let me grow a little more into my body so I don't have to live for eternity as a seventeen-year-old girl?'

'And you'd do that?' the puppet master had asked, 'give up years of your life?'

'For you, yes.'

'Your mother, your "Daddy"? your friends, everything?'

'Yes! I love you Danny…'

He'd smiled, his eyes soft. 'My brave girl,' he had whispered, 'It won't be all bad either, obviously you'll have to go and live with my friends – but I'll visit you, we'll have whatever time we can before he comes to "rescue" you…'

The two men pulled Reuben past Bree and dropped him down in the corner. He looked exhausted, frightened and depressed. He didn't even fight, just slumped. He was shivering – Bree had never seen him do that before, never seen him cold. It made her stomach hurt. Bree was suddenly cold too, her body shivering almost in sympathy on the cold floor onto which she'd slid down. Her head pounded and reality swayed again, a pressure at her nose made her put up a hand. It came back bloody.

'Beatrice?' Damien said quietly, 'Bee? Are you with me?'

Reuben's head snapped around as he spoke. His eyes darkened, 'If you even so much as touch her, Damien...' he growled.

'Says the man who just tried to eat her...' Damien laughed. 'but then you never could face up to what you are.'

Reuben closed up at once, anger and pain shining on his features. Damien moved over to Bree to take her by the arm and pull her away from Reuben. Blood spilled from her nose as he pulled her about, dribbling to her top lip. Bree wiped it away on her sleeve, still too disorientated to resist as the memories flooded back, ripping through her mind and leaving scratches and wounds where they went. Danny sat Bree down, then gently rubbed the blood away from her lips. He glanced up at the two men stood on either side of Reuben both strangely quiet and subdued, and flicked a wrist at them. They both paused, but then wordlessly departed.

'Why are you doing this?' Reuben asked at last, 'What do you want with Bree?'

'With her? As if. No, you know what I want, Preacher...'

He moved to kneel before Reuben and then, to Bree's utter shock, he kissed him softly on the lips. Reuben drew back so quickly his head hit the wall behind him with a thud.

'Don't!'

'Still? Ah, oh well. It doesn't matter.'

'There never were any slaves, were there?' Reuben suddenly said, his eyes closing with the realisation. 'All this — you've planned every bloody step of this!'

'Nothing, in my entire experience on this earth has ever been as strong or as powerful as you are. Yes, I planned this. I knew you wouldn't come back willingly but I want you back. I want your offspring, preacher, and if it has to be this human girl you love, so be it! I'll take that to see you reproduce that gift I gave you so long ago.'

'I have given you what you need to make a fucking army of half-breeds, every twenty years I've bled for you...'

'And yet it doesn't work,' Damien interrupted, 'Dead blood thus loses its potency.'

'I won't turn her,' Reuben said, 'not even her!'

'And if I told you she's dying?'

Reuben's eyes ran over Bree's face, she chewed her lip, her eyes leaking water and her nose leaking blood. Half of her wanted to continue the lies, wanting to avoid at all costs letting him realise the truth of her deception, but the other half of her battled. He deserved the truth!

'I don't believe you,' not even Reuben sounded like he believed that.

'A ticking timebomb. Some asshole has gone and fucked about with her brain a bit. Made a bit of a mess in there... sorry about that!'

Bree put a hand to her head, the pain was intense and she didn't doubt that what he said was the truth. So much for being Damien's sweet girl – his true love. He'd used her, but then of course he had. Her mind took her again to those "forgotten" years. To the fear and loneliness as he'd grown bored of her, as he'd abandoned her to become the plaything of his debauched friends. Bree's heart ached, not for Damien or even for herself, but for poor Reuben – the target of this puppetry. He was in pieces and she'd helped to do this, she'd voluntarily participated in his downfall. The emotions churned so violently that her belly hurt.

'You... why?' Reuben whispered, his eyes shining with tears.

'Because I wanted you to have to face this exact dilemma. You swore never to reproduce my gifts but now you have no choice. Turn her, or watch her die.'

Reuben slumped, he looked so broken, lost. Anger began to flare within Bree, burning and turning to molten fury. Still wrapped about her wrist was the silver chain, and attached to that was the crucifix. It wasn't much, not against a creature powerful enough to bring Reuben to his knees. It was a chance though, a chance as long as she lived long enough, to allow

Reuben to regain some control. Bree had never seen her lover look so defeated.

'Bree,' he whispered, 'This is my fault, I've brought you into this.'

'You have, but you can save her from it,' Damien cajoled him.

'I... I can't...'

Bree's eyes filled with tears at the torment on his features. She shook her head, no longer able to watch the performance before her. 'Reuben, he's lying to you,' she whispered.

The silence that fell was tangible, thick and cloying.

'Beatrice...' Damien warned.

'He... Reu, I'm sorry, but he is the one who took my memories. I have them back now, I-I... this is all part of his plan, even still – he's playing you. I'm no innocent victim – I asked him to... I loved him...'

'Beatrice, I am warning you...' Damien's voice, a growl, but Reuben was looking at her face, his eyes growing angrier. Good! He was going to need that fury, and very soon if Bree's guess was correct.

'He's puppeteering you,' she gasped out, 'Both of us. Everything – even sending Max to push us back together! ...and I was a willing participant, don't feel sorry for me. This is Damien Danvers – Reu – *Danny*! I... I was a part of this... I... I didn't know, I swear, but...'

She was stopped by a roar of anger from Damien. His eyes squinted, and his teeth were barred almost like an animal. Bree started towards Reuben but Damien grabbed for her, throwing her aside.

'He's done this on purpose!' Bree screamed, hoping the urgency of her tone would force Reuben into motion, 'Reu! You can take him though – he told me as much! He told me that you are-are strong enough to...' but then Damien was upon her. His hands went around her neck, not even attempting to feed but instead throttling her. Bree gasped and threw up the hand with Reuben's crucifix in it, aiming for

Damien's eyes. Then things blurred, a splitting pain in her head, and then a grunt from Damien. Bree's heart pounded, her lungs gasped for the sweet inhale of oxygen after the shutting off of her windpipe.

Damien roared again and ripped free the crucifix from where it had sunk into his skin. The pressure on Bree's throat reasserted, bringing sparkles to her eyes. His face was set into a grimace of fury, and his hot blood dripped down onto her upturned face. Bree struggled, trying to gasp through his fingers. Her hands came up to fight him off, scratching and batting at him as her body arched towards him. Bree forced her eyes to Reuben, sensing a movement there. He had stood, eyes glaring and lips pressed. He seemed almost unsure for a moment, but then he too roared. Bree, moving as best she could, put out a hand to him and that was enough for him to lose control entirely. The pressure on Bree's windpipe released again, giving her a painful half-mouthful of oxygen, as Damien sensed the danger. Reuben's face was changing, not the drinker but not to wolf either, instead it was a hybrid of the two – not the werewolves of Hollywood, but scarily not far off. His eyes turned not silver, but yellow and his jaw had enlarged, not enough to be a snout, but enough to pull his lips back from a mouthful of sharp teeth. There was nothing of Reuben left, not even a glimmer of humanity, instead the beast – for it was that at least – growled and then sprang. Bree felt her airways clear even more so, as Damien swung around.

'Reuben,' her voice was a croak, 'end him now!'

The beast looked to her, and then to Damien, then, to Bree's horror, he paused.

'Do it!' she cried out, 'Reuben?'

Still the beast paused and Damien suddenly softened.

'Reuben,' he all-but whispered, 'Oh you are glorious! You can't kill me – you won't, you love me just as I love you! we are bound in this…'

But he was wrong and Reuben, or at least the beast which was within his form, suddenly pounced.

The end came quickly for Damien. He scrabbled against Reuben but his strength was nothing like enough to push away the assault. Reuben tore out his throat with his teeth, bathing his face in the blood, and then knelt over him as he fell. From the pocket of his jeans he pulled an item – the silver penknife he used to cut his own flesh, Bree realised, they'd neglected to check his pockets! – and used it to plunge into Damien's chest. More blood spurted, but then slowed almost at once to a trickle as Reuben cut out Damien's heart, then, not even glancing at Bree, he put the flesh to his lips.

'No… Reuben! No!' Bree cried out as best she could through the pain in her throat. 'Don't! It's not… not worth it!'

The beast paused and spun about to look at Bree. The change in him was so drastic that her breath caught in her still painful chest.

'Reu, if you're… if you're in there…' she stuttered, 'Please, put that down. Don't… don't eat flesh, remember – you told me? Don't eat flesh! Don't feed it!'

Reuben eyed her with confusion in his eyes, but then dropped the bloody meat to the ground. He crouched and glanced about the room like a trapped animal. Bree forced herself to her feet and moved to kneel before him. She slid a hand up each side of his face and looked deep into those old, frightened eyes. Whatever had come to the surface, it was newly formed, confused and afraid.

'Reuben, my love,' she whispered, ignoring the caution in his eye, the blood pooled below him, and the crushing pain in her throat, 'Please come back to me, Reu, come back now.'

At first he did not even react, but then his eyes focussed on her face.

'Please, Reuben. Close your eyes and… and ground yourself my darling. Here, five things that you can see, four that you can hear… listen to me. Now close your eyes, come back! Three things you can touch or feel, two you can smell,' she paused again, 'And now one thing, other than blood, that you can taste.'

Her hands shook, her heart pounded and for a moment she didn't think it had worked, but then, slowly and gradually, Reuben's face began to reappear on those grotesque features. Bree sucked in painful breath and let it out again in deep, slow waves. At last, though, Reuben was entirely Reuben again.

'My love, I am so, so sorry,' Bree whispered again but Reuben didn't speak. His eyes searched hers, then dropped, unable to hold her gaze. He moved away and pulled himself into the corner in which he'd been sat before, hands over his ears and face hidden behind his arms as his body curled.

Bree scrabbled on her hands and knees, moving across the floor as best her tired limbs would allow. Her hands hurt from the roughness of the ground below, her weight grinding the dust and grit firmly into her palms and knees. Reuben remained sat in silence in the corner of the room. His legs were pulled up before him protectively and his hands slid down over his face. Bree could feel the tears before she even saw them, a ripple in the energy about him. His shoulders were tense, his body drawn away.

'Reu... please forgive me...' Bree's voice was a whisper. More blood dripped from her nose, and her ears still rang with tinnitus. She knew it was nearly done; she didn't have long. Reuben looked out at her. His eyes were wet, as she had suspected, and his lips pressed tight. Despite it all, despite his confusion, he opened his arms to her. Bree went, not speaking – there was no need for that – and curled her body in next to his bare chest. Reuben held her and put down his chin on her hair. Bree wondered if he realised she was dying in his arms. In the end it didn't matter, she supposed, he'd know soon enough. Reuben's arms pulled her tighter, his head moved so that his cheek rested on her hair. And then there was silence. Reuben's heaving sobs quieted, his gasping breath smoothed and his exhaled air was warm on her skin. Bree closed her eyes. There was blood everywhere, she could feel it, could smell it, it was on her clothing, her face, her hands. Most of it was her own. Her head felt heavy suddenly, and the urge to suck in mouthfuls of air was fading. She allowed her body to go limp, allowed her head to droop. Somewhere, out in the distance, she was aware of Reuben's form stiffening once more, his hands holding her, shaking her. It didn't matter, nor did his murmur, and then his cry of shock.

'Bree! Bree, wake up!'

No, not this time, she said, inwardly, *not this time* and then let go of consciousness.

ЗІ

Reuben looked down at the girl in his arms. Her lips were turning blue and her eyes were closed. For the first time, he really began to see the truth; the blood at her nose, the way she'd stumbled and clutched her head. Whatever Damien had done, it had broken something inside of her, irreparably. Reuben gently pulled her hair from her eyes and shook her form, she didn't respond. His breath caught, he wasn't ready for her to die, not now, not yet – they had so many unused years yet. His mind flit to Lucy, to losing Lucy. His last companion, his last love. Lucy had defied all the odds of their dangerous lives and had lived to be nearly seventy. She'd been his companion since he'd rescued her in 1918, an orphan in the great war, just sixteen years old when he and Izzy had found her starving, half-dead on the side of the road. After Damien, and Lizzie before him, Reuben had sworn never to love again, but Lucy had gotten under his skin, much as Bree had.

The dementia had hit early.

By then she and Reuben had moved from being lovers to being fond companions. In what seemed like such a short time, the girl he had loved had fallen away to an angry, confused old lady. She remembered the kin and what they were – what Reuben was – but she couldn't remember him as a person. She'd attacked him with her blade, one modelled on his own silver knife. If Izzy hadn't intervened, breaking her neck in one fell swoop, his beloved Lucy might well have killed him there and then. It was the very worst memory of his life, seeing her sprawled, dead at his feet, with Izzy screaming in panic in the background at what she'd been forced to do to save him. If Reuben could have turned Lucy, he might have done – especially in the early years of her illness – but he couldn't. To do that would be to pass on Damien's evil experiment and he would not wish his torn and broken existence on anybody. He looked down at Bree, dying in his arms and the same dilemma pulled. There were other means, other ways, though, and he'd try anything before he tried turning her. Not off the table, but a last resort.

Reuben pressed his lips to her brow again, and then tried again to wake her, shaking her and calling her name but Bree was out for the count, floppy in his arms. She was still breathing though, her pulse weak but still a little thud against her throat. Reuben put his lips to his own wrist, pulled through the teeth of the demon which craved the blood, and bit his own flesh. As long as he was in control, held the demon back, she'd be safe – just like last time. Reuben held his wrist out over Bree's lips and allowed the blood to fall. At first she didn't respond but then, like a babe to suckle, she opened her lips and took it in. Not much, just enough to stabilise her. Still she didn't wake up though and Reuben's senses were keen enough to feel out that he'd not healed her fully. He sucked in another long, deep breath and then sighed, holding his girl in his arms. He'd done all he could and she was coming back to him. He hadn't cured her though, he knew that much too.

Once Bree was stable, Reuben gently set her down on the cold earth and went back into the antechamber where he'd turned. The wolf form he was used to, had given himself over to many a time. The half-thing, the merging of them both, that was new – more like how Samuel Haverly had described it should be after observing another who had been made in a similar way – a female called Frances. As far as Reuben knew, there were only the two of them so far in existence which carried both curses simultaneously. He pushed the thought back and moved into the darkest corner, looking for his shirt. It lay where he'd discarded it and just a few inches further into the dark corner lay his phone. Reuben pulled on his shirt and then picked up the phone. The screen was cracked, but it was still usable. Reuben brushed it clean of the dirt it lay in and then went back to Bree. He pulled her up onto his lap again, laying her head against his shoulder and inhaling the scent of lavender in her hair, then looked at the broken phone for a long moment. With something of a sigh, he dialled the number for Sam – he couldn't deal with Hugh, not right now.

'Hello Reuben?' Sam's voice was deep and soft.

For a long moment Reuben was silent, that voice stirring up another myriad of emotions but finally he found his voice. 'Yes, it's me. Your London job… it's done.'

'You got the leader?'

'Yes.'

'Good. Anyone we know?'

Reuben licked his lips, then sighed, 'yeah, my sire... my *real* sire…'

The silence from the other end of the phone was deafening for a long moment, then Sam's rich tone, 'I… are you all right?'

'No, not really. I will be though.'

'Was it… as Hugh and I suspected? Slaves?'

'No actually, it was personal.'

'Personal?'

'A trap, for me. It's done now though and perhaps we can rest easily that it was nothing like we suspected.'

'This is true. Are you going home to Devon?'

'Yeah.'

'Maybe take some time off?'

'Yeah.'

Another long pause, then, 'I'm sorry, Reuben. You know where we are if you need us. I know you don't see us as family, but we are.'

'I know. Bye Sam.'

'Goodbye, come and see me soon!'

Reuben let out a long breath, that was the hard one done, then dialled Chris's number.

'Oh, thank Christ, Reu! Is Bree with you?' Chris didn't even bother with "Hello".

'Yeah.'

'Jesus! Tell her I'm pissed at her. She just vanished and we couldn't track her phone…'

'She's… she's not quite with us, currently. I'll tell her when she wakes up. It was Damien b-but he's dead – the club is ours for the taking. Wanna come claim it?'

'I… er… yeah, no worries.'

'Good. I'm heading straight back down to Devon. I'll have Josh do the legal stuff.'

'Ok,' a pause much like Sam had given, 'Ben, are you good, man?'

'Yeah, I'm good,' he said, 'I'll be home soon.'

Back in the other room, Bree was waking up. Reuben stood in the doorway, looking down on her tearstained and bloody face. He already knew he'd not healed whatever Damien had done, that was beyond him. She had spoken of lies, of being in cahoots with Damien and within him the beast asked him why he didn't just leave her there to rot. He couldn't though, he already knew that. Her eyes followed him as he made his way back to her and sat down beside her. She tried to take his hand but he shook his head.

'I think I am owed some explanations,' he said softly.

32

Bree looked up into Reuben's eyes, and she wanted to sob at the distrust now locked away in there. She wet her lips and looked at her hands. From behind her she heard a murmur, and then another. Her spine pricked, in so long the voices had left her alone but now, suddenly, they were returning – those eerie murmurs – the "not there" people. Deep within, the mechanisms for quieting them began again and Bree combined these with Reuben's grounding to push back the noise.

'Bree?' Reuben pushed, still gentle but firm.

'I… I first met Damien at a party when I was sixteen,' she spoke softly, once her head was clearer. 'He used a house close to ours – it was empty so I guess he was dossing there. He was interested in me at once. He had just been hunting – looking for sport but I…' she broke off, realising she'd have to go back further, 'Ever since I was a kid, I heard… like… voices… the dead…'

Reuben's face paled but he said nothing.

'I… I can hear them again now, starting up again but he… he repressed them. He… Reuben I was so young… naïve… I know that's no excuse! But I was… I was obsessed with vampire novels anyway – probably because of my own dark gifts… so I was… when he showed me what he was…'

'I understand,' Reuben said but still his eyes were dark.

'I asked him to turn me but he refused. He told me about you. He said if I wanted to stay with him forever then I had to persuade you to... to give me your blood.'

'Another of his damn experiments.'

'Yeah...' she paused.

'And so your abduction?'

'Staged, but it was then... then he started fucking about with my memory... I still don't really have enough of it to really piece it together but I... I need you to know that... that I didn't know! From the minute I awoke – every moment you have spent with me – I didn't... didn't know,' Bree couldn't hold back the tears anymore, 'I am... am appalled with myself, with what I have done!'

Reuben was silent for a long time. Bree cast her eyes over him and tried to stem the tears which were falling almost unheeded from her eyes. She put a hand down on his arm and he did not shake it off. Inside her head the voices began up again and in her weakened state it was harder to push it all back. As she tried, another shot of pain pushed through her temples.

'I...' Reuben began suddenly, looking up, 'I of all people understand regret, and I of all people understand the spell Damien could cast on a person's senses.'

'I... I can't... can't apologise enough. If ever I can make up to you what I have done just tell me what to do... and I... I guess I understand if I can't...'

'A young girl did a really stupid thing, for the sake of her first love,' Reuben said softly. 'If I could not understand such, then I would be a hard man indeed.'

Bree said nothing, her heart beginning a hopeful thud once more. 'Will you forgive me then?' she whispered.

Reuben finally softened and slipped an arm around her shoulders. He didn't speak but then he didn't need to. His arm tightened, holding her safe and his lips moved to kiss her forehead, just a soft, tender kiss. Bree lay her head on his shoulder, spilling the last of the tears and holding tight to his hand.

'My head hurts,' she finally whispered.

'I know – there's something… I could feel it when I tried to heal you… my own instincts tell me that…'

'That my brain is fucked from Damien's interference? Whatever he did, it's killing me?'

'Yeah.

'Can you cure it?'

'No. If I could, I would…'

Bree sucked in a deep breath, then sighed. 'Then let me stay with you, now, until… until the end,' she whispered, 'please? I… I love you Reuben, I don't want to die with Damien between us!'

Reuben looked down on her face, his eyes were still dim and his lips still pressed but a tiny glimmer of something started up in his eye again, a flicker of love in the sombreness of the moment.

'Ok,' he whispered, 'Ok, that I can do. Come, let's get us home.'

The orange glow of October's rusty flame bathed the house in an autumnal cosiness. Bree sat quietly on the sofa, her legs curled up beneath her and her book set aside on the leather sofa arm. She'd spent the day slowly but steadily cleaning out the flue of the fireplace with a long brush on a big stick, exhausting, but satisfying despite that she was paying for it now, shaky and feeling a bit sick. Afterwards, she had laid a little fire to put some warmth into the cold stones of the house. This fire now crackled and popped, giving off a little smokiness but not enough to stink out the house. Bree glanced into the flames, then back up at her mother who was sitting by her side, and pulled her blanket more so over her legs. It was nice to have her mum there; she'd arrived shortly after Reuben and Bree had contacted her, and hadn't left yet – some three weeks later. Despite the company of her mother, Josh, Jess and Izzy, Bree missed Reuben. He had been gone a few days again this time, not working now but exploring old stories, myths, trying to find the ever-elusive cure to what the doctors had diagnosed as a brain tumour on the amygdala – the memory centre of the brain. All of them knew it was hopeless, but Reuben needed to be doing something, and so still he went off looking, still he spent days with his head in musty old books then went off on treks to buy random potions and powders, refusing to give in. Despite how Bree missed him though, she knew the time was coming when she'd have to leave, her health was in a fast decline, especially that week: dreadful headaches which kept her awake at night, the constant mutter of voices and the panic as the instincts tried to invade her form. She was beginning to suffer more major memory loss too. At the moment she felt serene and just tired but she'd read enough to know that the end of her disease was anything but calm and she sure as hell wasn't going to let Reuben see that. He could claim her body, after, bury her in his little private graveyard, but those last few weeks or days, however long it took, she wasn't going to allow him to have to witness that. He'd finally told her about Lucy too and the tale had made that decision even more salient.

'I want to be buried here, Mum,' she whispered suddenly, the thought becoming salient, 'in the churchyard around the back, when the time comes.'

'Let's not talk about that, Bree.'

'No, Mum, you need to listen to me before the cancer grows any further and I begin to rant and rave and whatever else. I want to come home with you, now, so Reuben doesn't have to nurse me through that, but when I'm gone, bring me here – bring me home to him?'

Her mother's hand shook where it held hers and her eyes blurred with tears, but she nodded, 'Ok, ok sweetheart, we'll do that!'

'Thank you… I need to pack my things… Reuben will be home soon and I… I want to be ready to go so that I can just say… say goodbye and then leave…'

'He won't want you to go,' Izzy whispered from across the room where she sat knitting, 'I think he sees himself curing you still.'

'We all know it's too late for that and if Reuben doesn't know it, then he's in denial.'

'Still…' the girl argued, pausing in her knitting to glance up, first to the door, then to catch Bree's eye. 'There's still stuff you haven't tried. Will you really go? Really give in?'

Bree clutched her mother's hand. She swallowed the lump in her throat.

'I never, ever thought I'd want to leave Reuben,' she whispered, 'but the truth is that there is no cure for me. This cancer does things to a person's sanity – makes them crazy – and I don't want him to remember me like that! I want him to remember his girl, not some… some… raving husk who doesn't even know him.'

'Like Lucy,' Izzy almost whispered.

'Yeah, like Lucy, I guess.'

A silence fell for a moment, there was a shuffling of movement behind, Josh making himself more coffee probably, and then the sound of an owl hooting, out in the night somewhere. Bree swallowed the suddenly excess liquid in her mouth and swung her feet out from under the blanket, ready to stand and pack – pushed on by the passion of her words.

'You know there is a cure… an answer…' Izzy said, glancing behind them quickly again, but then taking Bree's eye.

'What? There is?' That was Bree's mother.

'I know. But it's not an option,' Bree interjected.

'If it could save you it very much is an option! What is it?' her mother snapped.

Bree glanced over to Izzy with something of a scowl, annoyed that the girl had given her mother false hope. 'Not an option.' she said again.

Izzy looked over at her mother. 'Bree could be turned,' she said. There it was, out in the world.

'Turned?'

'Made like us.'

'Oh? You can do that?'

'I can't, I don't know how and anyway its forbidden, but Reuben, he could…'

'He never will, and for good reason,' Bree interjected, 'And more so, I'll never ask.'

'What? Why not? I don't understand! Bree if this could cure you?'

'Mama, I can't. Reuben is not like the others here, not like the ones you've met! Nobody knows what it would do to me if he tried to turn me – it might just kill me outright anyway, and even if it doesn't it's not an easy life. Reuben trains and meditates every day of his life to calm the beast within him. He is more disciplined than I could ever be!'

'You could train? You could learn? Honey, the alternative is death! For God's sake!'

Tears sprang from Bree's eyes as the frustration built. 'I know, Mum, but Reuben has sworn off it. He's too afraid of birthing a monster… I… I couldn't ask him, I couldn't make him relive the pain of telling a loved one that no, he can't save them. I love him too much to put him through that! I can't do that to him, even if the alternative is that I have to go!'

'I think that's the most selfless thing I have ever heard a person say,' Izzy said, glancing up again from her knitting.

'I agree,' a broken voice came from behind. Bree spun about to see Reuben standing leant up against the door behind her. The electric light behind him bathed his body in a glow which contrasted well with the darkness out of doors. He was still wearing his coat, obviously just returned, and his boots still held the mud from outside where he'd not yet tapped it off by the door. He'd loosened his hair from its usual tail though and a few strands frizzled with static from the hairband. His eyes ran over Bree, then he put out his hand. 'Come with me? If you are feeling well enough?'

'Another cure?'

'Yeah… this one will work.'

Bree's heart thudded. Her mother helped her to stand and wobble over to Reuben. There he lifted her up, one hand under her knees, with her head on his chest.

'Mrs Morgan,' he said, holding Bree's weight with ease. 'What I am about to do is going to cure Bree. There is a slight risk but I am convinced it will work. You can rest your pounding heart now, your girl is safe.'

'Thank you,' her mother whispered.

'She'll be very different when it's done, she won't ever be able to come home.'

'Here is her home.'

Reuben nodded and then indicated the door; Bree slipped her arms about his neck as her mother opened it for him to carry her outside. The night was a little chill but Bree didn't shiver, taking warmth from Reuben's body. Outside, he carried her into the glade where he had his dojo and there he sat, her still in his lap. Reuben exhaled, then laid back slightly, his back on the trunk of a tree behind. He slid his hands up over her eyes and Bree closed them.

'Long inhales, in and then out,' he murmured.

She obeyed.

'I've never done this before,' he said, 'and I wasn't made this way, so I don't even remember it from your side of things.'

'Reuben… What…?' Bree sat forward a little.

'Come back here, lean on me and close your eyes.'

Bree did as she was told, her heart racing.

'Changers just swallow a few mouthfuls of blood and it's all good,' he went on when she was settled again, 'Drinkers don't work that way. With me, I have no idea, so I think I'll go for the more extreme way, just in case.'

Beside her face, Bree felt him begin to shift, his features to change. She risked a look and there saw he was letting both the demons shine through together, just as he had when he'd killed Damien. She drew in a sharp inhale, it was still so alien to her, that odd face, more so than his drinker face.

'Don't be afraid of me,' Reuben whispered, still himself despite the deformity. 'I have control now, of both. I spent my whole life trying to keep them at bay but I never needed to, together they are easier to control. Keep breathing, relax and begin to ground yourself. You are going to need all your serenity for this.'

'Reuben, you don't have to do this!'

'Hush and listen. The process is to remove your blood, until you reach the point of death, and then to cheat it, by reviving you with my own blood – the demon exposed. I have two demons within, and I have no idea which one will take you, or if you will get both too. You ingest the blood though – somehow that is the key.'

Bree just concentrated on her breathing, allowing his voice and the touch of his hand on her face to soothe her. Her bladder felt weak and she knew that her legs would not hold her if she tried to stand.

'When a human being bleeds out, there are symptoms to be aware of. I took, I suppose, a pint or so at a time when you were coming to me at the club. You know how that feels. As I go on, your body will start to feel cold. Your breathing will feel heavy and you will become confused. You'll start to lose consciousness, but your brain will fight it and you might have a few moments of clarity as your adrenal glands release the adrenaline. It might hurt, it might be frightening, I don't know. Eventually though, you'll fade. You'll weaken until your chest is heaving. Your vital organs will begin to close off and you'll go to sleep. At that point, I'll bring you back. You'll sleep for a time – it varies from person to person – and when you awake, you will share my blood, my curse.'

Bree continued her grounding exercise, but fear clenched her shoulders again.

'I am not going to let you die though,' Reuben's voice softened, 'and I will try to get it done quickly so the discomfort is minimal. Do you understand all I've just said?'

'Yes.'

'Ok,' he took a deep breath.

'You don't *have* to do this Reuben.'

'I do, because I actually can't bear to watch you wither and die in front of me like this.'

'This way, even from his grave, Damien wins.'

'I'm past caring. Let him win.'

'But I'll be your first offspring, after so many years...' Bree wriggled but he gently held her still where she was, kissing her brow with his deformed lips.

'I know, be calm sweetheart. I am aware of that. I've put more thought into this than you know. I have been away meditating and preparing for this moment, I guess I knew it was coming. You have to ask me now though; I can't do this unless you ask me.'

Bree held back yet more tears, scolding herself for them, she wanted it though, she knew she did and in the end it was only Reuben's reluctance which had held her back.

'Reuben... will you... will you turn me?

'Yes,' he whispered, his own voice cracking to say the word. He took in two long deep breaths, she could feel his chest and belly both expand and deflate, and then that familiar pain of his bite to her throat. This time though, his teeth sank deeper, going for her jugular; he was set not for a feed, but to kill. Bree's eyes flew open and her hand flew up to grasp the back of his head. Reuben's fingers tightened in her hair, but he didn't stop, not until her gasps were subsiding into the darkness. His tears mingled in with the blood which trickled down her neck and his shoulders shook as he tore her life free. Bree allowed the darkness, allowed the serenity and peace even as a hot trickle began to burn her lips. His blood. The transfusion was beginning. Bree moaned. More blood fell onto her lips, and then once again her consciousness wavered. Bree used every ounce of strength she had, and pulled the demon into herself, then the darkness took it all away.

Epilogue

Reuben's body moved effortlessly from pose to pose. The moonlight shone down on him, illuminating the small but heavily scented garden in which he stood. Pots after pots, with not a blade of grass in sight. Bree had insisted, when they returned to London, that Reuben had a garden of some type and so she'd built him one here up above the city. A roof garden, she'd called it, convenient and trendy. It was better than nothing. Reuben paused and allowed his mind to flit over the past six months. At first he'd been sure it hadn't worked. Bree had laid like the dead for so long, too long, but then she'd opened her eyes and he'd been able to breathe again. She'd taken both, half and half, just like he was. It was fine, he kept an eye on her and it was blissful to have someone to run with when the other form pulled – not as often as it did for the pure changers, but just once every couple of months or so. Bree had good control too, better than he'd had when Damien had first turned him, better too than the other one of his kind that Sam had created a couple of years earlier.

That had been the main experiment, to mix the changer blood and the drinker blood. Reuben strongly suspected that it was his inner guide, his inner voice, which had helped. Perhaps he hadn't been entirely human to start with, and Bree, he now understood, had been the same. If nothing else, his old lover had brought them together, had given him one final gift. It was about all he'd done.

Reuben moved to the edge of the roof, looking out over the city. He still hated it but at least this was only temporary again. It had been Bree's idea to come back – just for a year or two, she'd promised – to clear her head and adjust to what she was now. To learn to accept that she no longer aged but that those she loved, her mum for a start, would grow old before her, would die, and she would go on. Reuben wished he could take the pain into himself for her, but he knew he had to let her feel it, in the end, just as he had. At least they had each-other now.

Downstairs, Bree stood in Reuben's old spot behind the bar. She loved the feeling of having a purpose, even if it was just to serve beer, to stack the dishwasher and to keep an eye on the patrons. The club wasn't what it had been, but that message was still not entirely out there and so it was her job to ensure people weren't dying in the feeding rooms – now all properly furnished with easy-wipe vinyl sofas and black-tiled floors – and to ensure that those entering knew the rules. Barnes had gone, as had the rest of the guys who had attacked her, who had actively participated in Damien's false plans for slavery. Across the bar, the door which led up to the living quarters opened and Reuben came in. Six months hadn't altered their affections much, aside for a move into a more comfortable place – a partnership which was equal. Reuben smiled when he saw her, winking and then letting himself out of the back door. He often went out, walking the streets at night, still ever troubled but calmer than he'd once been. The man he called sire, Sam, had a house close by and sometimes Reuben went there too – Bree had an idea that Sam helped him more than he let on with controlling the bubbling blood within him. His whereabouts didn't trouble her though, she knew he was careful, and she knew that as the day began to break, he'd return and take her hand, lead her up to their little flat above and hold her in his arms until the following evening. Life was steady, but Bree was content.

'Love you,' she mouthed, but the door had already swung closed behind him. It was ok, though, he knew, and she knew he loved her back. They didn't need words for that.

Author's Note

Hi, I'm Emma. I'm an author and local historian from Plymouth, in the UK. I write under various genres: Historical Romance, Supernatural Romance, Dark Fantasy and Historical Fantasy. My background in Psychology (educated to Msc) combined with my love of history, (educated to Ma, PhD underway) influence and intertwine in everything I write. I am local to Plymouth, UK, and both work and study at Plymouth University. My PhD is focused on insanity and asylum care in the long nineteenth century, something I find to be fascinating, as I do with a lot of the darker side of history. I run a historical blog which explores some of these themes from a historian's perspective.

I started writing at a fairly young age, 18 or 19, but didn't publish my first novel for some years. Ella's Memoirs was released in May 2014 and after a short social media campaign, it was found to be a success, making it into the top 10,000 best-selling ebooks overall on kindle for new releases, and the top 1000 free ebooks on kindle during a free promotion shortly after release. This led then to the full proof and edit of novel number 2, The Blood of the Poppies. This novel was somewhat delayed and was released a year later than planned in the May of 2016. Since then, I have released the sequel to Ella's Memoirs, "The Black Marshes" as well in 2018 and my first fantasy novel, The King's Idiot, in 2019 and now this one in 2020. I aim to bring you guys a novel a year for as long as I can!

This novel, Donor, was the novel which was never supposed to happen. After I shelved the Haverleigh series in 2018, I did swear off writing any more vampire romantic fiction in a world/market which is saturated with it, however Reuben and Bree would not leave me alone and so I allowed them to tell their story through me as my final bow to this genre. I have not, however, ruled out writing more vampire-led historical fiction in the future so look out for that!

https://emmabarrettblog.blogspot.com/
https://www.facebook.com/EmmaBarrettBrown/

Also by this Author:

Ella's Memoirs
When Ella rescued the injured wolf in the forest, she had no idea of the events that act would set in motion. In the eyes of a creature, she saw the glimmer of humanity, she acted on it and was rewarded with a curse which would leave her ageless and lonely throughout the centuries. As she sits, lonely and forgotten, she begins to write her memoirs. A journey written by the hand of a woman who has survived the odds. From the witch-hunts of sixteenth century Germany, to the brothels of nineteenth century Paris. A tale of werewolves and vampires, of hopes dashed and of a love which refuses to die, even as the centuries pass.

The Blood of the Poppies
Jessie was just eight years old when she found the dead body of a woman in the woods. The corpse which she stumbled upon, decayed and forgotten, fast becoming the key to a life she'd never have lived otherwise. Through this, she learns to love Ethan, the strange boy who moves to the village with his aunt and no other family, and apparently no history.But Ethan has a secret, one he will defend to the very end, and one which could get them both killed.

The Black Marshes

Frances Hodge was just a child when she met the man in the marshes, a man who gave her a gift which would stay with her and shift the whole course of her life. No longer entirely human, she stumbles into the world of the drinkers and the changers, into a life where fear and hatred is the only motivation for survival. As the seasons change and a new century falls, Fran's group come head to head with a powerful enemy, an enemy which has already killed her husband and some of her closest friends. For Fran, the changers are primal, unfettered and viscous, but then she meets William Craven and everything begins to change. This book is an indirect sequel to Ella's Memoirs.

The King's Idiot

In a world of peace and prosperity, a golden king sits on the throne of a land once ravaged by war. His illegitimate daughter, Niamh, a solitary and quiet girl, often jeeringly called "the king's idiot" by her peers, begins to find where the cracks form in the gilt of the golden keep. A pressure is building below a façade of gentle rule, and the king's new ideas on religion are driving the Woldermen – the wild savages of the marshes – back into the kingdom. Led by desperation as their temples are torn down, their sacred forests are felled and their priestesses murdered, the Woldermen are gathering their forces. When Niamh is taken hostage by a group of Wolder, led by a familiar face from her past, she is faced with a choice. If she takes one path, it could lead to the destruction of her kingdom, but if she takes the other, a whole new world awaits her. Torn between two worlds, the princess must make her choice quickly. On one side is her father, a man beloved by his people and who raised a bastard child as though she were his true daughter, but on the other is the man she loves, a man with a cause, with a motive to bring it all down around them. Whichever path Niamh chooses, conflict is imminent and the golden reign is at risk.

Printed in Poland
by Amazon Fulfillment
Poland Sp. z o.o., Wrocław